I0452084

The Keepers

Things Left Unsaid

JJ Hull

Paranormal Crossroads & Publishing

The Keepers, Things Left Unsaid

Copyright © 2012 by JJ Hull

All rights reserved. No part of this book may be reproduced or transmitted in any form or by any means without written permission of the author. For information, address Paranormal Crossroads & Publishing, Po Box 5056, Bella Vista, AR 72714.

ISBN 978-0-9849879-5-5

www.paranormalcrossroads.com

This work is fiction. All of the characters, organizations, and events portrayed in this novel are either products of the author's imagination or are used fictitiously.

The publisher does not have any control over and does not assume responsibility for author or third-party Web sites or their contents.

The scanning, uploading, and distribution of this book via the Internet, or via any other means without permission of the publisher is illegal and punishable by law. Please purchase only authorized electronic editions and do not participate in or encourage electronic piracy of copyrighted materials. Your support of the author's rights is appreciated.

Image copyright AISPIX by Image Source, 2011 used under license from Shutterstock.com.

Table of Contents

Dedicated to...

My Uncle Ralph

The Keepers

Things Left Unsaid

JJ Hull

CHAPTER ONE

Elizabeth

There seemed to be no end to the night. I was relieved to see daylight streaming through my window. I quietly rose, preferring my room mate and best friend, Tilly, not to hear me. She had protectively guarded the door and window late into the night explaining that the ratty haired young man with the crooked smile and black, lifeless eyes was a true dark soul. My worst fear was realized, he was a Dweller. The Dwellers wanted nothing more than to over throw the Keepers and rule Home and the Earth Plane with evil. This ratty haired dweller used the full force of his dark eyes upon me. This intent stare left me terrified and totally unable to move last night. Marvin and Tilly rescued me and pulled me away from his black, scowling eyes.

Upon fleeing, Marvin offered himself as a decoy leading the group of Dwellers that were tracking us in a completely different direction. Tilly and I were left with no choice but to confide in Rhett, Marvin's uncle, about our illegal adventures outside the protection of the Keeper dome in hopes of getting Marvin help. Then we found ourselves locked away in our room with no hope of escape. Today, I planned to visit Rhett alone and inquire as to Marvin's whereabouts. I begged to go last night, but I couldn't get out of the Hall of Knowledge undetected by the gum popping Tilly. I couldn't risk leading her unintentionally to Dwellers. Not to mention, she kept repeating that the allusive guards, which I had never before seen, were on high alert and I wouldn't be able to pass them undiscovered.

As I neared the door to Rhett's house, I was flabbergasted to see Albert Solliday, the leader of the Keepers, exiting his it. As he passed, he gave me a warm smile and continued walking down the badly cracked sidewalk. I knocked on the door.

After a moment or so, Rhett answered, "Good morning!"

"Is he okay?" I questioned as Rhett waved me in with the expression on his face shifting to sorrow. I bolted past him down the dark, creaky hall finding Marvin seated in a big comfortable chair in the living room. He looked heavy hearted and odd with a bruised face and a swollen, black eye. "Marvin," I kneeled before him and gently touched his bruised face, the outward proof of his commitment to protect me. I flung my arms around his neck saying, "You don't know how worried I have been and how relieved I am to see you." I expected his arms to wrap around me. Instead, they unlocked my grip from his neck. He struggled out of the chair and immediately moved away from me.

"Elizabeth, you need to go," Marvin stated as he stood next to Rhett who placed a hand on his shoulder appearing to give the visibly shaking Marvin support. I was at a loss for words when he pleaded, "Don't make me do this here."

"Do what?" I stated feeling bewildered. "What you are talking about?"

Marvin inhaled a deep, and what appeared to be, physically painful breath. "Elizabeth, I don't want to see you anymore." Marvin flatly stated as he peered directly at me.

I gasped and stood dazed while Rhett excused himself from the room. "What?" I stammered as a rattled panic swept over my body. "Why are you saying this?" I questioned as my hands began to tremble uncontrollably like the quivering of my chest.

"I've lost my interest," Marvin shrugged looking at his feet.

"I know you have feelings for me," I strongly disagreed.

Marvin simply ignored me appearing uninterested as he shuffled his feet.

"Marvin, we are meant to be together! Remember, right here," I patted my chest over my rapidly beating heart.

"I have been granted opportunities my family never had," Marvin stated obviously assuming this statement countered my feelings. "They all work for the Department of Ghosts."

"What does your family have to do with us?" I questioned feeling confused.

"I am the first in my family to be Keeper," Marvin coldly continued. "You do realize I should stand before the Council for our trip outside of the dome, don't you?"

"There are bigger problems than just our leaving the dome," I answered trying desperately to keep my voice from cracking. "They were Dwellers!"

"They were," Marvin coldly agreed as he looked away. It was obvious this wasn't news to him. "My point exactly. We shouldn't have left the safety of the dome. Now..."

"I'll tell them it was my idea," I interrupted in a begging voice.

"No!" He shouted across the room shooting me a stern look. "I don't want you drawing attention to yourself." These words instantly bothered me because they were similar to what Dustin always told me. "You're a trainee. I'm the Keeper." Marvin threw his hands up in exasperation. "I knew what the consequences were for illegally leaving the dome. I'm a man and can stand on my own two feet. I will carry the blame for my actions. But in doing so, I only have one option to keep myself from the Council."

"Not to see me anymore," I surmised. "Someone is forcing you to do this."

"I have given you the wrong idea," Marvin disagreed with his fists clinched. "I. Don't. Want. To. See. You!" He had methodically pronounced each word in a stern voice.

"Please, don't," I pleaded as my voice began to crack with the seriousness behind his voice. Every heart beat, every breath taken, belonged to him. "Marvin, please! Please. Don't do this!" I begged as it sunk in. I could feel the first tears roll down my face. "I'm in love with you!

"Just stop!" Marvin said as he turned to trudge away.

"Did you hear me?" I asked as I rushed him, grabbing his arm. As his head spun around to look at me, I peered into his eyes. "I love you. Forever and a day!"

"Nothing you can say will change my mind," Marvin harshly stated. He looked resigned to his chosen path. "I'm moving on without you." Pulling his arm from my grip he coldly continued. "I don't want to be tempted to get into anymore trouble. I'm doing this for my family."

"You're letting them come between us?" I mumbled while attempting to wipe away the tears streaming down my face. "Don't you think they want you to be happy?"

Marvin stared eye to eye with me. "In life, you make choices. I am choosing my family because my appearing before the Council would crush them."

I placed my hands on his chest as tears began to roll down my face. "Please, don't do this," I sobbed. "I'll do whatever it takes to make this right. Please Marvin, don't do this."

He took a deep breath, grabbed my wrists in his hands, and held them away from his chest. "It's over."

"What happened last night that could possibly make you do this?" I demanded in a shaky voice. "I don't buy it was our venturing outside the dome!"

He released my wrists spouting, "Give it a rest! You already know what last night was about."

"I don't know," I disagreed as I wiped my tears on the back of my hand. I followed him to stand before the window.

"Yes you do," he growled revealing a hint of true annoyance with me.

Great, now he sounded like Professor Zirak. Remembering nothing about yourself while everyone around you had answers they wouldn't share with you could be very tiresome. "You know why the Dweller attacked us?" I questioned as I ran my hand down his back.

"Yes, I now know," Marvin said as he flinched and moved away from my touch. His hand found its way to his forehead. "I guess I knew all along. I simply didn't interpret what I was seeing."

"You knew all along?" I questioned while holding my chest and stepping back. "What have you been hiding?"

"I saw you once prior to meeting you that first day at work," He exclaimed as he looked away.

"What!" I half yelled feeling suddenly unable to breath. This blow hurt because I had confided in him. He knew how important finding my past was to me. The overwhelming feeling of betrayal swept over me. "Why did you not tell me?"

"I was somewhere I shouldn't have been," Marvin paused appearing to be deep in thought.

"Was I alone?" I demanded as the full sting sunk in. "Who was I with?"

"It doesn't matter," he nonchalantly replied.

"It does matter to me!" I screeched as I backed further away from him. "Well then, tell me what was I doing?"

"It doesn't matter," Marvin casually replied.

I couldn't hold back the tears or help spit out, "You let me go on and on about not remembering… about my family… I trusted you."

My hurt must have been visible as he crossed the space between us. His voice softened and he genuinely said, "I'm sorry." Then as if a switch had been flipped he intently added, "It's in the past and I'm done looking back." He paused sharing the look of sorrow Rhett had across his face when I entered the house. "The best thing for you is too move on."

Move on? Where would I go from here? The internal struggle was instant. How could I forgive him for not telling me? However, could I hold this against him when I couldn't live without him?

"You're foolish to think our love could last," Marvin coldly interrupted.

Foolish or not, my love for him would never change. "I will love you… forever and a day," I sobbed as my legs began to quiver.

Marvin shook his head with clenched fists and muttered, "My life is ruined!"

Rhett strolled into the room and Marvin promptly stepped back from me. Rhett had probably been listening and was attempting to end our conversation. "Elizabeth, may I escort you safely back to The Hall of Knowledge?"

"No, I can make my own way back," I snapped at him as if he were the one that betrayed me, the one that had crushed my heart. I wiped my tears on the back of my hand and tried desperately to pull myself together in front of Rhett.

"You shouldn't wander around by yourself," Marvin said under his breath.

"What difference does it really make to you at this point," I threw out while doing my best to keep my voice steady. "I ruined your life!"

Rhett shot Marvin a glance like he had said too much and then stepped towards me saying, "Marvin, I will walk her back."

I wasn't three and there was no need for anyone to see me back. I threw my hands up and stormed down the hall, out the door, and up the cracked sidewalk. Rhett jogged to catch up as I began the trek down Dogwood Trail towards the park. I felt content to ignore him as I desperately tried to breathe deeply in an attempt to control the tears welled up in my eyes. As they made their way down my cheek, I tried to quickly brush them away. I had no desire to cry in Rhett presence. However, I was having no success.

"She looks really upset," I heard Dustin say in my mind.

I scanned my surroundings, relieved in the knowledge I could always hear Dustin's thoughts when he was near.

"What are you looking for?" Rhett asked breaking the silence.

"Nothing really," I stated as I felt myself smile. Dustin was perched on a bench, under a tree. I once again wiped my cheeks on the back of my hands and inhaled a deep breath. "Dustin," I yelled as I waved him over.

"Rhett, have you ever met Dustin?" I asked while I watched Dustin sprint towards us smirking.

"Umm… Never been introduced. Is he a friend of yours?" Rhett asked.

"Elizabeth, I see the smile on your face but you look…" Dustin started. He raised his hand to brush the remaining wetness from my cheek. I glanced at Rhett who looked a little aghast at him brushing my cheek.

"What did they do to her?" I heard him ask with a small sigh.

Turning my focus back to Dustin, I interrupted, "Never mind how I look. I would like you to meet Rhett."

"Hello, nice to meet you. I am Dustin Farris," Dustin stated while extending his hand to shake Rhett's. I couldn't help recall my own introduction to Dustin and how he refused to shake my hand claiming he didn't like to shake hands. How odd…

"Very nice to meet you Dustin," stated Rhett as he clearly hesitated to shake Dustin's hand.

"She has something up her sleeve," I heard in my mind as he stared at me.

"Well, you see Dustin…," I hesitated. Now was my only chance to shake my escort. "Rhett didn't want me to walk alone. He felt obligated to see me home."

"That was very considerate of you to want to see Elizabeth home," Dustin stated while looking at Rhett as if they both perceived something I did not.

"But that's the problem," I stated once again catching Dustin's attention. "Rhett is so busy. I was wondering if you might walk me to the Hall of Knowledge. Rhett could then conclude his obligation was filled since I would be in capable hands."

"I see, trying to ditch her escort," I heard in my head.

I fought the urge to smile. Dustin sometimes amazed me with his understanding.

"No, I don't mind to walk you back," Rhett insisted as he stepped towards me.

Dustin seemed to ignore Rhett's comment, "I would be delighted to accompany you." He then offered his arm for me to take.

"Thank you," I sheepishly said as I took his arm while glancing between the smiling Dustin and the stunned Rhett.

As Rhett disappeared from sight, Dustin looked at me, "What was all of that about?"

It was futile to attempt to hide my tears under Dustin's stare which felt as if he saw right through me. The thought of Marvin and I caused a tear to roll down my face. "Rhett is Marvin's uncle."

"So?" Dustin asked while focusing intently on me and brushing my tear away.

The words tumbled out, "Marvin no longer wants to see me! He said…" I cried out as a deep sadness overwhelming me. "He said I ruined his life!" That was all it took. I could hear myself sobbing uncontrollably.

"If I get my hands on him," I heard Dustin growl in his head as he pulled me close to him wrapping me in his arms. "I wish I could tell her, convince her that it will be okay." His hand rubbed my back in a consoling manner as we stood and I cried into Dustin's chest. "Ruined his life. The nerve of him. He was never strong enough for her."

When my tears had lessened, he once again wiped my face. We then traipsed in silence on our slow trek back to The Hall of Knowledge. I leaned over against him as his hand circled my waist. Standing so close, I couldn't help but inhale Dustin's scent. It was a sweeping, relaxing mist that swept over my body. I never appreciated someone's silent presence as much as I did this morning. To my surprise, he guided me through The Hall of Knowledge and all the way back to Keeper House. This left no doubt in my mind that his catty girlfriend, Tiffany, would be informed about this. All the Tiffany spies we passed stopped to gawk. Once inside the door, he rounded the corner and led me up the staircase.

I couldn't help but inquire, "How do you know where you are going?"

Dustin looked over at me with a smirk, "I was trained in Keeper House."

Before I could ask anything else, we halted at the second landing.

"Look what the cat drug in," Destiny teased while appearing stunned at the sight of Dustin standing with me.

"Go find Tilly," Dustin demanded in a stern voice.

"Why?" Destiny disagreeably retorted.

"Because, I don't belong on the girl's floor," Dustin coldly answered.

"Hmm…" Destiny hummed as she backed down the hall with big eyes taking in Dustin's arm around my waist.

"You shouldn't be here," Shannon stated from the doorway to her room.

"Like I care what you think," Dustin sarcastically stated in his head.

"Stuff it," I managed to croak out.

Shannon annoyingly rolled her eyes. Beyond her, Tilly's head popped out from our door. She did a double take with her head shaking negatively back and fourth over the surprise. Destiny followed on her heels as she made her way down the hall.

"Are you okay?" Tilly asked while intently glancing at Dustin and his arm wrapped around me. As her eyes grew bigger with the sight, so did the bubbles she was blowing.

"I'm fine," I stated as I stepped away from Dustin.

"Like I buy that!" Tilly sarcastically said under her breath.

Ignoring my bubble blowing friend, I placed my hand on Dustin's arm saying, "Thank you."

"Anytime," Dustin's mind stated.

He leaned forward, looked me directly in the eye, and whispered, "The way I see it… The only thing ruining his life is not having you in it. He is foolish."

A slow grin crossed his face as Tilly firmly grabbed my hand and roughly pulled me down the hall.

I could hear the other girls whispering, "What did he say to her? What did he say?"

As we neared the door of our room, Tilly glanced over her shoulder and mumbled, "He's still standing there."

I followed her gaze to see Dustin watching us. Tilly jerked my arm forcing me to enter the open door of our room. Destiny was directly behind me as Tilly warned her, "Get lost! You're not welcome in our room this morning."

Destiny appeared angry and countered, "I just wanted..."

"Out!" Tilly firmly shouted as she pointed towards the hall. Once she began to shut the door, Destiny was forced out. As Tilly spun around, I was her focus. "How in the world did you end up with Dustin in Keeper House with his arm around you? What are you thinking? Do you have any idea the storm that's going to brew when Tiffany finds out?" Tilly wandered over to her chair and plopped down. "It appeared he was whispering sweet nothings to you!"

"He sort of was," I admitted to Tilly's look of horror and gaping mouth.

"Someone I know is foolish for not having you in their life?" Tilly asked rolling her eyes. This is just great Elizabeth! If Dustin was talking about himself, Tiffany is going to slaughter you! Have you considered Marvin?"

"Dustin's words were a friend sort of comment," I countered.

"Friend," Tilly repeated. "This is bad! Really bad!" Then deep in her thoughts, she murmured, "I need time to think." Her mind seemed to be deep in thought as she then began to loudly and methodically chew her gum.

I pulled the only things of Marvin's that remained from the closet. I held to my heart his T-shirt and sweats combo from the fateful night when Tilly dressed me up and Marvin found me looking like a clown in her skirt and high heels. I felt destined that night to find Dustin. Instead, I found true love. I found my soul mate, Marvin.

Tears once again fell down my cheeks. Tilly from her place across the room asked, "What are you doing? Changing into sweats? Then she noticed I was changing into Marvin's clothes. "Wow, I hadn't considered Marvin. What are you going to tell him?"

Internally my mind screamed, "Nothing." I began to change my clothes thinking I could not function with the way my heart ached for Marvin. Numbness spread over my body with the realization he was gone.

Ignoring Tilly, I could hear her jump up asking, "What about class?"

I turned to face her with my tear stained face and choked out, "I can't go to class today."

"What happened this morning? Where did you go?" Tilly asked as she began to pace between our beds while popping her gum. As if a light bulb suddenly went off she inquired, "Has something happened to Marvin."

I crawled into my bed and tried to inhale what scent of Marvin that remained on his clothing and refused to talk. At the moment, I couldn't hold a conversation with Tilly. I buried my face in my pillow and let the tears flow.

I wouldn't have noticed Tilly excusing herself if it weren't for the sound of the door closing behind her. With her absence, the constant knocking on our door began. I ignored it. My mind kept repeating, "Could I ever love again?" Marvin and I were soul mates. The void in my chest was beginning to ache. I sobbed into my pillow. My soul felt numb and shattered. Not only due to loosing Marvin, I was crushed with his deception. All that was left was to drown myself in my tears.

After awhile, Tilly returned. Her unusual quiet demeanor forced me to look at her.

"I'm so sorry about Marvin," Tilly sympathetically said as she sat on the edge of my bed and loudly chomped her gum.

"I guess Dustin is still out there?" I assumed out loud.

"In Professor Zirak's office," Tilly answered while nodding. "He told me."

Caught off guard, I returned, "What is he doing in the Professor's office?"

"Hello," Tilly said like I missed the obvious. "Dustin went beyond the common area. Zirak's idiotic rules." Tilly mimicked the Professor, "Rule Number Two, guests are only to be in the common area of this house."

I couldn't help but smile at my friend who could lift anyone's spirits.

"I'm here for you," Tilly reassured me.

"Marvin says I ruined his life," I blurted out as another tear rolled down my face.

"What?" Tilly questioned as she jumped up and once again began to pace between the beds.

"You heard me," I stated as she dug in her pocket for a fresh piece of gum.

"Now Dustin's comment makes sense," Tilly said while chomping her gum. I watched her pace back and forth for a long time. Eventually she plopped on her bed disagreeing, "You didn't ruin his life. Do you really think he meant that?"

I began to answer, "Well, he must…"

"Deep down?" Tilly interrupted me. "Think about it. He offered himself up as bait for the Dwellers. He lured them away from you so that you would be safe last night." When I didn't have a response she continued, "I don't understand it. However, the best medicine is to get back out there and enjoy life. When Marvin comes crawling back, and he will, show him you are strong and moving on. A little jealousy is good for a man's soul!"

That was classic Tilly. The answer to any problem was a date.

CHAPTER TWO

Tilly

Who could miss the annoying sound of taping at the window or the sight of Trevor hanging from the rope ladder? Although the ladder was the only way to escape our curfew and this prison, tonight wasn't the best night for an adventure out or an unwelcome visit. Even if the visitor was Trevor, I was exhausted and emotionally drained. Consoling Elizabeth was out of my realm. It was no mistake that I didn't have a lot of girls who were my friends. Who wanted to deal with their drama? I slid the window open asking, "What?"

"May I come in?" Trevor asked.

"Whatever... Just don't wake her," I said as I stepped aside and plopped down on the end of my bed knowing that my statement was crazy. Elizabeth was a sound sleeper and could sleep through a tornado. Even her heart break wouldn't bother her now that she was asleep.

Trevor swiftly dropped through the window and knelt in front of me. He pushed my hair out of my face. "Are you okay?"

"Are you saying I look less than perfect?" I sarcastically retorted in a huff.

Trevor grinned at me before answering, "Of course not. I would never..."

I smiled to myself. Trevor would always be mine and wrapped around my little finger. Even on my worst day, he couldn't resist me. "I'm fine," I interrupted him as I pushed his hand away.

"Is it true?" Eddie asked as he too slid through the window.

"If you're asking about Marvin breaking up with her, yes it's true," I growled as I picked up my back pack from the foot of my bed and begun to dig for a fresh stick of calming gum. Marvin was toast! Crossing Elizabeth was the same as crossing me. One way or another... he would pay. Toast!

"So that is why Dustin brought her home," Trevor interrupted the ranting in my head as he stood and retrieved a piece out of his own pocket.

"Hold on," I replied as I let the bag drop to the ground. "You didn't know about Marvin?"

"Nope," Eddie replied. "All we know is that the grape vine says Dustin brought a distraught Elizabeth home."

"Not just brought her home," Trevor paused as he handed me the gum. "He came up the stairs and stepped into the girl's hall with his arm around her."

"He did not come down the girl's hall," I disagreed. Gossip! The cackling hens loved to spread drama and gossip. Only this time it was untrue. "They stopped at the end and waited for Destiny to get me."

"That's not what Destiny is spreading around," Trevor seriously cautioned.

"Destiny! Of course, where else would that lie come from," I growled. "She has some nerve. I'm going to strangle our no good, nosy neighbor."

"She must be bummed," Eddie stated as he eyed Elizabeth and appeared baffled. "Why would Marvin or anyone dump Elizabeth?"

"It's a long story," I replied under my breath as I threw my hands up.

"We have all night," Trevor stated while peering intently at me and plopping into our comfy arm chair under the open window.

"I'm just relieved she stopped crying," Eddie said as he stood staring at Elizabeth.

"You could hear?" I asked watching Eddie who seemed out of character for himself. Usually nothing fazed him, so why in the world was this bothering him?

"For awhile," Trevor replied.

"When the sound ceased we figured you had closed the window and that she was beat down," Eddie added.

"She insisted the window be closed," I said. For the night, I had abandoned my need for calming, cool night air and had reluctantly given into Elizabeth's window paranoia. She finally had managed to cage me in this cell of a room.

"I want you to level with me," Trevor seriously stated as he sat forward in his chair.

"Of course Dad," I sarcastically replied back. "Let me spill my guts. Where should I start?"

Eddie chuckled a little as Trevor gave him a small glare before returning his attention to me. "What is going on?"

"I've told you exactly what went on," I replied as I shrugged and purposely blew a big, pink bubble. There was no guilt in not finishing my sentence… I did tell him what went on this morning. My gut screamed that at all cost, I should leave him out of the loop about last night.

"You never know what is lurking around," Trevor sighed clearly not buying my innocent act.

"Bro, it's all about the dark side," Eddie said in a pestering manner.

My eyes flashed from Eddie to Trevor. Before last night, I would have thought Trevor was spending too much time with Elizabeth and that she was rubbing off on him. She was the most paranoid person I knew. Caught a little off guard, I asked Trevor, "Are you worried about Dwellers?"

"No," Trevor too quickly responded. "Are you?"

"Don't let him fool you," Eddie disagreed. "He talks all night long."

Trevor often chattered in his sleep on the Earth Plane divulging situations that bothered him. If he thought it while he was sleeping, it came out his mouth. If he was spouting about Dwellers in his sleep, then he was worried. Since I understood the man under the skin, he couldn't play it off with me. Some things never change and he knew more than he was letting on. Since when did he keep secrets from me?

Trevor glared at Eddie saying, "I've told you..."

"Dude," Eddie interrupted. "You spout about Dwellers walking amongst us every night."

Trevor knew. I blew a big bubble as the realization hit me that I wouldn't be able to skate around this one.

"Tonight isn't about me," Trevor glared at Eddie for saying too much. Eddie shrugged and went back to watching Elizabeth sleep. Trevor sat back in his chair peering at me. "Let's have it. You went out last night with Marvin and Elizabeth. Today they break up and Dustin brings her home? I must be missing a major piece of the puzzle."

I purposely blew another perfect pink bubble and popped it. Since I understood him as he understood me, there was no way out of this conversation. "Well, there's no need to loose your mind."

Eddie's attention focused on me as he pulled the chair from under my makeup table and turned it around to face me. He loved gossip and was worse than any of the girls combined.

"We used our destination cards," I said to Trevor's huge frown.

"We weren't going to share them with anyone outside of our little group," Trevor reprimanded.

"Don't give me grief for Marvin knowing," I retorted. "Remember in the beginning we were going to shop them around to everyone." As he stared me down I added, "Remember, the plan was to sell them for favors?"

"She's right," Eddie agreed.

"Until we decided it was best to keep them our secret," Trevor contradicted me.

"He's right," Eddie agreed playing both sides.

"Elizabeth is my best friend and I thought the square was here for the long haul," I defended. "How could I have known what a rotten square he was? Do you think I could foresee their break up?"

"Where did you go last night?" Trevor asked steering the conversation back to what he wanted to know.

"To Anthony's house at Lakeland," I admitted bracing for the undeniable fall out which was to immediately come. Clearly Trevor was green with envy. Who could blame him? I was a goddess.

"That Humling is not good for you!" Trevor half yelled making Eddie and I both jump. The jealous fool was wearing his heart on his sleeve again.

"Shh," I hushed Trevor. "You know better than to tell me who I can and can't date."

"That's a bogus thing to say to him," Eddie immediately chimed in.

"I've already lectured her about the Humling," Trevor spouted to Eddie. "You know reasoning with Tilly is like talking to a wall."

"Dude," Eddie said shaking his head.

"Talking to a wall?" I repeated feeling the tips of my ears beginning to burn as I loudly popped another bubble.

"You won't listen to me anyway. Isn't that right?" Trevor pointedly asked. With my non-response he relaxed back in the chair obviously feeling he had won that small battle. "Humling's shouldn't be trusted."

Back to the fairy tale about Humlings not being able to be trusted. Anthony was no less trustworthy than Trevor. Whether I could make Trevor see that or not, I knew… "I won't be seeing Anthony any time soon," I said under my breath.

A cocky grin crossed Trevor's face.

He was misguided to believe I was not seeing Anthony due to him. "It has absolutely nothing to do with anything you've said," I adamantly interjected. "I can't go back to Lakeland because we were attacked there by Dwellers last night."

Trevor sprung up from his chair and ran his fingers through his hair before questioning, "How many?"

"Only one that I saw," I replied stunned at his uncharacteristic reaction. Trevor's mind always collected all the facts before returning a well thought out response.

"But you thought there were more?" Trevor questioned.

"Yeah," I replied watching him once again ruffle his hair with his fingers. "Marvin thought so too."

"There walking all around us," Eddie mindlessly hummed with a new found realization that maybe Trevor's nighttime rants weren't crazy.

"How did they attack you?" Trevor methodically asked as if he were a detective collecting the facts.

"They attacked Elizabeth," I stated as my mind shifted to how helpless Elizabeth was. "His hand was griping her arm and she couldn't move. It was like she was paralyzed."

"Couldn't move at all?" Eddie asked in dismay.

"She couldn't lift a finger," I replied. "Even had trouble breathing."

"How did she get free?" Trevor asked.

I closed my eyes and took a deep breath. I couldn't tell Trevor that I flirted with the Dweller as a distraction. Actually, I completely wrapped my arms around him. Even the Dweller found me breathtaking. He was male after all. As my eyes opened, peering at Trevor I knew, maybe a little editing was in order.

"Mathilda…," Trevor stated in a firm demanding voice.

"Mathilda?" I repeated.

"How did she get free?" Trevor again questioned.

"If you must know Dad," I began in defiance. Calling me Mathilda. Who did he think he was? "I tickled him."

"You were that close to a Dweller!" Trevor exclaimed with a new found, pure panic behind his eyes.

"Trevor," I reprimanded. "Don't forget you are standing in my room! Be quiet! Let me add that I'm not scared of a Dweller. Remember, I married one on the Earth Plane."

"And you shouldn't forget he caused you a lifetime of trouble," Trevor added. "I don't like you being up close and personal with a Dweller here at Home."

"Did he follow you?" Eddie asked.

"We escaped across the lake in a boat," I answered as I nervously blew another bubble.

"A boat? At night?" Eddie returned totally shocked.

"You crossed the lake?" Trevor asked in disbelief.

Trevor knew me as well as I knew him. The water did terrify me. Its icy and cold darkness called to me. My Dweller husband had failed to drown me in a lake. Every since then, all bodies of water knew they were cheated from taking my life when I was on the Earth Plane. However, last night I had no choice but to place my trust in Marvin and Elizabeth to see me across the icy, black water.

"For you to cross the lake there must have been no other option," Trevor unhappily concluded.

"Technically there was another option," I disagreed.

"You can't be serious," Trevor threw out as his hands ruffled his hair once more. "Face them?" To my shrug he added, "Mixing with that Humling brought you all this trouble."

"Actually Marvin sent us with Anthony to the neighboring subway station," I stated feeling highly irritated with Trevor's digs at Anthony. Jealous or not, Trevor had no right to judge Anthony.

"Marvin left you?" Trevor questioned in apparent disbelief.

"He rowed back across the lake to meet them," I answered. Watching the square row the small boat to meet the Dwellers as a distraction had given me a new respect for Marvin. My gut screamed last night that there was nothing he wouldn't do for Elizabeth. How was my radar so off?

"He must have been amped cause that's crazy," Eddie chimed in with big eyes.

"I know," I admitted. "That is why I don't get Marvin breaking up with her today. If he would face Dwellers for her last night, then why the sudden change of heart?"

"There's more to that story," Trevor said under his breath. "You've seen Marvin today?"

"No," I replied. "Elizabeth went by herself. She says he's beat up and looks awful."

"Huh," Trevor said. "As far as your concerned, you are not going back to Lakeland because of the Dwellers?"

"I don't want to face that Dweller again," I said as I shivered. He couldn't help but stare at me, but I would never forget how cold his stare was.

"What did he look like?" Trevor asked as his angry demeanor suddenly turned to concern with my apparent shiver.

"Tall, ratty, curly brown hair, pale with a crooked grin," I answered.

"You hadn't seen him before?" Trevor questioned.

I looked away. Of all the things for Trevor to ask. Of course he would ask exactly what I didn't want to tell him.

"Was he the same one from the Hall of Records on the Humling side?"

Trevor asked as he concluded this to be true.

"What?" Eddie asked.

"Remember when Elizabeth and Tilly adventured out the first night of our training," Trevor asked to Eddie's nod. "They thought they were being followed."

"Narly," Eddie stated.

"Have you ever seen him in the dome?" Trevor asked.

"No," I replied. Luckily, I could leave out the fact that Elizabeth had twice. Trevor should know to order his words better around me.

"We should discontinue using the destination cards," Trevor concluded.

"Sure you can," I replied.

"Tilly, it's not safe outside the dome," Trevor shook his head. "Use your brain! He stood again and appeared agitated. "I simply won't make anymore cards for you. Then you won't have any choice."

"Trevor Stillholm, you can't stop me from leaving the dome," I defiantly replied. "I can use the subway, swipe a destination card from my mother, or simply ask Barrett for one."

"Who could forget about bow tie freak," Trevor said as he threw his hands up.

"Good one," Eddie stated with a smirk.

"He spends all his time outside the dome," Trevor said as if the thought of Barrett disgusted him.

Although, I didn't have a lot of romantic feelings towards Barrett, he was another sore subject for Trevor. He was totally jealous. Well… "At least he's not a Humling," I replied.

"No, he's much better," Trevor replied. "He's old!"

"Bro, I think it's time to bail," Eddie said as he stood. "You're about to launch yourself into another chick problem."

"Great idea," Trevor instantly agreed. Caving to Eddie caught both of us off guard. "You go on up. I'm going to play some ball down at the court."

"Again?" Eddie asked.

"Play ball?" I questioned.

"His new past time," Eddie shrugged. "Basketball at night."

"Tonight, I need to blow off a little steam," Trevor said as he glanced my way. "Not to mention, I need to formulate a plan as to how to handle Tiffany."

"Tiffany?" Eddie questioned.

"She's going to loose her mind over Dustin," Trevor stated the obvious. "It's inevitable that we are all going to pay."

"We're not going to let Tiffany get to Elizabeth," Eddie firmly stated.

What were they talking about? They were both my followers and always had been. Trevor was uncharacteristically standing up to me while Eddie was unusually protective over Elizabeth. He was still staring at her. "I'll worry about Elizabeth," I said with a sense of finality while waving Eddie away from my sleeping friend. Once again, she proved she could sleep through anything.

"I have one more question," Trevor said as he moved to look me directly in the eyes. "If Marvin hadn't broken up with Elizabeth, you didn't intend to tell me, did you?"

I didn't say anything as my eyes spoke the truth. No, I wouldn't have said a word. For the first time in a long while I saw true disappointment in Trevor's eyes before he proceeded towards the open window. "Trevor…"

"Awkward," Eddie hummed as he waited for his turn to straddle my window. He peered over his shoulder one more time at Elizabeth. "Do you think…?" Eddie pointed between himself and Elizabeth.

"You and Elizabeth what?" I responded.

Trevor disappeared out the window shaking his head while mumbling, "Dude."

"Date," Eddie matter of fact stated.

"Not unless you learn how to use a fork," I responded in utter disbelief.

I watched as Eddie shrugged and crawled out the window.

Trevor was walking across the lawn which surrounded The Hall of Knowledge when I peered out. I really disliked that gut wrenching feeling that had swept over me. Guilt. My irritation over Trevor's nagging jealousy was nothing compared to the feeling of disappointing or hurting Trevor.

CHAPTER THREE

Elizabeth

I was still in bed and didn't want to face the world without Marvin. So, I decided to not attend class again. Professor Zirak told everyone I was ill after visiting me in my room. I was convinced he must know the real reason. However, I don't understand why he is going along with my walk through sadness and seclusion. This was day two of my missing classes. The topic of the week, according to Tilly, was how to help your Humling cross over. Professor Presnell lectured on the topic yesterday. Professor Kegley was lecturing today on turning the small bound recorded sections, which the Keepers maintained during the Humlings earth life, into the final chapter. It would then be shelved at the Hall of Records. Under normal circumstances I would have found this interesting. Tilly told me I could borrow her notes. However, I grasped how few notes, if any, she normally took. It would be essential to get a copy of Trevor's class notes.

Tilly had left exhausted due to our staying up most of the night. For a second night, I needed her shoulder to cry on and her ear to sing my sob song into. She really was my best friend, letting me vent and cry until it was all out. Today I had an agenda that I felt certain Tilly would not be happy about. I was going to find Marvin. I knew in my gut that we were meant to be together. I couldn't explain why Marvin had told me I ruined his life. I simply didn't believe that we weren't meant for each other. If my disappointment repeated itself, I would need to find the strength to move on. However, the longing for Marvin would never subside.

The landing seemed very quite and still. Usually it was filled with the muffled sounds of others exiting from their rooms. Thinking back, it seemed Dustin arriving at our landing was a topic of conversation with everyone itching to ask me directly about it. Tilly stood guard for most of the last two days, successfully turning them all away. I hid under my blanket enjoying the peace. I really did need to retreat, just to be alone. It was late when I finally cried myself to sleep.

Startled, I heard a knock at the door. Slowly, it pushed open with Dustin saying, "Good morning," from my doorway.

I sat straight up and could not believe the grin on his face or that he was standing there.

"Interesting," I heard his mind say.

I instantly knew what was interesting, my disheveled look. "Umm, what are you doing here?" I asked while pulling the covers up under my chin and trying to run my fingers through my hair.

"Messy hair in the morning," I heard in my head.

"You were so upset yesterday, I wanted to make sure you were okay," he replied.

"Why didn't you wait like a normal person for me to come down?" I questioned, annoyed.

"I did, but you never came down," he replied. "Then, Tilly informed me you were sick and shouldn't be bothered."

"A white lie," I heard his mind say.

"You still shouldn't be on the girls landing," I responded. "If Professor Zirak finds you, I will be in trouble."

"All the trouble she gets into, and this is what she is worried about," I heard his mind say.

"You might be in trouble as well," I countered his thought.

"Would you like me to go?" He questioned.

I thought for a moment, No. But then I remembered the reason he should go, Tiffany. "And what would Tiffany think if you were found here," I asked.

"Wouldn't matter," I heard his mind say.

"I think we are in the same boat," Dustin replied with a grin as he came in and shut the door.

"Same boat?" I questioned and thought for a moment. "Did she hear about you bringing me home yesterday?"

"Yes, and she was extremely angry," Dustin replied not looking bothered at all, but extremely happy. "She dumped me!"

"Oh happy day!" I heard his mind sing.

"Sorry," I replied but understood it really wasn't necessary.

"No worries," Dustin smiled as he dug a small brown bag out of his coat pocket. "I brought you some ginger candy."

"Why?" I asked off the top of my head.

"I thought the sweets might cheer you up," Dustin said with a shrug as he tossed me the bag.

"Dustin, I must be honest with you," I began under his stare. "Today, I am going to find Marvin. I just know we are meant..."

Dustin interrupted me, "You can't do that."

"He won't take you back," I heard his mind say.

"Give me a good reason why?" I questioned.

"He's a jerk and you could do better," Dustin said in his head.

I could see him trying to think of something else to say when, "He dumped you." Dustin set on the end of my bed as he continued, "Someone who hurt you so badly isn't right for you."

"Then what do you suggest I do today," I asked.

"Besides pretending to be sick?" He inquired with a grin.

"Yes," I replied.

"I have one errand to run, which should give you time to get ready," Dustin started. "After that, let's go out to the lake."

I thought for a moment. How could I possibly let him derail my plan? "Dustin, I can't. I really appreciate the invitation, but I just can't. I'm sorry."

"Eventually you will," Dustin voice rang in my head.

"Okay, may I ask you again tomorrow?" He asked. "A rain check?"

"Tomorrow," I repeated. "I will be back in class. Won't you have work?"

"You are more important than work," I heard his mind say.

"I will continue to ask the next day and the day after that," Dustin responded as he jumped up. He turned to peer into my eyes continuing, "Eventually you will say yes and I have a lot of patience."

"You may need it," I responded.

"Let me know when I can be your slave for the day," Dustin said as he turned and left the room.

Tilly

All I felt were hands shoving me from behind and an irate voice questioning, "Where is she?"

After unexpectedly face planting the wall, I swirled around to see Tiffany with Janelle supporting her in flank position. "What the hell?" I spewed at them as I felt my face go flushed and my temper sky rocketed. "What was that about?"

Tiffany shot daggers at me with fury in her eyes. She charged me again screaming, "Your boyfriend stealing tramp of a friend."

I braced for the hit and batted her hands away.

"I'm only going to ask this nicely one more time," Tiffany spewed. "Where is she?"

I leaned in face to face and answered, "That's none of your business." I couldn't help the giggle that escaped me as I checked out her look. Tiffany was unkept today with no makeup, wrinkled clothes, and frizzy hair. "Couldn't find a brush today?"

I couldn't help but giggle. Then I giggled a second time and then a third.

"This is no laughing matter," Tiffany spewed as her hands curled into fists. In a flash she lunged at me, swung her arm around to hit me, missed, and then grabbed my hair. She yanked with all her might making me gasp with pain. I wrapped her long, curly, black hair around my hand and returned the favor.

Tiffany groaned a little and screeched, "She took Dustin!"

"Fight! Fight! Fight!" A few boys were chanting. "Cat fight!"

I clawed Tiffany's arm with my well manicured nails as I returned, "Elizabeth is not interested in Dustin!"

"Fight! Cat fight!" I could hear the crowd yelling.

The pain of my nails made Tiffany let go of my hair as her hand flew to her arm. I jerked her hair hard forcing Tiffany to lean over.

"Her boyfriend dumped her and she moved in on mine!" Tiffany countered as her hand opened and she slapped me across the face.

As my face stung, two sets of strong hands were pulling at my arms. I didn't let go of the final strands of hair which were intertwined around my fingers. I heard them break and rip from Tiffany's head. Two sets of warm hands suddenly drew me back with force and I realized it was Trevor and Eddie. Trevor ran his fingers over my cheek which was throbbing as Eddie released my arm.

As I scanned the crowd encircling us, I noticed they were all standing stunned and whispering amongst themselves. I honed in on Tiffany who was being held by Rodger and one of his cronies.

She struggled against them spouting, "Let go of me! I want to finish her off!"

"Finish me off?" I huffed offended. "Clearly, I had the upper hand." I taunted her by holding up her long strands of hair still in my clenched hand.

"Ladies, what is going on?" My mother inquired as she pushed her way into the circle. I wondered what in the world she was doing here.

Tiffany jerked free from her captors and flung herself into my mother's arms. "Mrs. Bradford, I'm so glad to see you!" Fake tears started rolling down her cheek as my mother embraced her. "She attacked me again!"

"You're a piece of work!" I spewed. "Who pushed who first?"

"Look at my hair in her hand," Tiffany countered swinging the conversation back in her direction.

"Yes," I replied as I held my hand out in-front of me letting her hair drop to the floor. "I can defend myself!"

"Mathilda," my mother reprimanded.

I pulled my arm free from Trevor as I said with exasperation, "Of course, take her side."

"Mrs. Bradford wouldn't dream of not taking your side," Trevor piped up from behind me. My head swiveled to look at him. Had he lost his mind? Did he not remember this was the Queen he was talking about, the mother who would disown me if she could? Trevor was intently staring at my mother. I followed his gaze and she was peering back at him.

"What is all of this about?" My mother questioned.

"Tilly's friend, the tramp, stole my boyfriend," Tiffany replied while pretending to wipe away tears.

"If this is about Elizabeth, I don't understand why the two of you are having a disagreement," my mother stated as she rolled her eyes.

"Disagreement?" An unknown girl questioned.

"It was a cat fight," piano boy interjected.

"Tiffany dear, anyone who would be interested in Elizabeth," my mother paused. You could see her ordering her words. "You can do better." My mother gave her a motherly hug. She peered at me saying, "I don't think this disagreement has anything to do with you."

"Anyone who threatens Elizabeth, threatens me," I stated.

"You shouldn't choose that rough girl over a friend you've had since child-hood," my mother reprimanded me. "I expect the two of you to apologize to each other." My mother gave Tiffany another motherly hug and smile. Then she peered at me demanding, "Now!"

If my mother wanted the perfect show, a perfect show she would get! "Oh, yes. I'm so sorry," I replied as I moved to embrace Tiffany. Buried in her frizzy hair I whispered, "Bother Elizabeth and I will take you down."

She returned the whisper, "It's on!"

She gave me a devilish grin as I pulled back questioning, "Friends?"

"Of course," Tiffany replied with her arms across her chest.

"See," my mother said as her hands clapped together. "All's well that ends well." She then surveyed the gaping mouths around the circle. They too knew she was choosing to ignore the obvious. Tiffany and I were enemies. "Everyone, go to training," my mother demanded. "Right now!" She waved for the crowd to disburse.

I moved around Tiffany and my mother. As I passed Rodger and Janelle, she grabbed my arm. She leaned over and whispered, "I feel the same way about Tiffany. Mess with her and you mess with me."

"Like you scare me," I huffed back at her.

"Do I?" Rodger asked as he stood in an imposing and threatening manner.

I playfully ran my fingers down his chest, "Of course, your little crush on me is terrifying."

"Shut up!" Janelle demanded as her skin instantly flushed . "You're going down."

Feeling Trevor standing protectively close to me, I knew him and Eddie followed on my heels. Once away from the crowd, I glanced over at Trevor and said, "Thank you."

He grabbed my arm and pulled me to the wall. After giving Eddie a get lost look he focused on me saying, "Would you expect any less than my having your back?"

"You weren't happy with me last night," I countered watching Eddie pull his hoodie over his head as he walked away.

"It's true. However, lately I can say I don't like all of your decisions," Trevor reasoned. "And I wish you would tell me everything. Nothing you could do will ever chase me away. I'll always be there for you." His hand gently stroked my stinging cheek. With a sigh suddenly he held up a stick of gum for me as he said, "Okay?"

"Okay," I replied as I snatched the calming gum with a smile. He would always be wrapped around my little finger.

CHAPTER FOUR

Elizabeth

I leaned against the wall as the group disbursed from Elephant Room after the morning cheer. The night crew challenged the day crew that they couldn't recover more hangers. The number hovers around nine hundred. As usual, the day crew accepted the challenge, betting dry cleaning of work coats. The usual routine was always maintained within the Department of Ghosts. They called it tradition.

I watched as Tilly bid Andy goodbye with a peck on the lips. I had no idea what she intended to do about him. He was her day puppy and oblivious to her nightly dates with Anthony. Tilly had spent weeks pining away over Andy, while he ignored her. Now Andy wanted Tilly, but she was now obsessed with Anthony. I wasn't even sure it was legal for Tilly to date Anthony! He was a Humling living outside the dome. She was a Keeper and forbidden to leave the dome. Thinking about her revolving love life could make your head spin.

I had my own issues that weren't unlike Tilly's. I had spent weeks dreaming of Dustin before becoming Marvin's girlfriend. Even with dating Marvin, the thought of Dustin intrigued me. He was sensually delicious. His cologne had always drawn me in. Now he and I were free and he was clearly showing interest in me. Only, I no longer had any interest in dating him. The grass isn't greener on the other side.

Marvin was the only one for me. I tried to find him yesterday, only he was nowhere to be found. My heart simply didn't buy his reason for our break up. I was sure of nothing else in my life except that I belonged with Marvin. I was just as certain he felt the same way. It was undeniable. Without him, I would never be whole again.

"Tilly," I could hear Ruthanne calling as she jogged across the Elephant Room towards us.

Tilly turned and muttered under her breath, "What is she doing here?"

Ruthanne came to a stop in front of us, out of breath. She leaned over clutching her chest while breathing deeply. "Harmony. They're meeting right now. Tiffany…"

"Catch your breath," Tilly said as she placed her hand on Ruthanne's back.

Ruthanne took a couple more deep breaths saying, "Your mother, Mrs. Raderton, Presnell, and Tiffany are ordering Professor Kegley to allow Tiffany to take over as conductress."

"Over my dead body!" Tilly instantly spewed.

"Heads up," I warned Tilly as Rhett was closing in.

"Miss Jones, is everything okay?" Rhett asked.

Ruthanne appeared suddenly like a frantic deer caught in headlights. She gulped saying, "Please don't say you saw me here."

Rhett scanned all of us demanding, "Spill the beans."

"Same old thing," Tilly mumbled, clearly in thought.

"Professor Presnell is trying to make Tiffany conductress of Harmony," I explained. "I guess they're meeting right now."

"Where?" Rhett asked.

"The rehearsal room," Ruthanne said looking sick.

"Miss Jones, thank you," Rhett stated catching her off guard. "I don't like injustice. Thank you for bringing this to my attention."

Ruthanne's wide eyes peered at the two of us as Tilly smiled, nodded, and said to Ruthanne, "Go!" When Ruthanne was a few steps away, Tilly told Rhett, "I don't need you to fight my battles."

"Conrad," Rhett called waving over Marvin's father.

Mr. Lagedge focused on me with that same fascinated gaze as he answered Rhett, "Are you ready to get started?"

"Go on without me," Rhett told him. "I'll be along in awhile. Some unexpected business has popped up."

"I didn't ask for your help," Tilly growled as she pushed past Rhett walking towards the lift.

Mr. Lagedge assessed the demeanor between me and Rhett before saying, "Sounds like your morning will be interesting."

"I'll catch up with you," Rhett reiterated as he followed quickly after Tilly.

My standing with Mr. Lagedge was awkward. "You know," I began. "I better catch up with them."

"Tell Marvin hello," Conrad said.

I stopped in my tracks and my eyes flickered to his.

"Yes?" Mr. Lagedge asked expecting who knew what.

"Marvin didn't tell you we aren't seeing each other anymore?" I questioned.

"He didn't," Mr. Lagedge answered now appearing uncomfortable. "You better catch up."

I gave him a faint polite smile as I moved to the lift in a hurry. Marvin neglecting to tell his Dad about our break up baffled me a little since his reason for dumping me was to protect his family.

As I made my way past Rhett's crew, I overheard Jason complaining as he sat to put socks under his sandals, "Man, where is he off too? We need him this morning."

"He's obsessed with those two trainees," Luke responded.

"You heard the change of shift bet," Jason stated. "I want my coat cleaned. We need to focus today, not run after the trainees."

"Don't get your knickers crossed fellas," Billy stated. "If we lose, we'll be sendin' our coats home with Conrad. His Misses will clean them up right."

They all chuckled. I pushed the button for the lift and peeked over my shoulder at Conrad and then at Jason, Luke, and Billy perched outside Rhett's office. Conrad did appear clean and pressed compared to the rest of them. Billy caught me looking. He tipped the brim of his cowboy hat towards me. I smiled and waved bye as I stepped onto the lift.

Elizabeth

I couldn't believe we were all standing lined up shoulder to shoulder in Grand Hall. We were anxiously waiting for Tilly and Tiffany to begin choosing their Harmony choir members. Alternating, they would each make a selection until we were gone. This was the nightmare Rhett negotiated much to everyone's dismay. Well, it was technically less negotiating and more interjecting himself into the process and demanding it go his way. The agreement terms spread like wildfire amongst all the trainees. I wasn't the only one who dreaded Harmony practice this evening. Rhett had single handed made Tiffany, Mrs. Raderton, Mrs. Bradford, Professor Presnell, and Tilly angry. Even Professor Kegley seemed unsure about the plan.

Tiffany and Tilly were up on the stage picking a number between one and ten. Rhett, Professor Presnell, and Mrs. Raderton all agreed upon the number and none of them were budging from their spot to assure fairness.

"Three," Tilly stated.

"Four," Tiffany said.

Rhett had a smile cross his face as Professor Presnell said, "Mrs. Bradford will choose first. The number was two."

Tilly gave us all a reassuring grin as she faced the line of us. Everyone was nervous not wanting to be on Tiffany's team. Tiffany looked pleased with her devilish grin and ready to create havoc.

"Elizabeth," Tilly called to my relief.

Trevor shoved his hands into his pockets as I passed him to hop onto the stage. He must have believed he would be chosen first.

"Who do I pick," Tiffany began as she left the stage to saunter down the row of fellow trainees. Tiffany halted before Trevor questioning, "What did you do for Tilly?"

"You should have picked Trevor," I whispered to Tilly as I watched Tiffany. I was fearful for Trevor.

"I was one of several on the tech team," Trevor stated while rolling his eyes at Tiffany.

"Hmm," Tiffany hummed.

Tilly shook her head, gave me a knowing look, and whispered back to me, "She would have picked you to carry out her revenge on you. Couldn't chance it."

She spun around to peer up at me spewing, "Too bad! My first choice for tonight was already picked."

Tiffany stepped to Ruthanne. "You were the band manager?"

"Yes," Ruthanne answered as she clung to Trevor's arm.

"What exactly did you do?" Tiffany questioned.

"Look who the cat drug in," Tilly whispered as she nudged me with her elbow.

Dustin entered through the doors in the back of Grand Hall. I did my best not to check him out as he took a seat in the back row. The fact he walked through the door seemed to agitate Tiffany. I breathed a sigh of relief at already being picked. Tilly was right.

"I was the coordinator," Ruthanne answered as her eyes flickered to Tilly's.

Poor Ruthanne, she thought Tiffany's changed demeanor was in correlation to her.

"You were the brains then," Tiffany said as she gave Tilly a devilish smile. "Brains under all that red hair."

"Just pick already," I heard an exasperated Dustin in my mind.

"I pick Ruthanne," Tiffany said peering directly up at Tilly. "Sorry, now you'll have to do something other than pick trashy attire."

Poor Ruthanne.

Janelle stood picking her nails as Tilly ignored Tiffany and instantly chose, "Trevor."

"A no brainer," Dustin responded in my head.

Trevor helped Ruthanne onto the stage and then took his place next to me.

Tiffany stopped before piano boy saying, "I choose you …."

"Gregg. My name is Gregg," he stated.

"Great," Tiffany sneered at him. "You'll look great in the back."

"In the back?" Piano boy questioned. Gregg crossed his arms across his chest appearing offended.

"She doesn't care who you are dude," Dustin's mind said. "She only cares about herself."

"You don't think I chose you for your magic fingers, did you?" Tiffany countered. "O cappella doesn't need a piano."

Tilly mouthed to him, "Sorry." Then from her spot next to me on stage she said, "I pick Eddie."

"Where are the guys who played the guitar and drums?" Tiffany questioned as she sauntered down the line.

"They're not down with the whole picking process," Tilly stated and brazenly popped a huge pink bubble.

"Brace yourself," Dustin's mind warned. "Princess complex will be making an appearance."

"What?" Professor Presnell questioned peering over the rim of her red glasses at Tilly.

"They aren't under your control," Tilly stated. "They just play with us because they choose too."

"Can they do that?" Tiffany whined and stomped her foot.

"Here it comes," Dustin's mind thought with a hint of joy at Tiffany's dismay.

"They won't play for you," Tilly said directly to Tiffany. "Even if you picked them, they would quit."

"That's not fair," Tiffany complained sticking her lip out to pout. She was as capable of acting as Tilly herself. "It's like you're two picks ahead of me."

"Good grief," Dustin said in my head.

"Then you take your current turn plus two more before Miss Bradford picks again," Rhett stated as he stepped forward purposely cutting Professor Presnell off while giving Tilly a knowing glance. "I'm sure Miss Bradford will be fine with this arrangement."

"It is only fair," Tilly said as she grinned at Tiffany with a sticky, fake smile. "You don't want musicians anyway."

I watched as Tilly and Tiffany took turns picking their band and choir members. With each passing round, the sour look plastered on Janelle's face grew more putrid. Tiffany showed no interest in choosing her best friend who was clearly irked and disappointed. Maybe a little in fear of being on a team with Tilly loomed as well.

Dustin was unusually quiet with his head resting against the wall and his eyes closed. He wished to cash in his rain check and catch some real life at the Hall of Records tonight. I threw out every excuse I could think not to go.

My ploys fell on his deaf ears. Here he was, publicly waiting for me, taunting anyone with his presence.

When it was down to the last three people, Tiffany was scanning them. Janelle began to squirm as Tiffany passed her standing in the middle to demand the mousy girl on the end, "Sing a few lines of any song for me."

"You can't be serious," Janelle spouted before the girl could sing a note. "Are you seriously considering picking either one of them?" Janelle pointed to both standing beside her in a condescending demeanor. "A mouse and a… um… dork? Really? You would consider one of them before choosing me?"

"Don't question me," Tiffany cut her off. She once more pointed to the mousy girl. "I choose you."

Janelle crossed her arms and stared Tilly down. I couldn't believe Tiffany hadn't responded to Janelle. How could she be so cruel to her best friend? The mousy girl shyly made her way around Janelle while intently watching her feet.

Tilly pointed between the two and started reciting, "Eney, miney, miney, moe."

"Hell, pick me or don't," Janelle snapped with her arms crossed interrupting Tilly's musing at her predicament.

"I can't have anyone with a potty mouth in my band," Tilly reprimanded. She turned to the young man from the Department of Records saying, "You're in."

He appeared relieved, almost as if he had just won the lottery. He happily sang, "Thank you…" He hit a high tenor note to everyone's pleasure.

"Miss Fairfield," Professor Presnell called. "The choice is yours."

Janelle apparently was still reeling from being slighted as she shot daggers at Tiffany.

"Don't stray from the plan," Tiffany coldly warned.

"Whoa," Dustin seemed to come to life in my head. *"What did I miss?"* Dustin sat up straight in his chair with a shocked but smirking look upon his face.

Janelle stood staring Tiffany down. You could see Tiffany had challenged her. Out of pure spite she said, "I choose team Tilly."

Gasps and shock spread through the room.

"What are you doing?" Rodger spewed from his place on stage.

"Dude," I heard Dustin say in my head. *"Don't get involved with this one!"*

"Don't be so dense!" Rodger condescendingly said as he shook his head clearly exasperated with her. "So stupid."

Janelle stood silent while gaping at him. Her anger filled eyes were showing a hint of hurt after Rodger's harsh public outburst.

Dustin was sitting with his hand across his forehead. From my viewpoint on stage, I could see him chuckling under his shielded face.

"She's lost her mind," Tiffany said as she confidently strolled up to greet her new choir members leaving Janelle to stand alone. "Forgotten who's in charge," Tiffany mumbled. Like sheep being led, everyone surrounding Tiffany snickered at her comment.

Janelle peered up at us and slowly joined our group as Professor Presnell said, "Professor Kegley, please lead your Harmony members to the rehearsal room. Your group will practice there nightly."

Janelle walked a few steps ahead of us and disappeared behind the black curtain at the back of the stage. I waited for everyone to follow Professor Kegley and Tilly through the curtain and the door leading to the rehearsal room. I couldn't help but think how great an actress Tiffany was. The warning to not forget the plan bothered me. Was there an established plan to get Janelle on our team as some kind of spy? Was she to sabotage us from within? More importantly, where did she go?

I peeked back through the black curtain and Janelle had not doubled back. I moved to stand in the rehearsal room door and scanned the room. She wasn't in there either. I walked over to the curtain which hung in front of the props room and jerked it back. Janelle was taken back by my uncovering her hiding place. Before either of us could say anything, we heard Tiffany talking loudly on the other side of the black curtain. Janelle peered at me with her finger to her lip clearly gesturing to me, be quiet.

"What was that about?" Tiffany asked.

"Don't look at me like that," Rodger responded. "I have no idea."

"All I need is someone going renegade," Tiffany coldly spewed.

"Don't worry," Rodger said. "I will reel Janelle back in."

"She has forgotten her place," Tiffany spewed. "Have you forgotten yours?"

"No," Rodger immediately answered. "My allegiance is to you and no one else. Don't you know that by now?"

Tiffany cackled answering, "And I'll pay you good on our next moonlit walk."

"Maybe now that Dustin has bugged out we can have more fun together," Rodger returned.

"Absolutely," Tiffany returned.

Poor Janelle. When I glanced at her I saw a brief moment of shock. I felt sorry for her. No one liked a cheating boyfriend. The snake in her group was Tiffany and she just received a deadly bite.

"Hey man," Rodger called. "Where are you going?"

"Do I need a reason to taunt the tramp," Mike answered with a chuckle.

"I love it," Tiffany replied.

"Professor is looking for you," Mike warned.

"My work is never done," Tiffany sighed.

Rodger and Mike chuckled. I could hear footsteps walking away. All of a sudden Mike came through the curtain running right into Janelle. "Oh, geez. Sorry," Mike said.

"Run me over why don't you," Janelle snapped as I backed against the wall unnoticed by Mike.

Mike's expression turned serious. I watched as his hand reached out and gently touched her arm saying, "I wanted to come find you."

"Why would you want to do that?" Janelle asked. "I thought you wanted to taunt the, um… Tilly."

It was obvious that she was editing her words since she knew I was listening.

"Nah, it's just I'm not interested in telling Tiffany everything on my mind," Mike answered. "I don't need Tiffany's approval to breathe." From my profile view of Mike, I could see he appeared genuinely concerned. "I was worried you might be upset."

Janelle sheepishly grinned up at him as I tried to slide down the wall to escape my eavesdropping place. Mike noticed my movement as he asked, "What are you, the fly on the wall?" His hand dropped from Janelle's arm. Clearly he didn't appreciate my intrusion into their moment. "It's rude to eaves drop."

"You should talk," I retorted. "Rodger might find your moment with his girlfriend rude."

"Actually, I'm a free woman," Janelle spoke up as both of us turned to peer at her. "Rodger is history."

I never considered that Janelle might be as miserable in Tiffany's clique as we were on the outside. Also, I never dreamed that Rodger was anything less than a doting boyfriend. Good grief. Who could blame Janelle for her normal disagreeable attitude, or for dumping Rodger!

The curtain ruffled again with Dustin stepping through.

"She is incredible to think that we could start over," Dustin stated in my mind

oblivious to my being able to hear his private thoughts. "*I learned my lesson the first time.*"

When Dustin saw me perched against the wall he instantly grinned at me. There was no way out of accompanying him tonight. We would definitely be catching some real life after practice. A prospect I might look forward to, if I were going with Marvin. All those around me were sure to misunderstand my longing for Marvin when I appeared to be stepping out with Dustin. Mike and Janelle gawked at the sight of Dustin and me. Great!

CHAPTER FIVE

Marvin

Hanging the last of my clothes in the closet, I was officially moved in. I leaned against the door frame in thought. My world had completely changed in three short days. Mom and Dad didn't really understand my moving out. I played it off that I was simply spreading my wings. They might have understood better, if I hadn't moved to Rhett's. It wasn't natural to move from your parent's home to your uncle's. My life was no longer normal without Elizabeth. She hadn't left my heart or my dreams. I felt like a broken hearted walking zombie.

In my decision, there was no choice in the matter. Mr. Solliday assured me I was on the radar of the Dwellers, maybe even marked. The words I said to Elizabeth rang in my ears, "I'm doing this for my family." When looking in my mother's eyes, I kept repeating this to myself. I couldn't chance drawing Dwellers home to my parents. Making the whole situation even more painful was the mix of recalling my words and the heartbroken shock spread across Elizabeth's face. While standing and looking at my Mom, Elizabeth's tear washed face just kept flashing in my mind. The painful memory of hurting her was forever seared into my heart.

Even more confusing for my parents was my change of job. As a child I spent every waking hour studying to be a Keeper, spurred on by Uncle Rhett. Not in my wildest dream did I ever think I would do anything else. Mr. Solliday said I was now in the inner circle. I will work directly for him behind the scenes on all matters concerning Dwellers. I told my parents I was promoted and would now be working for the Administration Complex. This didn't wash with my Dad. He kept staring at Rhett who tried to look anywhere but at my Dad. The only up side was not having to face Elizabeth in the morning at the Keeper Complex.

"Marvin," Rhett called from the first floor.

I closed my bedroom door as I quickly descended the stairs.

"We have company," Rhett stated from the kitchen as I stepped off the last stair.

There set both my parents. I crossed the room saying, "Hey Mom." I had never seen her visit Rhett's house. She was perched on a chair that I was sure she wouldn't have sat in normally. I could almost hear her call it unclean and full of germs. My eyes moved past my Mom as I said, "Dad."

"We need to talk son," my Dad stated in an even tone. "You've moved, changed jobs, have a bruised face, and today I find out you have broken up with your girlfriend."

I looked over at my Mom feeling a little bit of panic. Since Mom didn't handle strangers well, I had never built up the nerve to tell Mom about Elizabeth.

"The cat's already out of the bag," my Mom unhappily said. "Might as well sit." She pointed to the chair beside Rhett. "I can't believe you didn't tell me about your new girlfriend."

"I was going to," I hem-hawed feeling the weight of her disappointed stare as I sat down. I had always imagined taking Elizabeth home and introducing her properly knowing full well the fiasco it would be. I always envisioned them accepting her because in my heart I thought we would spend eternity together. "Then we broke up and it doesn't matter anymore."

"Broke up or not it matters to me," my Mom stated as she placed her hands upon the round table top. I couldn't fathom that she hadn't noticed the visible coffee stains under her hands. My mom looked between Uncle Rhett and Dad. "As for the two of you, I am equally disappointed that neither of you said anything sooner."

"Susie," Uncle Rhett called in a remorseful tone.

"I know," my Dad interrupted whatever Uncle Rhett was going to say.

"You know what?" I asked.

"After what we went through as kids," my Mom said shaking her head with pure grief filling her eyes. "How could you let Marvin get involved?"

My Mom's statement took the wind out of Uncle Rhett's sails as he looked deflated at having to face her.

"Son, we know you are joining forces with Rhett and Solliday," Dad said.

I fidgeted popping my knuckles as I sat.

"Rhett, I have known all these years there was more to what you did than appeared on the surface. All four of us on your team have chosen to overlook some of the oddities. We simply want to be Ghosties and we enjoy hunting lost souls." He shook his head, "I know you chose to be a Ghostie for some reason which had nothing to do with the work itself, something left over from your childhood."

Uncle Rhett sat speechless.

"But you Marvin. You wanted to be a Keeper. So, if you are not in cahoots with the two of them, if they haven't wrapped you up in something you shouldn't be into, then tell me why all the change?"

"Maybe you're better off not knowing," I countered.

"We are your parents," Dad disagreed clearly irked at my snappy response.

"I need to tell him," my Mom piped up while looking at Rhett. "He needs to understand before he gets consumed in whatever the two of you are doing."

"It won't matter," Uncle Rhett warned.

"I have never worried about you Rhett," my Mom stated in a motherly fashion. "We grew up knowing the consequences of the paths we choose. However, we chose to shelter Marvin. You know he doesn't understand." She paused as Dad grabbed her hand with a sign of support. "It's time he knows."

"You start," Uncle Rhett said looking resigned.

"Rhett and I as children lived next door to each other in a town called Bella Vista," my Mom began. "This was before the dome when the Keepers lived with the Humlings. Bella Vista was considered a safe place and my early childhood memories were great up until the event."

"The event?" I questioned.

"The day the Dwellers came," Dad answered. "You know the story about the Keeper souls who vanished."

"I ran out the back door of my house to flee from the Dwellers," Uncle Rhett recalled. "I hid around the edge of the neighbor's house. When my neighbor..."

"My father," Mom interjected.

"He took me by the hand and pulled me inside," Rhett finished his thought.

"I was at home with my mother when my father burst through the door," Mom said in a robotic manner. "He was yelling frantically for my mother. When he appeared in the kitchen doorway, he was holding Rhett's hand. Instantly he demanded that everyone hide. I can still see the confusion on my mother's face as she asked why. My father steadily informed her that there were Dwellers next door."

"I remember your father peeking out the window panicked due to the house being surrounded," Rhett stated to Mom.

"My mother placed us into a cabinet which normally held our pots and pans," my Mom remembered.

"I was scared and starting to cry," Rhett admitted staring off into space.

"So, my mother gave us a bag of suckers and told me to give you as many as it took to keep you quiet," my Mom said as she reached towards Rhett.

"How old were the two of you?" I asked.

"I was six," Mom answered.

"Four," Uncle Rhett said.

"My mother made us promise not to come out until we heard her calling," My Mom said.

"Gram and Gramps," I mumbled.

"My grandparents. Your great-grandparnets, who you know as Gram and Gramps, raised me instead of my parents," Mom stated from across the table.

"Your parents never came back, did they?" I asked.

"No," Uncle Rhett answered as my Mom looked into her lap. "They disappeared with all the other Keepers on that fateful day."

"It took awhile for the guards to realize what was happening," my Mom stated.

"Longer for them to look for us in the cabinet," Rhett added.

I was at a loss for words. What could I say? My life held as much mystery as Elizabeth's. Only I hadn't realized it.

"I need a moment," my Mom said as she stood and walked towards the hall allowing her hand to drag along everything along the way. She was so germ phobic I couldn't believe my eyes. When she turned the corner my eyes scanned her crisp white shoes which she always wore. I had never seen her wear shoes inside. The front door closed as she stepped outside.

"Son," my Dad called capturing my attention. "Have you never wondered why your Mom is so obsessive about cleaning?"

"Her mother told her, as she closed the cabinet door, to clean to keep the Dwellers away," Rhett explained.

"All the cleaning," I mumbled. "It's all been to keep Dwellers at bay?"

"All done to keep the Dwellers away," my Dad reiterated. "She always cleaned, but didn't clean so obsessively until we had you. In her mind she was keeping you safe by cleaning." Dad banged the table with his fists, "Don't you see! She has lived her whole life in fear they would return. Her whole life focus has been to keep you safe and now you run off and get yourself involved somehow!"

"Calm down Conrad," Uncle Rhett said.

"Calm down?" My Dad repeated. "How can I calm down? This is my son!"

An unusual silence prevailed. There was nothing Uncle Rhett could say and he knew it. "Why did they focus on both sets of your parents?" I asked Rhett breaking the eerie silence.

"They weren't focused on your grandparents at all," Rhett sighed. "It was my Dad who was marked."

"Why was he marked?" I asked.

"Because of his job," Rhett automatically answered.

Chances are I was already marked. Even though I had been left to day-dream and constantly think about Elizabeth, I wouldn't change a thing. If I was marked due to even one moment spent with her, it was worth it. One moment with her defied rational thought. I knew full well that one moment would never be enough with her. I yearned for eternity together, but knew it couldn't be.

"I just want the truth," my Dad began. "Level with me. Marvin, you're marked aren't you?"

"I think if they really wanted Marvin, they would already have him," Rhett stated.

"It is what I feared," my Dad said in a dejected tone. "A Dweller did all that to your face?"

"I was just at the wrong place at the wrong time," I replied.

"You're marked," my Dad hummed as he placed his head in his hands.

"We don't know for sure," Uncle Rhett countered.

"We can't tell Susie this," my Dad said as he stood and paced a few steps back and forth. "This would make her crazy. She'd have a breakdown."

"Please understand Dad," I countered. "If I am marked, then or now, I won't chance bringing them home to you. Do you now see why I had to make changes?"

"All you ever wanted was to be a Keeper," Dad hummed. "And your girl-friend."

"Albert thought making some changes was best," Uncle Rhett stated as the door opened and closed again.

"Is that why you live here?" I asked Uncle Rhett.

Mom reappeared and instantly asked Dad, "Why are you standing?"

"Coming to find you dear," my Dad said with a warm smile.

"Aren't you going to answer Marvin," Mom said to Rhett as Dad pulled out her chair for her to sit.

"I asked if it's why you live here," I repeated for him.

"I was raised by Albert," Uncle Rhett said.

"In Dogwood Estates?" I asked feeling shocked. It hit me instantly that he had known every detail about Elizabeth from the beginning. The first day I saw Elizabeth standing in the garden with Mr. Solliday and Dustin, it was Rhett whom I was following. He was raised with Elizabeth's mother. That's why he gasped when Solliday placed the locket around her neck. He must have understood the magnitude of the situation.

The locket which hung around her neck was the key to her lack of memory. She had used the locket to enter the world of the Dwellers. The thought of her being in the darkness made my stomach churn and my hands nervously begin to sweat. Although her mission was unknown to me, the trip had been a total disaster. I couldn't imagine what they had hoped to accomplish by sending her there.

Then I remembered Uncle Rhett's warning that Elizabeth was trouble. Since he already was at a place of understanding, he didn't want me involved with any of this. However, this was bigger than him or me. I glanced over at him and could see the regret oozing from every pore. Uncle Rhett had desperately wanted and tried to keep me from this heartache. His disapproval of my relationship with Elizabeth all made sense now.

I peered around the table. Dad was looking for a way out now that he had a better understanding of the situation. Mom had an uncharacteristic blank stare. Although I now comprehended why, germ a phobic was the only words which could normally describe her frenzied cleaning behavior. I had never seen her sit in such a dirty room since she usually wasn't able to visit other's homes due to their conditions. The only place she went regularly was Gram and Gramps.

"Everything I have done in my life has been to protect you," Mom stated from across the table.

If only I could tell her how I understood. I had given up everything, my whole life, to protect Elizabeth. Just as she had done for me. Most considered Mom to be a little touched. For the first time I viewed my Dad differently. I never gave him credit for all he put up with. He loved her so much he put her first and outwardly showed his love daily by shouldering the jabs from others concerning her. He reinforced my decision concerning Elizabeth. When you love someone, you put their welfare first.

CHAPTER SIX

Elizabeth

"Tilly, where have you been? Dale is angry about your not showing up for work at the office," I reported as I placed a couple books on the shelf in the Hall of Records. My part time gig as a library assistant sucked.

"Training is the last thing on my mind today," Tilly responded as she plopped her backpack on my cart.

"Mrs. VanCues didn't sleep well," I informed her. "She kept repeating one of her angels was missing."

"Of course she would miss me," Tilly responded like the thought of anyone not missing her would be crazy. With a quick shrug she blew off my concern saying, "I had something more urgent to tend to."

"Hopefully, it was really important. I feel the Professor, Jacob, Dale…" I couldn't help but recall the flashy smile and slimy persona as I thought, "Mr. Brassbuckle… They are all going to make you pay," I responded.

"It doesn't matter," she simply stated. "You can't get bogged down with consequences."

"I know," I responded leaning against a shelf of books. "Throw caution to the wind."

"I couldn't have said it better," Tilly said with a devilish grin. "Do you want to know what I did today?"

"I can only imagine," I responded. What could be more significant than our commitment to sing to Mrs. VanCues?

"Elizabeth, I have observed you mope over Marvin for days," Tilly began without looking directly at me. "Equally frustrating was the fact that Marvin didn't even tell you what happened." She looked up at me, "I don't know which bothers you more, the break up or the lack of information."

"Put him out of your mind, he doesn't matter anymore," I stated as I began to push the cart to the next aisle.

"Sure," Tilly replied stepping in front of the cart. "Sell that to someone who will buy it. You are still sleeping in his clothes every night, right?"

"Let it go," I demanded. I had no desire or energy to explain that the clothes were all I had left of Marvin and my sense of security and belonging.

"So what are you doing with Dustin?" Tilly asked catching me off guard. "Just throwing caution to the wind and letting go?"

"Don't," I warned. "Dustin and I are only friends."

"Hmm…" Tilly hummed as she unwrapped a stick of gum.

I knew she didn't believe me. My heart belonged to Marvin. Dustin wasn't the one. Wait! "You didn't go and approach Marvin, did you?" I questioned in horror.

"I tried," Tilly responded with a shrug, popping the gum into her mouth. After chewing a minute she continued, "I marched over to the Department of Keepers Complex and up to his new office. Are you aware he is no longer assigned there?"

"No," I replied as I pulled the cart of heavy books around the corner.

"It's only been two days. I had to wonder how he messed that up." Tilly seriously questioned. "His buddies couldn't tell me what his new assignment was. So, I went downstairs and asked Dan."

"Who?" I questioned scanning the shelf.

"Dan, the guy at the turn styles. You know, he's tall and really handsome," Tilly began.

I held up my hand to stop her. She was always interested in the opposite sex. I just didn't seem to view guys in the dreamy way she did.

"Anyway, it's beside the point. He could not find in the information kiosk that Marvin works as a Keeper anymore," Tilly stated.

"That makes no sense. He told me he only had to stop seeing me," I responded looking directly at Tilly pausing from my work.

"I know it makes no sense," Tilly agreed and blew a big bubble appearing deep in thought. "It's like he thinks he's been marked."

"Marked?" I questioned.

"They say those tracked by Dwellers are marked," Tilly answered. "The changes would make sense if he has been marked."

Marvin was truly a great guy and destined to become a great Keeper. I had fowled that up for him. His destiny now apparently, was a life of being chased instead of a life filled with helping others. He should be walking the halls of the Keeper Complex.

"This is why I had to do the unthinkable," Tilly continued and then blew another big bubble.

I held my head in my hands, how could this get any worse? But somehow, with Tilly, I knew it could.

"I went to his home and spoke with his parents," Tilly bravely stated as she placed a book away on the shelf for me.

"Oh no, please tell me you didn't," I cringed.

"Don't worry, his Mom assumed I was a friend who hadn't seen him in a long time. She probably thought we went through training together," Tilly stated.

"His Dad didn't say anything or let on that he knew you?" I questioned in disbelief.

"Not a word," Tilly said clearly in thought.

"So he wasn't home?" I asked once again pushing the cart towards the next aisle.

"That's the thing. He came home earlier in the week, packed his bags, and told them he was moving out," Tilly said.

"Did he tell them why?" I asked.

"His Mom said he got a new job with the Department of Administration which would require a significant amount of time. They lived too far away from the Administration Complex," Tilly stated. "This is the oddest part. When she asked him where he was going to live, he told them with his Uncle Rhett."

"You didn't go there did you?" I questioned as I stopped abruptly.

"No, I thought if Rhett caught wind of my trying to talk with Marvin, one of us might get into trouble," Tilly responded.

"You're probably right," I agreed. "Were his parents okay with his abrupt decision?"

"I don't believe they understand it, but they seem okay with him living with Rhett," Tilly stated. "His dad didn't say much. I get the feeling he knows something he doesn't want Marvin's mom to know."

"Odd," I agreed. "Out of curiosity, what is his mom like?"

"You never met her?" Tilly questioned.

I shook my head no.

"Well…" Tilly hem hawed and blew a bubble to buy time. "His mom seems obsessed with cleaning anything that gets touched."

"Maybe that is why he never took me home," I replied leaning against a shelf and scanning the few books that remained on my cart.

"You haven't heard it all," Tilly replied in a girly gossiping manner. "She is scared of germs. I had to wash my feet, put on socks which were deemed as clean and then wear latex gloves to keep my skin from touching anything. Then she placed plastic over the chair I was to sit in."

"Don't kid," I replied.

"Who said I was kidding?" Tilly seriously retorted.

"Poor Marvin," I replied recalling him with his dog. Banjo had played in the mud and Marvin had been clearly worried about it.

"No! No poor Marvin!" Tilly demanded. "He has chosen to no longer be a part of your life. I don't want to hear any more sympathy for him."

"That's not fair," I countered. "I told you he didn't have any choice."

"That's not true," Tilly disagreed and seemed to hesitate in her thoughts. "Never mind, I don't want to hurt your feelings."

"Just say it," I spouted.

"You always have a choice," Tilly answered. "Don't defend him. He chose to dump you."

I could see she did not agree with me, but it didn't matter. I knew in my heart Marvin would never stop loving me. "Tilly, my life isn't complete without him," I countered.

"What about his deception?" Tilly demanded as her hands found her hips. "He had seen you before and didn't say anything to you."

Even though I had no answer for this, in some crazy way I knew I loved him despite it. "Tilly, you must understand…"

"Don't defend him now that you are… forgetting Marvin with Dustin," Tilly interrupted. Before I could answer she continued, "Actually, one question has been burning in my mind. Why him? I told you to find someone new and move on… However, I never dreamed you would take my advice. Much less choose Dustin to be your rebound guy."

"Stop!" I demanded. "Just stop. Dustin and I are only friends. I don't know why I went with him last night. I really don't have any feelings for him."

"Okay," Tilly hummed with big eyes.

"Tilly, did tracking down Marvin take you all day?" I questioned.

"Of course not," Tilly said with a devious smile. "I had to have lunch with Andy. Then I carved out a little time for an afternoon stroll with Anthony."

"Your one to talk," I countered. "What are you going to do with two of them?"

"Great!" Tilly stated peering past me. "We've got company."

I turned to see Janelle making her way toward us. "Be nice," I mumbled as Tilly rolled her eyes at me.

"I'm surprised to find you here," Janelle began. "I want to talk to you about Harmony."

"What made you cross over from the dark side?" Tilly pointedly asked.

"This shouldn't come as a surprise," Janelle began. "I quit!"

"You chose my band to quit?" Tilly asked confused.

"Of course," Janelle answered. "You didn't really believe I wanted to be on your Harmony team?"

"You are under the assumption that Professor Kegley will let you quit the choir easier than Professor Presnell. Right?" Tilly instantly understood.

"For once," Janelle giggled a cat like laugh. "We see eye to eye. Look, I have no desire to monkey with your band."

"What's your motive," Tilly said catching me off guard. "You and I aren't friends."

"Enemies are the best way to describe our relationship," Janelle pointedly agreed. "Look, I should want to dismantle your so-called band. However, you're on a lucky streak because I have a bigger fish to fry than you at this time. Just don't expect me at Harmony." She spun around on the spot and walked away.

"Can you believe that?" Tilly huffed.

Actually, I could. I knew exactly who the big fish was, Tiffany. The next few weeks were sure to get interesting.

Tilly

Here it comes! I blew into the conference room with Elizabeth on my heels. Dale was seated and methodically tapping a pencil against the table. I plopped down in the chair next to him holding my head high and saying, "Hey!"

"Good morning," Dale returned.

Elizabeth sat in the chair next to me everyone we seemed to know streamed through the door. Jacob and Professor Zirak were joining our party. The more the merrier.

"This entire fan fair is because I missed yesterday?" I nonchalantly asked. Really who wouldn't miss me? I was a beauty. With a giggle I added, "Couldn't live without me, huh?"

Every eye turned to look at me, but no one said a word.

Judging from all the unhappy stares from around the room, I conceded, "Let me have it."

The conference room door flung open. Mr. Brassbuckle strutted in flashing his perfect pearly whites. "Good morning," he stated as he rounded the table to sit. "I was under the assumption that the two of you where satisfied with our arrangement. Do you not want to work with Mrs. VanCues?"

"Of course we do," Elizabeth too quickly answered.

It didn't matter how much I coached her, she still didn't grasp how to be cool, calm, and collected when staring authority in the face. "Leave her out of this," I replied to the serious looks from around the table. "She didn't skip yesterday, I did."

"Why were you unavailable," Jacob patiently asked.

"I just had something personal to take care of," I responded as I dug in my pocket for a stick of gum.

"Miss Bradford," Zirak began. "If you have something personal that arises, you need to tell someone."

"I thought you understood how important the connection between you and Mrs. VanCues is," Jacob countered.

"It was me," Elizabeth spoke up. "She was running an errand for me."

"Stop," I sternly told Elizabeth as I stared at her. "What are you doing? Don't get yourself in the middle of this."

"You wouldn't have been out if it wasn't for me," Elizabeth nervously countered. "You know that it's true." She turned to Jacob adding, "We both know how important the bond we now share with Mrs. VanCues is."

Mr. Brassbuckle leaned back in his seat with a grin plastered across his face. "Ruben, what are we going to do with the two of them?"

"First things first," Zirak stated. "Is the office still willing to work with them?"

"No them," I chimed in unwrapping the gum. "Elizabeth didn't miss yesterday."

"I don't see an option," Dale sighed with a non-smiling face.

"Oh, come now," Mr. Brassbuckle said. "There is always an option."

"No," Jacob disagreed. "We can't forget that Mrs. VanCues has been ill. She is top priority."

"If you're going to punish me, or Elizabeth, get it over with," I replied and popped the first calming bubble. "I have other things I'd rather do than sit here and amuse you." Noticing a chipped nail I added, "I could be doing my nails."

"Shall we go with what we talked about?" Zirak asked Mr. Brassbuckle. He held up his hand a gesture saying sure. "Great. Miss Bradford Jacob and Dale didn't have the heart to punish you for skipping. Unfortunately for you, I happen to be in charge of grilling some character into you."

"Why are you intent to punish us at all," I said between chewing my gum. "We have been to sing to Mrs. VanCues almost everyday. We come on our lunch or in the evening, whenever Jacob and Dale send for us. Yesterday should be considered comp. time for me."

I couldn't help but notice the slight grin on Jacob's face as Zirak continued, "Each of you will do eight hours community service in the Soul's Nursery."

"When will I find time for that?" Elizabeth asked in a complaining voice.

"I already told you she had nothing to do with my missing," I objected. "I'll take all sixteen hours."

"One hand washes the other," Mr. Brassbuckle interjected. "If you're involved, she is too. You might consider this the next time you plan something. Whether Miss Cantrell is involved or not, she goes down with you."

"That is really not fair," I objected.

"Well, the way I see it, we need something to tame you," Mr. Brassbuckle stated.

"Tame me?" I questioned. He had nerve. "You want to tame me!"

I could feel Elizabeth's foot stomp the top of mine while her fingers dug into my arm.

Mr. Brassbuckle flashed his grin before saying, "I think you might care more about the welfare of Miss Cantrell, than your own. Time will tell."

Elizabeth stood, roughly pulling me to my feet, while questioning, "So, we are free to go?"

"Of course," Mr. Brassbuckle stated. "I suspect we will be graced with your presence all day today."

"And when do you think we will find time to monkey around at the Hall of Babies?" I sarcastically asked.

"Saturday," Zirak answered.

"What?" I loudly returned.

"Sounds great," Elizabeth said as she jerked my arm to pull me out of the room.

CHAPTER SEVEN

Elizabeth

Our punishment for Tilly's adventure had forced upon us a long boring day of laboring at the Hall of Records. The supervisor, who was dressed in a head to toe white dress, placed me behind the circular desk which loomed in the middle of the gleaming white, hospitable, circular room. Humlings and Keepers alike made their way to me and placed their hands upon the small, metal box scanner to find their assigned office. As the light scanned one of their hands, it radiated through their skin allowing me to see the bones in their hands. A beeping sound signaled that their palm was read. The small electronic screen in front of my seat would flash the Hallway and office assignment. Then, I would relay the information.

I referred a few around the desk to the informational layout which displayed under glass the diagram for the building and corridors for viewing. Then there were those who couldn't read the map, or would come back to ask which of the six corridors was the one they were looking for. The layout was now ingrained in my mind. The Corridors were labeled; Hallway A – Administration, Hallway B – Keeper Chart Creation, Review, and Returns, Hallway C – Humling Review of Charts, Hallway D through F – Humling Chart Creation. The six corridors jutted off the main circular room like legs of a spider. I couldn't fathom why those who came back to me for help couldn't read the sign hanging over each of the six corridors which announced the corridors by letter, A through F.

As I plugged away behind the desk, the blinding light from Hallway A was much brighter than the light coming from the other corridors. I attempted to ignore it, but it called to me. The only person to enter the hall was the supervisor. From the angle where I stood, I could see her sitting in her chair behind her desk in the first office. Distracted by the last few souls which I helped, I missed her disappearing from her office. I left my post and made my way around the circular desk. I sauntered across the circular room and into Hallway A. The familiar surge of warmth and love washed over me. I briskly walked past the four dark offices setting on either side of me. I stepped over the bench and through the mirage of a wall which acted as a barricade for those who couldn't see the angels beyond or the continuance of the corridor.

The corridor came to life as I caught sight of the breathtaking, ghostly figures as they glided across the corridor. The long hair of different hues flowing around their shoulders, stunningly beautiful faces, and long bodies covered in robes of fine material were just as I remembered. I was still in awe of the energy emitting from their backs reminding me of streams of heat circling their backs. As my presence was noticed, a ghostly figure glided to me with the grey silk of her robe flowing around her body.

"Excuse me, may I help you?" The ghostly figure enquired with a musical voice as she stopped before me. Her beautiful facial features were extraordinary. With long wavy red hair, rosy cheeks, and crystal blue eyes, she was breathtaking.

I had no reason to be here, other than the corridor seeming to call to me. It was a mystery as to why I could see the light of the corridor or even enter it. I was sure the angel hovering before me was capable of answering all the mysteries in my life; my missing family, the journal entries, and my true identity. Worst was the Dweller that was chasing me. I wished someone could explain Marvin's dumping me. This was the story of my sad life. All of this and the truth I should be working my post at the desk. What could I say, "Um…"

"You have visited before, have you not?" She inquired.

"Yes, once before," I replied.

"Then the corridor is open to you," she surmised.

"I feel drawn to its light," I said under my breath.

"You have favor in God's eyes," she answered giving me a motherly grin. "Making your way here is never by mistake."

I didn't know about that because my life was a mess. I responded, "Why would you say that?"

"Only those who have favor have the sight to see us," she answered peering at me deeply. "Angels serve the pure. It is not everyone who can see the light of the Nursery." As she studied me, I began to feel subconscious. "I sense heartache," she stated with a knowing look. An understanding smile crossed her face as she seemed to read my mind, "You believe I am capable of only answering questions about the workings of this corridor?"

I began to answer, "Well, yes. The last time I was here…"

"The corridor called you here," she interrupted. I nodded in agreement. "Last time, it was out of curiosity for the corridor itself. Today, I simply sense unrest and heartache."

I walked a few steps away from her. I had no desire to spill my guts about Marvin. I ignored her comment and peered through the floor to ceiling glass wall in front of me. The blinds were open as I viewed the rows and rows of babies nestled into their beds and peacefully sleeping. I couldn't forget that the corridor was a nursery and the ghostly figures were angels entrusted to watch over the baby's soul. The babies before me were Keepers and Humlings who had made their official life chart and departed for their earth life. This was best described as a holding nursery since the souls live simultaneously. Once conceived on the Earth Plane the baby's body grows in their earth mother's womb as your spirit is tended to in this nursery. The body of the baby spirit I was viewing mirrors the body in the womb.

"The souls lying in the beds before you are untarnished and perfect," she said as she took her place beside me.

I scooted down the corridor and ran my hand along the glass wall. Baby after baby was perfect.

"They have no memory of who they once were at Home," she began as she followed me. "And have made no choices for their earth life. A soul is its purest when in the form of a baby."

I stopped and peered through the glass at the baby lying asleep before me. This baby was different from the rest. Across its face was what could best be described as a huge red birth mark. I couldn't help but ask, "What is the mark on the babies face?"

She followed my gaze through the window answering, "The birthmark?" I nodded. "Do you understand the significance of birthmarks?" She asked.

"Not really," I replied.

"They are a carry over from the previous earth life," she stated with a blank stare. "Caused by a trauma in that life. This baby or soul died in a fire during a previous earth life." Silence fell until she questioned, "Why are you ignoring the reason you were called here?" She asked.

I stared off. I couldn't bare anyone telling me that Marvin and I weren't destined to be together. My gut was screaming that she knew more than we were simply broken up. I couldn't shake that she could tell me about my future. And the thought of a future without Marvin terrified me.

"I'm going a little off script," she said with a smile.

"Off script?" I questioned.

"Normally, I would talk to any visitor about the Nursery itself," she replied. "With you, I know you have been called for a different reason." She intently looked at me.

"The light was just so bright," I countered.

"No one comes into our corridor by accident," she reassured me. "Your fears are unwarranted."

"What?" I questioned.

"Look within yourself," she said. "What does your heart, or your gut feeling say?"

My gut screamed that Marvin and I were soul mates. Simple and true.

"Don't get derailed from your path young one," she replied with a motherly grin. "More importantly, when the time comes, forgive those who stray from theirs."

"Stray?" I repeated.

She closed her eyes and hovered quietly intently waiting. A smile crossed her face as she lovingly looked at me saying, "Time will tell. Be patient, child of God."

As with everyone in my life, I was always left with questions. "But..."

"Oh dear," she said. "Someone is looking for you."

She pointed back towards the lobby where I could see Harry peeking in the offices. I had ignored him all day. However, he must have noticed my absence. "I better, you know, go," I hem-hawed.

The warm motherly grin crossed her face again. "Go with God's love." I smiled at her as she added, "Visit anytime the light calls you."

"I will," I assured her. As I gave her my own smile, Harry had left the corridor. As quickly as I could, I crossed the mirage of a wall and back into the world of the Keepers. I glanced back as the angels returned to their ghostly forms and were gliding down the corridor beyond the wall. I felt they had knowledge that went well beyond what had been shared with me.

"Where have you been?" Harry asked catching me off guard from behind.

I took a deep cleansing breath and sprung around answering, "Taking a break."

"A break?" Harry repeated. "You can't take a break anytime you choose." He pointed towards the circular desk. "They've been looking for you."

"I'm found," I cut him off and began to walk around him.

He was on my heels as he asked, "How is Tilly?"

Good grief. You couldn't beat the guys off with a stick. "Ask your sister," I responded.

CHAPTER EIGHT

Tilly

Last weeks brunch had been odd. Professor Zirak ignored the fact Elizabeth did not participate on Monday morning. He didn't assign any additional work and the room breathed a sigh of relief. However, today was sure to be back to normal. Zirak would load us up due to the fact Elizabeth was still no closer to remembering anything about herself than she was on the first day of training. Her memory fog was more of amnesia at this point.

"How's Andy?" Trevor inquired as he sat down next to me.

"Huh?" I huffed in return. Andy was highly annoying me, wanting to spend every waking moment with me. He was acting like a boyfriend. Ugh! Juggling him with Anthony wasn't the problem. I could juggle men. It was that I longed to spend all of my time with Anthony. Hmm, Anthony and the word boyfriend had a nice ring to it. Either way, I needed to cut ties with Andy.

"Pay him no attention," Eddie leaned over to say to me from the other side of Kim who seemed to be batting her eyes and doing her best to give Eddie a flirtatious smile.

"What's wrong with you?" I whispered to Trevor.

"Did you forget?" Trevor pointedly asked.

"Oh no," I instantly said as my hand flew to my head. "The Harmony meeting. Yeah, I forgot."

"It's no big deal," Trevor stated looking directly at me while handing me a stick of my favorite pink gum. "Ruthanne and I didn't mind the alone time."

That stung. Of course Ruthanne didn't mind spending the time with Trevor. Who would? And, of course, Trevor knew how to make me pay for standing him up. Flaunting Ruthanne in front of me hurt. I simply tolerated Ruthanne and didn't' care to hear details. We knew each other too well. He knew how to push my buttons.

"Look at that," I heard Eddie mumble.

I turned to see Elizabeth bidding Dustin goodbye. He was a new burr under my saddle. Anyone who would date Tiffany couldn't be worth seeing. He was a rebound guy and Elizabeth was wasting her time. However, she apparently did not view it that way. No matter how many times I told her, she ignored me. She had always been fascinated with Dustin. With the whole love sick over Marvin thing, I wasn't sure what she was doing or feeling for Dustin. Holding my breath, she broke free without getting any type of kiss. Any romantic display in front of this room of our fellow trainees would be like thunder warning of a lightning storm to come. Tiffany catching wind of a passionate kiss would bring the world crashing down on Elizabeth. It was a good thing we were already dead. I was fully aware that at some point, Tiffany would try to find a way to seek revenge.

"Where's my chair?" Elizabeth asked.

"I've got your chair," Destiny stated as she patted the chair next to her from across the table.

"There is one down here," Eddie piped up as Kim let out a huge sigh. I would need to enlighten Eddie. Apparently, he could not see that Kim was trying to get his attention.

"Hands off," Shannon stated from the other side of the empty chair which set between herself and Eddie. "I was here first and I'm saving this chair."

"Don't worry about it," Elizabeth said to Eddie who appeared peeved at Shannon and disappointed. I saw a hint of a smile cross Kim's face at Eddie's lack of luck and her good fortune. Elizabeth began to make her way around the table to the empty chair across from me.

Piano boy entered, stopped, and leaned down asking, "Where were you?"

"You knew about our meeting?" I asked in return as I looked at Trevor.

"We have a plan," Trevor whispered and flashed a confident grin.

The boy who followed my every move suddenly appeared so confident flashing me that grin. Looking at him I could see for the first time that he had finally grown into his skin and was taking responsibility for his world around him. He did learn from the best. After all, I was a great teacher. However, when did this happen?

"Get together after brunch?" piano boy asked.

"Sure," I said and blew a big pink bubble.

"You're going to love it," Trevor hummed.

"Good morning class," Zirak stated as he breezed into the room and stood at the head of the long dining room table. When he spied Elizabeth, he added, "Welcome back Miss Cantrell. I assume you are feeling better?"

"Love sickness doesn't last long," Shannon threw out.

"Not if you're Elizabeth," another girl further down the table added.

"Ladies," Professor Zirak called in a reprimanding tone.

"Well, she did get dumped and instantly moved on to someone else's boyfriend," Shannon qualified her statement.

"She did no such thing," I loudly disagreed slinging a book down the slick table at her.

"Enough!" Zirak yelled as he caught the flying volume and then slammed the book onto the table. Silence fell over the room as most stared at the table. It was obvious most of those gathered agreed with Shannon, but no one dared to catch the Professor's eyes.

"I feel fine," Elizabeth piped up looking directly into the Professor's glare. "I'm sorry I missed the last meeting."

"Since you were absent, we didn't collect the two assignments which were due last week," Zirak stated. Sighs broke the silence from around the table. "Please pass in the paper due on the life theme of justice. Please pass in the paper due on how your life plan interacted with a family member's life plan." Papers began to shuffle around the room as he continued, "Miss Cantrell, are you ready to share you life plan or life theme with your fellow trainees?"

"I have repeatedly explained to you why I can't," Elizabeth countered in an exasperated tone.

"Very well," Professor Zirak said. "Everyone is well aware of the punishment for not turning in the assignments." He paused and took in all the angry stares directed towards Elizabeth. "This week the training group will write an essay on the life theme of poverty. In addition, you will each complete an essay on the life plan of your parents and how you fit into it." I was stunned to see a hint of excitement cross Elizabeth's face. "Miss Cantrell, may I suggest you complete your assignments. If not for your benefit, then for the benefit of your fellow trainees. I'm sure they would appreciate not having the extra work each week."

Elizabeth seemed caught in her own thoughts as Destiny elbowed her. When she looked up at Zirak she mindlessly said, "Okay. Fine."

"Miss Cantrell, do you have the additional assignment to turn in today?"

She waved the paper containing the fifty people and their exit points and passed it to Destiny to pass on. The assignment would have taken her hours if it weren't for Trevor and Eddie taking fifteen names each and researching them. I had taken ten myself which left ten for Elizabeth to research. Trevor, Eddie, and I always did this when we were kids. Trevor always said any punishment was easier to bare when divided. Trevor offered to do this for Elizabeth which meant to me that Trevor and Eddie fully accepted Elizabeth. She was really one of us.

"Continuing our assignment from last week," Zirak began. "This week has been about researching how to help Humlings cross over. I would like to hear your observations." As he looked around the table at us, he asked, "Who would like to go first." When no one readily volunteered, he asked, "Miss Stone, I regret calling on you first..." He paused. "However, you did have a great opportunity this week."

Kim looked sick at being called upon as she began to stutter, "I... I... we... wen..."

"Take off your glasses," I leaned forward and mouthed.

"We," Eddie piped up and gave me a dirty glare from her other side. "Kim and I viewed Kassidy."

"Who?" I interrupted off the top of my mind.

"Kim's older sister," Eddie answered not missing a beat. "We were out on the golf course."

I couldn't help but ask, "What were the two of you doing…"

Trevor elbowed me and gave me a hush look. The cat was out of the bag. Well it was no wonder why Kim had been glaring at Elizabeth.

"Kim's learning how to skate," Eddie said as he deliberately placed his hand on hers. The effect was visible for all to see. It was like the nervousness was butter and you could see it melt away. Kim didn't need to take off her glasses when she was lost in Eddie's small gesture of support.

"How romantic," Destiny said as she rolled her eyes.

Kim seemed to be lost watching Eddie as she clearly answered, "Riding clears my head. It makes me feel like I don't have a care in the world."

Eddie grinned at her continuing, "Kassidy is living her one life on the Earth Plane."

"Then how did you see her," Shannon said while tapping her pencil on the desk annoyed with their display of affection.

"Astral travel is more common in the world of the Humlings," Zirak stated. "Astral travel refers to the soul traveling home to visit loved ones or places while their Earth Plane body is sleeping."

"So anyone can do this?" Elizabeth asked.

"Yes," Zirak answered. "Although, most don't realize they can do this while they sleep."

"And this has to do with someone crossing over because…," Destiny prodded.

"Kassidy will be taking her next exit point," Kim said while still staring at Eddie and oblivious to anyone watching her.

"Probably it was her last visit before crossing over," Eddie said looking around the table. "Her soul had completed its lessons on the Earth Plane. Realizing she was done, she was too excited not to come find Kim to tell her."

"I thought this was a unique experience," Zirak stated.

Kim once again noticed the eyes staring at her. She blushed a little and retreated back into her shell realizing everyone was watching her and Eddie and knew they were spending time together. I wondered when all of this had happened and why Trevor hadn't said a word to me about it. Also, if Eddie was into Kim, why was he showing interest in Elizabeth? Now more than ever, I need to straighten Eddie out. I wouldn't have a friend who was a cheating fool. I couldn't have planned this budding relationship better if I tried. I was rubbing off on the new Casanova.

Elizabeth

As Tilly and Trevor were sneaking off after brunch, my gut screamed they were up to something. I would have followed them, if it weren't for Dustin waiting for me. Neither Tilly nor Trevor seems accepting of Dustin. Anyone who had dated Tiffany, they considered tainted. I couldn't blame them.

Dustin surprised me with a picnic lunch outside on the luscious grass under the massive tress surrounding the Hall of Knowledge. If I had been with Marvin and not directly after brunch, I would have thought lunch was romantic. I had wasted all those precious Marvin moments dreaming about Dustin, feeling totally drawn to him. Although his cologne was still intoxicating, now I could have him and he wasn't as exciting as I thought he would be.

Even though I enjoyed snacking on the ginger based lunch, I was relieved to bid Dustin goodbye for the afternoon. I passed Tilly on the stairs. She was off to an afternoon date with Anthony and covered from head to toe with thick snow bibs and a huge winter coat. Anthony planned to take her ice climbing and she was thrilled. This was the first time I saw her leave for a date in more than a skimpy skirt and low cut shirt. I was her cover for Andy.

I might have been upset about spending the afternoon alone, if it weren't for my looking forward to down time. Lately, every time I thought I had a moment to myself, Dustin would show up.

I entered the door of our room to discover that Tilly had left all of the windows wide open. I instantly shut them and plopped down in the chair under the window. As my eyes scanned the room, I saw it. The familiar simple beige envelope with my name scrolled across the front was propped on my pillow.

The journal entry, which I would find inside the envelope, was part of a story which someone was enticing me with. Deward and Piper Venema were the leaders of the Dwellers, the dark souls. Their son, Walter, married a Keeper and chose to live in the light. They had two daughters, Bethany and Tina. Walter was captured by the Dwellers and sent through the Dwellers black arch for his choosing light over darkness. He now lived eternally on the Earth Plane. Tina was captured and started to live her life in the world of the Dwellers. Bethany lived in the world of the Keepers. Bethany's Dweller guard was the author of the journal entries. He had infiltrated the world of the Keepers, lived amongst the Keepers unnoticed, and was in love with Bethany.

Tina had made herself at home with the Dwellers. The journal entries were filled with her cruel acts. None were worse than those inflicted on the slave named Grace who was once a Keeper.

Reluctantly, I moved to retrieve the envelope. I ripped it open and sat down on my bed to read.

Journal Entry #366

As I curled into a chair in Bethany's empty dungeon room, I was startled by Grace appearing and shutting the door behind her. She told a story of sacrifice for another. She began by telling me her and the others all woke up one day, sitting in the slave quarters, without any memories of who they were or where they came from. She only had one thought, one day a "girl" would come for her, so she held on to the hope during all of the years since.

Grace said it dawned on her, after seeing Bethany, who this "girl" must be. A family member of some connection who had came for her. But when they locked Bethany up in the dungeon, she could hear her cry through the walls at night and understood her desperation to leave this place. She also knew if Piper intended to lock her up forever, she really was never to leave the room again. How could she let this happen to the only light in her life?

Grace was in Piper's room and saw Bethany's missing locket which she put into her pocket and hid in her mattress, thus starting her plan. She knew the locket was the key to getting the "girl" home. She then set on Bethany's bed and pushed a block out of the wall and I could see a notebook, full of writing. It seems Grace and Bethany had been writing to each other and placing it into the hole. She told me Bethany really did forgive me and knew she was safe as long as I stood at the door. So they made the plan that if I ever left, she would disappear and then use the locket to go home.

Today, when I left, Grace had gone to Tina and made the comment that I was no longer guarding the door, but please not to subject Bethany to the outer rim of the grounds. Grace is more cunning than any of us have ever given her credit for. Collin, Tina's guard, refused first saying it wasn't safe. He often had his hands full when it came to the whims of Tina. When his reasoning fell on deaf ears he asked if she would really expose her own sister to the danger of the outer grounds. Then Tina threatened to go by herself. Collin gave in for fear Tina would be hurt by the dark souls which circled Venema House. They took Bethany and pushed her from the safe grounds and watched as she disappeared. Grace felt time would tell if they found her.

I asked Grace about herself and Grace told me she was old and no longer mattered. However, she felt Bethany was the future and needed to go on. Then she encouraged me, as she had promised Bethany, to use my locket and join her. Grace felt certain that I was the only one who could protect her from the family.

Journal Entry #367

Tina told the story of Collin and herself loosing Bethany when they took her to the outskirts of the grounds and shoved her beyond the safety of the Venema grounds. For fear of what was to happen to Collin, Tina admitted she made Collin do it. Deward intended to have Geren punish Tina when the search party returned. Piper had discovered the locket missing and told me if she went back to the world of the Keepers, she would have no memory of anything before the time she would wake in their world. This was because she was half Dweller and using a Keeper locket. The travel by Keeper locket, when she wasn't a full Keeper, would erase her memories.

I had waited long enough. I used my locket and was instantly walking down the familiar hall to the hospital. I was certain Bethany went to hospital which was the plan so she could then be placed into the Hall of Knowl-

edge. I went to the hospital, to see if it was true. Would she really not re-member me? She looked at me as if I were a stranger. I felt as if the air had been sucked from my lungs and that I would never breathe again.

Solliday tried to console me. He says one day we will tell her because we both know they will come for her again. For now, I will keep a safe distance from her and try to watch from afar. I am needed because I can hear when they come. I do believe one day they will figure out that I have stopped work-ing for them and will come for me too, and I know exactly what that means.

Maybe it was for the best that she remembered nothing of her family, of the tragedy. She loved her father dearly. Maybe it is better for her not to remember why her mother had to leave her to hide, better not to remember always being hunted, better not to remember me. We were never right for each other. I am meant to live in the dark, she is meant to live in the light. Two impossible worlds to merge.

All I can do for my love is protect what is left of her and the life she will now live.

There was no denying the facts. This girl was Home with no memory as to who she was. She had no parents because her father was gone, her mother in hiding, and her sister evil. The similarities to me were overwhelming. Is this why my chapter was empty? Did I belong to the world of darkness? Was this the reason the Dwellers were chasing me? The truth had to be dreadful since it had driven off Marvin. I certainly didn't feel as if I was filled with darkness. If this were the answer, only one question came to mind. How?

I walked over to the window discovering the ladder was down. Of course, the journal was left on my bed by someone using Tilly's escape ladder. I couldn't tell her, nor could I make her believe the ladder or our open win-dows were dangerous. My answer was simple. Trevor.

I took a deep breath and crawled out the window onto the swinging lad-der. As I climbed upward, it swayed back and forth in the sunlight. To mini-mize being seen, I attempted to climb it fast which only made it sway harder. Relieved reaching the top, I found Trevor's window open. I straddled it to enter his room. Crawling across Trevor's small cot of a bed I found the room to be empty.

I lay over on his bed thinking my being here might be a mistake. I should go find Marvin and convince him to level with me. I was in over my head with no memory as to why a Dweller was chasing me or why a Dweller was leaving me journal entries.

"Elizabeth?" Trevor questioned as he entered the room and then closed the door behind him.

"Trevor, did you put out the ladder today?" I asked pointing towards the window.

"No," Trevor said as he moved to the window and began to rapidly pull it up. "How did this get out? It's daytime. Someone might see it."

I threw my legs over his bed and stood demanding, "Trevor, I have something I have to confide in someone."

He turned to look at me concerned and asked, "What is it?"

"Someone is leaving me notes on my bed," I admitted.

"Those love notes that Tilly is always referring too," Trevor chuckled.

"I'm serious," I half complained.

"Sorry," Trevor said under his breath as he closed his window.

"I believe whoever is leaving the notes is using the ladder to get access to my room," I threw out.

"Don't be ridiculous," Trevor said. "No one knows about the ladder. Besides, I spend a lot of time watching it during the evening." He moved over to sit down next to me. "Isn't it more likely that someone in the girl's hall is sneaking them into your room?"

My complaints were falling on deaf ears.

"The notes are probably ending up on the wrong bed," Trevor seriously stated.

"You don't think someone would leave me notes?" I asked in a huff. "Like, I'm that repulsive?"

"Oh no, you're hot," Trevor quickly and mindlessly retorted. "Elizabeth, I'm not attempting to make a pass at you. I'm totally into Ruthanne. However, any male would be crazy not to see your beauty. My comment wasn't meant as an insult."

"You just assume the notes are meant for Tilly?" I questioned.

"Only because she draws guys like they are flies," Trevor said under his breath.

I couldn't disagree with his assessment. I guess I could see why he assumed they were for Tilly. Really, it didn't matter if he assumed they were for Tilly or me. I had to remember my purpose for coming up to see Trevor, the ladder. Maybe it would be better if he believed they were for Tilly. He was over protective of her. "I see your point," I conceded for his benefit. "Please see mine. I feel in my gut that the notes are being left by someone using the ladder."

"How long have you been getting notes?" Trevor questioned.

"Awhile," I admitted.

"That accounts for your fear of the windows," Trevor muttered to himself as if it suddenly made sense. "What am I going to do?"

The door opened with Eddie walking through. He shut the door exclaiming, "Crash!"

"Hey Eddie," I returned.

"Why the visit?" Eddie asked as he glanced between Trevor and me.

"She has a concern about the ladder," Trevor answered for me.

"Kim isn't happy with you," Eddie stated as he plopped on his bed.

"What did I do to her?" I asked.

"It isn't what you did to her," Eddie said with a chuckle. "It's what you do to all of us each week."

"The assignments," I said under my breath.

"Don't worry about it," Trevor piped up from beside me.

"Really crash," Eddie said. "Neither of us is upset."

"Professor Zirak is punishing me for no reason!" I huffed.

"Tell us about it," Trevor said slightly pacing in thought.

"There is nothing to tell," I stated noticing that Eddie appeared to be as eager as any big eared girl waiting to hear juicy gossip. "I assume Tilly hasn't told you why I haven't turned in my life plan or theme."

"Nope," Eddie answered while Trevor nodded no.

"I remember nothing about myself," I admitted to the two of them. "Tilly has kept assuring me that it's simply a memory fog."

"Those aren't uncommon," Eddie stated.

"I did know you had a fog," Trevor stated. "I just didn't know your memories hadn't returned."

"I'm blank," I stated. "I remember nothing beyond waking up in the hospital."

"The hospital?" Trevor asked repeating the words.

"I know," I answered. "It's not the normal place to return. I should have returned to the Hall of Babies. I didn't though. I returned to the hospital."

"Like a Humling," Eddie muttered to himself. Trevor's eyes darted to Eddie's. You could see the Humling statement hit home with him.

CHAPTER NINE

Trevor

"Trevor," Elizabeth called as I strolled across the foyer of The Hall of Knowledge. I grinned at her efforts trying to skip steps as she flew down the staircase.

"Hey," I greeted.

"I need a destination card," Elizabeth blurted out.

"Shh…" I hushed her as I glanced around to see if anyone overheard.

"Sorry," Elizabeth mouthed.

"Where too?" I asked and then added, "Not that Humling town."

"No," Elizabeth quickly replied. "I want to go shop where I can purchase vanilla ice cream and a bag of peppermints."

"That's a strange combination," I said watching a smile cross her face. "It doesn't sound very good."

"I don't know whether it's good or not," Elizabeth said off the top of her head. "I've never tried it."

"Elizabeth, is this a get Marvin back scheme?" I asked. When Elizabeth didn't answer, I spoke my mind, "This is unhealthy. Tilly and, well, all of us are worried about you."

"Would you give up if it was Ruthanne?" Elizabeth pointedly asked backing me into a corner.

"No," I answered fully understanding the point. "May I ask you one question that has been bugging me about the whole situation?"

"Sure," Elizabeth responded as I pushed the lift button.

I turned to look her dead in the eye, "What about Dustin?"

The lift door dinged as we both made our way in.

"Elizabeth!" The little man exclaimed excitedly.

"Hi Leo," Elizabeth returned as she took a brown paper bag which he was holding up for her. "Thank you."

"You're welcome," Leo said. When he noticed my watching the exchange he growled, "Put your eyes back in your head." Elizabeth crossed her arms across her chest frowning at him slightly as he said to her, "Sorry."

Elizabeth moved to stand beside me as she countered my question, "I don't have an explanation for him. He is just … Dustin."

"You've watched Tilly. You can't have your cake and eat it too," I said quietly to Elizabeth. "No man likes to be second fiddle or have a third party hanging around."

"I'll keep that in mind," Elizabeth sighed. "The card?"

It certainly was against my better judgment. However, all I could really do was give her my advice and the freedom to make her own mistakes. "I'll make it tonight," I said watching her swing the brown paper bag. "What's in the bag?"

"Gingerbread," Elizabeth answered. "Want some?"

"No, that's okay," I replied. "Leo makes it special for you?"

"He makes it fresh everyday," Elizabeth leaned over to whisper. "He always gives me a daily bag."

The lift dinged with the small man announcing, "Destination One, Administration Complex."

Elizabeth was a step ahead as she said in a friendly tone, "Thank you." The small man smiled up at her.

We were greeted by Tiffany and her crew who were hanging out in the center of the massive foyer. Janelle seemed to be disagreeing with Tiffany over something. I wanted to lean against the wall and observe for as long as possible. Unnoticed, I could watch.

"Where are you going?" Elizabeth asked as I stepped backwards.

"Forgot something," I said. "Go on without me."

"Okay," she replied intently watching me. I watched her give the group a wide berth as she passed unnoticed and unscathed.

With my back against the wall, I watched. I had learned to be quite and observant over the last month or so. There was more danger around than the normal Keeper realized. The little man passing Elizabeth a daily brown bag was odd in my thinking also.

My working to protect Tilly was where it all began. The morning I went to blackmail Mrs. Bradford into acting like a mother towards Tilly, my path was set. Shortly after the morning I blackmailed Mrs. Bradford, a knock came at my dorm room door waking me from a peaceful nights sleep. A stranger was standing in the boy's hall and handed me a small envelope with my name on it. He was gone in a flash, before I could ask questions. The note inside simply said, "Department of Ghosts, locker room. Isobelle." I was too intrigued to ignore the note. Like a curious cat, I was on my way as soon as daylight broke. The details of that fateful morning would be etched into my memory forever since my life changed on that day. I embarked on a mystical adventure to the Ghost Complex to see Isobelle, not realizing the journey I had started on was one of the biggest I had taken in my life. It was second only to my visit to the Earth Plane with Tilly.

Once inside the locker room at the Ghost Complex, I found myself staring at Tilly's Aunt Belle. I produced the note, but she kept asking me for my code. I had no idea what she was rattling on about. Startling me was the stranger who had appeared at my door spouting a code from behind me. He was like a spy with his sneaking around. It all happened fast at this point.

Belle typed the code into the panel on the front of the locker. The locker shook as if someone were hitting it with a sledge hammer attempting to get out from the inside. The door flung open and instantly the stranger and Belle shoved me into the locker. I pushed on the door from the inside in a panic, but I couldn't keep them from shutting me in.

I panicked feeling trapped as the locker began to rattle with me inside it. Frantically, I realized no one knew where I was. Usually, I had more control and didn't put myself into situations like that. The eerie feeling continued as the air swirled around me in a tornado fashion. As suddenly as the shaking began, it stopped. I could hear the electronic keys being pushed on the front of the locker and then the door popped open. With my hands made into fists, I shoved on the door and jumped out. I was ready to take on whoever was standing there to victimize me.

Words couldn't express my shock. Mr. Bradford was standing before me in a busy, cavern of a room with no windows.

Mr. Bradford reassured me, "Calm down. Everything is okay."

I now realize I must have looked like a caged animal that had been backed into a corner and was ready to pounce.

"Where are we?" I asked as I took in the rows and rows of desks filled with strangers.

"You are standing in the Underground," Mr. Bradford proudly replied.

"The subway?" I questioned.

"Follow me," Mr. Bradford replied to my stumped expression. "I will explain once we move somewhere more private."

"Why have you kidnapped me?" I questioned with my feet firmly planted not daring to bring up Mrs. Bradford.

Mr. Bradford intently peered at me. Then he moved to lean against the wall asking, "You want to talk in front of the whole room then?"

I peered out nervously at all the unknown faces in the underground cavern.

"Come on," Mr. Bradford waved as he stepped off towards the back of the dark room.

I followed him noticing that everyone in the room was a male. Odd.

He stopped at one of three office doors and held it open for me. Once inside, I found a normal enough looking office with a desk, chairs, and picture on the wall. A tall filing cabinet stood against the wall beside the desk. Mr. Bradford fiddled with some button on his desk and the wall behind his desk slid away revealing shelves and shelves of radio receivers. I only knew what they were because Eddie and I had bugged a couple of places within the Hall of Knowledge. These receivers looked like ours, but better quality.

"Do you have anything to admit?" Mr. Bradford asked as he rounded his desk.

I had a lot to admit, however I knew what he probably was referring too. "Before I admit to anything, I should ask what you have been listening too?" I stated as I pointed to the wall of receivers as I sat down in the chair across from him.

He turned to point at one receiver in particular saying, "This receiver is always interesting. In general, I use it like a radio. It has always been interesting to listen to my daughter plotting in the middle of the night with a boy down the street as to how to sneak out or make life miserable for her unsuspecting mother. My favorite night was when they plotted to go to the Earth Plane together."

I cringed in my chair.

"However, not to long ago I heard…"

I held up my hand interrupting, "Blackmailing."

"Interestingly enough, yes. A certain neighborhood boy blackmailing my wife early in the morning," Mr. Bradford stated. "That was when I realized the nuisance of a boy had grown into a man who could stand on his own two feet."

At this point, I knew I was definitely in trouble? Had he in a round about way given me a compliment? "I'm sorry you found out this way," I stated.

Mr. Bradford beamed at me before saying, "Don't worry, you didn't break the news to me. I knew long ago."

"What?" I questioned in disbelief.

"Let me explain all of this from the beginning," Mr. Bradford said as he waved his hand around the room. "When I was your age, I was part of Administration House. As a whole, I was top of my administration class and second only to one other in our training grouping. I was handpicked for this job."

"What exactly are all of you doing?" I threw out nervously, but trying not to show it.

"To put it simply," Mr. Bradford began. "We call ourselves the underground and we are gathering intelligence on Dwellers that are living in our world."

"Dwellers in our world?" I mumbled shaking my head and thinking he sounded like Elizabeth.

"I'm not crazy," Mr. Bradford said. "You know the story of those who disappeared, don't you? The event?"

"Who doesn't," I retorted. "The Keepers and Humlings lived amongst each other. Then one day Keepers, one by one, started disappearing when the Dwellers kidnapped them."

"Some Dwellers never left and new ones arrive from time to time," Mr. Bradford sighed.

"If all of this is true, then I assume you believe they are building up to something?" I questioned.

"That is why I have chosen you. You are smart." Mr. Bradford said with a smile.

"Mrs. Bradford?" I questioned.

"I met Olivia during my training and I adored her," Mr. Bradford said as the smile faded from his face. "When she was younger, she was a lot like Mathilda."

"Tilly," I corrected him.

"That nickname is a source of contention. Her mother doesn't want it used," Mr. Bradford said shaking his head. "Olivia was just as beautiful as Tilly. She could have the pick of whom she wanted to date. She always had raw determination to come out on top. She was driven. When she couldn't have who she really wanted, she settled on me."

He suddenly looked like the Mr. Bradford I was used to seeing; dejected, wimpy, and henpecked.

"By the time she settled on me, I had settled on her," Mr. Bradford stated. "It was necessary for me to provide the perfect smoke screen to camouflage my dealings with the underground. It was essential that I appear to take a submissive role to my partner in a successful and otherwise normal marriage. Olivia was perfect. She was strong willed and too self absorbed to pay too much attention to what I did beyond providing her the lifestyle she desired."

I sat astonished. To all who knew them socially, he was henpecked. It ended up they were more perfectly paired than anyone could possibly realize. I broke the silence saying, "It worked."

"It did," Mr. Bradford said as he seemed lost in his thoughts. Then his eyes flashed to mine, "Every good pairing comes with its own unique problems."

"Don't go there!" I growled.

Mr. Bradford held up his hand continuing, "All I will say, is I knew from the beginning. It just made it all more believable. Math… Tilly draws enough attention away from me that I have never had to worry that anyone was looking too closely at me."

"Now I have your side of the story," I stated. "Earlier, you said you chose me?"

"Yes," Mr. Bradford replied.

"I'm not sure I believe any of this conspiracy stuff," I retorted. "What if I don't want to be chosen?"

"Come on, don't play with me," Mr. Bradford stated. "Why would you think I would lie to you?"

"Lets see," I sighed. "You have lied to your daughter her whole life. I do think you would lie to me if it suited you."

I remember how he stood shaking his head and calling for the burly man who appeared. They took me to show me the underground's collection of documentation on Dwellers. Being a scientific mind, I couldn't deny it after seeing their evidence. I had been naive. I also understood for my own safety, Tilly's safety, and my family's safety, there was no choice. With the realization that this was much bigger than any one person, I became a member of the Underground. I would never be able to pretend what I had seen didn't exist. I also was bound to silence. No one else would want to share the horrors of what I had seen in their evidence.

Elizabeth was a growing concern of mine. She was taking some strange vitamins and eating ginger. During my time in the Underground network, I had learned ginger was key to the strength of Dwellers. Maybe it was just a coincidence, but this wasn't the first time I had seen her eat ginger. This was only the beginning of my concerns about her. Then there was her apparent inability to move when in the presence of a Dweller. This baffled me. Lastly, I would have to figure out the cause for her lack of memory. It had been too long for her lack of memory to be a memory fog. All mysteries to figure out.

Back to the spying at hand. Janelle appeared as if she simply couldn't take anymore of something. She seemed to storm off as Tiffany laughed with Rodger. It was odd that Rodger had so easily taken up with Tiffany. Maybe this was the reason for her storming off.

"What's wrong?" Ruthanne asked as she approached me with Eddie.

"Nothing," I sighed. As I peered at her I couldn't help but smile at the red headed beauty before me. I was a lucky man.

"Is Elizabeth still getting notes?" Eddie asked. "Where is she?"

"Notes?" Ruthanne repeated as she looked at Eddie. "What are you talking about?"

Eddie looked past Ruthanne and instantly apologized, "Oh, sorry dude."

"Elizabeth is getting love notes left on her bed," I explained covering tracks.

Ruthanne instantly frowned huffing, "Now you're her psychologist too?"

"Dude, you and your chick problems," Eddie mumbled as he put his ear buds in and pulled his hoodie up over his head. Chuckling, he turned to stroll away.

"I think whoever is leaving them doesn't know it's Elizabeth's bed," I plunged on. Why not give her the full picture and then she could be mad or not. "I think they believe Elizabeth's bed is Tilly's."

Ruthanne didn't look half as angry as she did now. "Harry," Ruthanne growled. "I'm going to hang him by his toes!"

"What?" I questioned.

"Harry doesn't know when to stop," Ruthanne said. "He gets attached too quickly and doesn't easily take no for an answer." She paused looking angrier by the minute. "I won't let him stalk another girl."

What? Stalk another girl? "Great!" I said under my breath. This was all I needed. The ladder was going to have to go. I never saw Harry as a stalker, but I wouldn't take any chances when it came to Tilly.

Elizabeth

"Tilly, could you occupy Rhett tomorrow night?" I asked. "Just keep him busy long enough to make him come home late."

"Are you going to try to see Marvin," Tilly questioned.

"She is," Trevor stated as he handed me a destination card.

"With a destination card?" Tilly asked as she glared between Trevor and me.

"I need to pick up a cold war offering, ice cream to take with me," I explained. "I need something to break the ice between us."

"Ice cream?" Tilly repeated.

"She is making his favorite treat," Trevor piped in.

"Marvin dumped you! Never crawl to a man, Elizabeth!" Tilly sternly spouted folding her arms.

"He has just strayed," I countered. "He's lost out there in a back alley somewhere."

"Strayed?" Tilly questioned as her hands flew to her hips. "Like an alley cat?"

"Stop," I demanded.

Tilly rolled her eyes saying, "I don't understand it. You have got to learn to be a dumper, Elizabeth, not be to a dumpee!"

"Please Tilly. You will detain Rhett tonight, won't you?" I begged.

"Rhett?" Trevor questioned looking a bit confused.

"Elizabeth wants me to run interference," Tilly explained. She then glared at me. "I don't agree with your madness, but I will and only because you're my best friend."

"How late will you be?" Trevor asked looking anxious.

"Don't worry about it," Tilly replied.

"I just wanted to warn you that the ladder was cut again," Trevor threw out.

"When?" Tilly asked. Before Trevor could answer she asked, "Aren't you going to fix it?"

"Not tonight," Trevor said. "I have a date."

Tilly just sighed as Professor Presnell entered the classroom. We were in for a long, boring day listening to her drone on and on.

CHAPTER TEN

Trevor

I reached the black curtain which ran along the sides of the stage in Grand Hall. Before I could push my way through its opening, voices carried to me. I stopped dead in my tracks.

"Shouldn't you be next door?" Andy's familiar voice boomed.

"Who are you to question me?" The familiar voice of Mrs. Bradford countered.

"Your daughter's boyfriend," Andy answered. If he only knew, I thought as I shook my head.

Then, I heard him half chuckle, "As for you, no one would know you were her mother. They might mistake you for Tiffany's instead."

"I could say the same," Mrs. Bradford taunted. "Who would know you were serious enough with Tilly to be considered her boyfriend?"

"What are you alluding too?" Andy spewed.

"You don't really think you are the only one, do you?" Mrs. Bradford stated and then cackled. "You're dumb to stand up for Tilly, just one of many idiots in love with her. It's too bad she doesn't really love you in return."

"She isn't dating Scott anymore," Andy spewed back.

"Really?" Mrs. Bradford innocently asked. "Scott ate dinner with her at our house not to many weeks ago, not to mention Doctor Barrett. He's kind of dorky with his bow tie, but he has a great job. Mathilda has a different date each night. I hear by the grapevine, she is seeing someone that she is keeping secret from her father and me." Mrs. Bradford paused.

Tilly was in trouble.

When Andy didn't say anything, she continued to taunt him. "Lastly, don't you know about Trevor? Mathilda plays him off as a friend, but one day they will marry. Remember the whole thing with the Council?"

I couldn't believe she pulled me into the conversation. I held my breath and backed up towards the rehearsal room door.

A red faced Andy burst through the curtain. When he saw me he asked me in an eerie, steely voice, "Where's Tilly?"

"I don't know man," I replied trying to play it cool.

Andy pushed past me into rehearsal room and briskly headed for the unsuspecting Elizabeth. He tapped her shoulder.

Elizabeth turned saying, "Hey."

"Where's Tilly?" Andy pointedly asked.

Elizabeth shuffled her feet a little. "Um… She'll be here before long."

Elizabeth's demeanor left me no doubt that Tilly was with Anthony. "Hang out with us," I began trying to draw attention away from Elizabeth. "You'll like the new songs."

"Sure," Andy spewed. "Play it off. Hide behind your friendship."

Elizabeth appeared baffled by his statement. "Wipe that look off your face," Andy stated. "You know!"

Elizabeth's eyes flashed to mine. Andy couldn't ignore the obvious. We did both know. An angry Andy stormed off.

Tilly

"You're as dumb as a box or rocks," Andy angrily yelled at Anthony as he charged across the lawn outside the Ghost Complex.

Great! Couldn't I sneak away for a secret rendezvous? Besides, how did he know where I was anyway?

"No," Anthony disagreed while shaking his head. "I just have a unique perspective. That's all."

"Man, you're a real dumb ass!" Andy snarled. "And you! I don't understand this!" Andy's fists clinched as he started to add something, but instead simply closed his mouth with the hurt screaming from his eyes as he peered at me.

What was with my sudden pang of guilt. I intended to end things with Andy, not by hurting him though. He had just begun to trust me again. If only I could find some way to make him understand. I began, "Andy..."

I knew it was all too much when he interrupted me.

"There is nothing you can say." He turned and walked away.

Once again, I left Andy with the knowledge I cheated on him with another guy. Now, I couldn't help but think Anthony would be leaving as well. Déjà vu. My world was imploding! I could now feel tears rolling down my face. I couldn't will myself to look up and see heartache in Anthony's eyes. I just stood while an uncontrollable sinking feeling consumed me. Anthony stepped closer to me and simply stood there. I kept waiting for his feet to disappear, him yell, and it all to be over.

Anthony broke the silence, "Tilly."

His seductive voice made the thought of loosing him unbearable. What in the world was happening to me? I was flustered and felt out of control. Then my heart knew what I hadn't had the guts to admit for weeks. Anthony was more than my simple boyfriend. I was in love with him! I gasped and held my chest. Panic and jitters began to take control of my body with this realization. Him dumping me was going to be unbearable!

Anthony grabbed both my visibly trembling hands and held them within his own. I still was unable to look at him. "If he knew what he had, he would have taken better care of you," Anthony stated.

"Huh!" My face lifted and I looked directly into Anthony's eyes. They were tenderly and lovingly filled with the view of me. I stammered, "What? You're not mad? Or leaving?"

"Not unless you want me too," Anthony quickly answered. "Look, your shopping in the sea of love isn't enough to chase me off."

I pulled my hands free as I wiped the tears on the back of them while I asked, "Why not?"

He let out a huge sigh. You could see his face searching for the right words. Suddenly he pulled me into his arms. His warm embrace melted away my fears of him leaving me. A sensation of sunshine and love washed over me and in the same instant, guilt. I, unfortunately, understood Andy wasn't my only problem standing in our way. I had another more serious issue to face. I stepped back, pulling away from his arms.

"What is it?" Anthony questioned feeling me becoming tense.

"Andy wasn't the only one," I openly admitted. "There's Barrett. Really, he's not my type. I was using him for lift passes."

"Hmm…" I heard him hum.

I closed my eyes, not wanting to see his reaction to how devious I could be. "Also, sort of a guy name Scott." Did he realize what he was getting himself into? "Scott is a guy my parents like. Every time I go home for a visit, they kinda invite him over. My parents say he is perfect for me."

"He's not perfect for you unless you are the one who decides so," Anthony reasoned.

I opened my eyes to peer at him after blurting out the array of guys caught on my hook.

"Why are you taking all of this so calmly," I inquired begging him to be upset with me.

"I already told you," Anthony answered.

This was too easy. "You're talking this in stride," I countered.

"You and I are uniquely suited for each other," Anthony added as his hands gently rubbed my arms.

"Wait," I said holding up my hand in front of him. "Are you telling me you are dating someone else? What's her name? Let me guess, Gina?" Suddenly I felt as if my skin were on fire.

"Gina?" He asked with a smirk.

"Funny is it?" I huffed.

"There's no one else," Anthony reassured me with a chuckle. "There has never been a Gina."

"Gina that Gary likes to mention is only a figment of my imagination?" I sarcastically inquired.

"Look, Gina is a girl who didn't exist," Anthony began. "Wyatt, Gary, and I always use her as an excuse to get rid of a clinger."

"A clinger?" I repeated.

"The girl who you can't get rid of," Anthony explained.

"Why did Gary tell me that?" I questioned. "Why does he keep mentioning her?"

"He likes watching your reaction and causing trouble for me," Anthony responded.

"Then, I don't understand," I told him. "How are we uniquely suited?"

He looked at me and chuckled under his breath. "I, not unlike you, have dated my share."

I couldn't help but glare at him. The thought of anyone else dating him made me crazy. I had to ask, "Will I one day be just another girl you have once dated?"

Anthony moved forward and once again embraced me in his arms. Then he whispered into my ear, "No one I have ever dated compares to you."

"Of course not," I mumbled feeling a little inadequate. I knew how many I had dumped over the years. I hoped I wasn't his Andy.

With my head against his chest, I could feel and hear his slight chuckle at my response. "Hey, one more thing," Anthony said as I listened secure in his arms. "No more home visits without me!"

"Sure," I half-heartedly agreed. With a heavy heart, I knew I would never be able to take him home. More importantly, there could be no real future between us. I was spoken for according to the Council.

Elizabeth

Standing in the shadows, I watched Marvin go inside Rhett's house. I knew Tilly was keeping Rhett busy claiming to have questions about our lesson today at the Ghost Complex. Marvin was mine. I happily carried my frozen ice cream and freshly crushed bag of peppermints and all but ran down the path towards the door. Rhett's house was always looking abandoned with the windows covered. I knocked and knocked with no answer. Fine. I was going in uninvited. I flung open the door.

Marvin was sitting on the bottom step of the stairs with his head in his hands. He didn't look up but stated, "Elizabeth, go away."

"I'm not going anywhere," I growled at him. I turned towards the kitchen and placed my freezer tote on the table and began to unpack the ice cream and peppermints. I then rounded the table to get the utensils and bowls I would need.

Marvin was now watching me from his step as he questioned, "What are you doing?"

"It must be my lack of cooking skills," I half admitted. "So, I'm committed to learn how to cook."

"It has nothing to do with your cooking skills," Marvin stated clearly exasperated.

"Let me finish," I demanded. "I know it's not real cooking. However, I figure I should definitely prove to you I can make your favorite treat, ice cream with peppermints."

"Where did you get the ingredients?" Marvin questioned. However, before I could answer, he said, "Never mind that, it's not important. Elizabeth, you need to go." He moved to hold open the front door.

"I'm not leaving," I repeated as I scooped the ice cream and turned away from him.

He moved over to me and began to place the lid on the ice cream. I grabbed the lid and when our hands met, Marvin hesitated. I knew it. Our eyes met and I could see behind them. The regret. The agony of our being apart.

We were lost in a forbidden moment standing there together, gazing into each others eyes. The brief moment seemed like an eternity. Then, I heard a familiar voice calling my name from the doorway, "Miss Cantrell, what are you doing here?"

Marvin jumped like he had been caught with his hand in the cookie jar. I grabbed the lid back and slammed it on the table. "I'm having ice cream," I stated to Rhett in a tone of annoyance. He was supposed to be detained. What happened to Tilly?

"Were you invited?" Rhett asked me, but looked at Marvin.

"No, I wasn't," I answered for myself. "I invited myself."

"Miss Cantrell, it's rude to invite yourself," Rhett stated.

"I don't see my presence as rude," I disagreed. "You did say once upon a time that your door was always open."

"Well, that was before..." Rhett trailed off.

"It's fine," Marvin said. "Make us all a bowl. But then, we have work to complete. You will need to get back to the Keeper House before dark."

"My curfew is my problem," I stated to be defiant.

"You scoop, I'll mix," Marvin stated ignoring my remark. He seemed to be resigned to get this whole affair over with.

"Your curfew may indeed be your problem," Rhett began. "Marvin and I do have serious work to do tonight." His eyes flickered to Marvin when he said, "Our project is giving us more problems than we expected."

"What project?" I asked to an awkward silence.

Whatever the project was, they were silent about it. I scooped the first bowl of ice cream. My hand brushed Marvin's as I handed it to him. It was as if I had stuck my finger into an electric socket. An instant jolt passed between us. Marvin instantly started scooping the peppermints and mixing them in. I scooped the second bowl as Rhett held his hands out for it. He began to mix the peppermints into his ice cream. I scooped the third bowl as Marvin handed me back the first completely mixed bowl. He grabbed the last bowl and diligently began to mix it. I waited until Rhett and Marvin were ready to eat theirs before I began. Marvin looked washed out and sad. I was disappointed when he pushed his ice cream around in his bowl and barely ate any of it. All the trouble I went too was for nothing. My plan had backfired because Rhett interrupted us.

As I finished my last bite, Rhett rose and said, "I need to talk with Professor Bungard. Going tonight will save me a trip in the early morning. May I walk with you back to Keeper House?"

I sighed. No one, including Rhett was going to derail me. "Actually, I was hoping Marvin would walk me back."

"Elizabeth... I can't," Marvin softly said. "Do you want me to do this again and in front of Uncle Rhett?"

"Do what again?" I asked being coy.

Marvin stood and in a frantic succession spewed, "I do not intend to date you! Please don't stop by anymore."

He, once more, had tried to crush what was left of my heart. However, I heard him loud and clear. He didn't deny the obvious electricity or feelings between us. I stood, picking up my freezer bag, and stepped past the chair between Marvin and myself. I leaned up to his ear on my tippy toes and whispered in his ear, "I understand." In a quieter voice I said, "That we are meant to be together." I let my hand brush his chest. Tilly had taught me a trick or two.

Rhett almost jumped out of his skin and was at my side in an instant, "Shall we." He held his hand towards the door.

Marvin plopped back down in his chair and simply said, "Goodbye Elizabeth!"

CHAPTER ELEVEN

Tilly

While standing in the shadows of the stage curtains, I couldn't believe I had been forced into hiding. What was happening to me? I wasn't weak, just in love. I couldn't be seen with any of my old flings, including Harry. My heart was set on Anthony and I wouldn't let anything or anyone come between us. I stepped behind the curtain into the props room to keep out of his sight. The back of Harry's red head was visible from the crack in the curtain. He was watching the rehearsal room door. What a way to end a long day after dealing with Mrs. VanCues. It was as if Harry was a stalker who couldn't take getting dumped.

This all reminded me of when I had purposely sneaked into another closet long ago. Trevor and I formed and were proudly the only two members of the Kissing Club when we were in the sixth grade. Deciding we needed more members, we dared Eddie and some girl to meet us in the closet in our classroom during recess. Trevor and I diligently crept up the three flights of stairs and past all the open doors which lead to our third floor classroom. We had done this many times. I was interested in Eddie proving he could be a part of our club. Kissing was the most rebellious thing Trevor and I had done back then. I, being the leader, needed Eddie to prove himself.

Once in the closet, Trevor seemed as interested in watching for Eddie as I had been. Eventually, I gave up hope and began to rummage through the mess of coats and backpacks. An unassuming, pink backpack called to me. It was Tiffany's. I picked it up as a loud thud hit the floor. Instantly, I looked to see what had fallen. It was a thick, hardcover diary. Trevor instantly told me no, but even then I didn't do or not do things because he said so. There was no way I wasn't going to thumb through it.

I cracked the book to about the middle. Shock was the only way to describe what I was viewing. It was all about me, a burn book. What was written was hateful and mostly untrue. It had never dawned on me that other girls could be so vicious. Tiffany and I had been what I thought of as friends. I felt betrayed. This was the beginning of Tiffany becoming my true nemesis. Eddie making it up the three flights of stairs paled in comparison to the light bulb revelation about Tiffany.

Snapping back to reality, I watched Trevor follow Ruthanne through the rehearsal room door chattering about the details for the music. Ruthanne was still helping my Harmony group. I figured she wanted us to succeed and Tiffany to fail. They both appeared surprised to see Harry hanging out at the door.

"What are you doing here?" Trevor pointedly asked.

"Rekindling an old flame," Harry shot at Trevor.

"No!" Ruthanne said with a loud boom. "It's true, isn't it?"

"What's true?" Harry asked.

"The love notes?" Ruthanne impatiently spit out. "You're not doing this with Tilly."

"You need to stay out of my love life," Harry growled back.

"And you need to stay off of the girls floor at Keeper house," Trevor returned as he seemed to puff out his chest.

"No more leaving notes on beds," Ruthanne added placing her hands on her lips.

"Leaving notes on a bed?" Harry repeated appearing confused.

"Yes," Ruthanne said.

"Man, don't play dumb," Trevor said in an annoyed tone.

"You've been leaving them on the wrong bed!" Ruthanne adamantly stated. "You're so incredibly dumb to think I wouldn't find out!"

"Wait," Harry said holding his hand up. "I haven't been leaving notes."

"Get a grip," Trevor growled. "Ruthanne has told me about your problem taking no for no."

Harry looked caught as he began to explain, "That was only with…"

"Stop," Ruthanne demanded. "Leave Tilly alone. You are as wrong for her as she is for you. Don't you see that?"

"Not really," Harry countered.

"Don't leave anymore notes," Trevor cautioned. "If you do, I'll be forced to turn you in."

"You wouldn't do that," Harry said challenging Trevor.

"Try me," Trevor challenged him back as he stepped closer to Harry.

"I should…" Harry paused shaking his head from side to side.

Trevor didn't back down as he shot back, "Should what?"

"Sis, you're the one who is dumb," Harry said. "Look at him standing up for Tilly."

"Don't disrespect your sister," Trevor said as he seemed to stand taller.

"Whatever," Harry said as he threw up his hands. "Like you aren't!" Harry paused a moment to peer directly in Trevor's eyes. "Dating two chicks isn't disrespectful? What about Tilly?"

Ruthanne instantly moved between the two of them as she warned Harry, "Don't."

Harry shook his head as he coldly replied, "Just don't run to me when the inevitable happens and he doesn't choose you!" With that he walked away.

Trevor instantly turned to Ruthanne. "You don't have to worry about Tilly."

Ruthanne stepped up to Trevor, placing her finger on his lips saying, "I know."

I scooted back, not wanting to watch their long, sloppy kiss. The thought of them kissing still made me feel nauseous and ill.

Elizabeth

I stepped into the lift at the Keeper Complex and was soon greeted by a sight that made me feel ill. Marvin was strolling with Tiffany and she was overly chummy. What were they doing? Appalled, I didn't want to hear their conversation. Quickly, I backed up until my body hit the back, metal wall of the lift as they too entered the lift. Standing behind them trying to hide, I watched Tiffany placing her hand on his strong arm that belonged around me…

"Office 7432?" Marvin turned to ask me in an emotionless voice.

The sight of them had distracted me. I forgot to punch my office number into the keypad. I opened my mouth but nothing came out. Marvin patiently and intently stared at me.

"Cat got your tongue?" Tiffany taunted with a devilish grin stroking Marvin's arm slightly.

Pull it together, I told myself. "Yes, office 7432," I replied.

With a smug grin, Tiffany turned back around focusing all her attention on Marvin.

The ride on the lift seemed never ending. I was in a perpetual hell watching Marvin with Tiffany on the lift. I had no where to turn, no escape. The brief ride was a reality check. My world and heart were falling apart. I stood helpless to put it back together. Marvin was really gone. He made good on his words to move on. The sickening thought of him moving on with Tiffany was overwhelming.

Pushing past everyone when the lift door opened, I exited with tears beginning to roll down my face. I didn't want the pair to see as I tried to breeze past them. I could hear Tiffany from the lift taunting, "Elizabeth… Sorry he doesn't want you anymore." After a catty giggle she loudly said for all to hear, "Who could blame him? I mean, look at her!"

I didn't turn to face them as I marched to the desk which I used to share with Marvin. I slammed my backpack onto the top of it. Every eye in the room turned to give me a dirty glare. My noise woke up the sleeping Mrs. VanCues. However, I didn't care. Marvin and I weren't supposed to end! We were forever and a day. I always believed I would be able to talk some sense into him.

I plopped down in my desk chair baffled. As I stared at my backpack, I wondered how he could want my enemy, Tiffany? Tears streaming down my face were mixed with raw emotion due to the thought of the two of them. I was equally angry as sad. How could he flaunt her in front of me?

Instantly, I stood and turned my backpack upside down, dumping the contents in disarray across my desktop. Out of the corner of my eye, I could see Jacob's cubby of an office door open. He stood there watching me for a moment or so. He wasn't going to stop me. I had a right to have an emotional break down. Tossing the backpack into the trash, I hid my face as tears ran like a water faucet.

Suddenly, I could feel warm hands on either side of my arms as Jacob leaned over and softly said, "Let's move to the conference room."

It was a blur moment, literally. I was crying too hard to notice most of the office staff. Jacob escorted me to a secluded conference room seat. Tilly was still missing in action and I really needed her. However, she probably was side tracked with Trevor, Anthony, Andy, or some random guy she just met. Where was she this morning when I so desperately needed her to lean on?

The door to the conference room opened. Jacob and Dale entered. They both sat down in the chairs beside me. It was Dale who began, "Mrs. Van-Cues is awake and the sound of your crying has made her extremely unhappy."

"So," I sobbed.

"We can't let you cause Mrs. VanCues any distress," Dale continued. "She is ill."

I tried to breathe deeply. Inhale. Exhale. The tears simply wouldn't quit flowing down my cheeks.

"Elizabeth," Jacob calmly said as I looked at him. "Dale heard the comment from the girl on the lift."

"Are you sure you want to be my shrink today?" I unhappily choked out. Watching Marvin with Tiffany was the equivalent of Marvin telling me again he didn't want to see me. My heart was shattered. Not even Jacob could reason it back together. Why try?

"No," Jacob answered as he intently watched me. "What we have decided is that you aren't emotionally stable enough today to work. Go back to Keeper House and sort out your personal life. Come back tomorrow when you are fresh."

"Why did Marvin transfer?" I blurted out while trying to dry my tears with the back of my hand.

"We aren't going to discuss employee work issues with you," Dale said as he produced a tissue from somewhere.

"Was it to get away from me?" I pointedly asked wiping my nose which was beginning to drip.

"Do you want someone to walk you back?" Jacob seriously inquired ignoring my inquiry.

"No," I instantly spouted. "I don't need anyone to see me home. Men stick together. You are just as bad as Marvin!"

I stood and left them sitting, staring at each other with big eyes. Chances were I would be in trouble for my remark tomorrow. My tears slowed. Numbness overtook me as I rode the lift down to the Keeper Complex lobby. I crossed it and waited for the normal lift which would take me back to the Hall of Knowledge.

The lift door opened and I was greeted by a smiling Leo. As he peered at me, his smile faded. He mumbled and asked with a concerned look, "Princess, what is wrong?"

"What!" I screeched at him. "What did you call me? How many times must I ask you not call me that?" I half shouted. My emotional fuse was short and it wasn't taking much to trigger less than desirable reactions.

"Oh," Leo said. "Sorry, I didn't…"

I turned to move away from the lift and those riding it.

I could hear him yelling across the foyer, "Wait! Come back! Come back!"

How could he call me princess in front of everyone? Today was shaping up to be bad, really bad! I stormed out the front door of the Keeper Complex. I had never actually walked to or from this Complex. My soul was in a pit as I wandered around in the dark alone. My soul would never be complete again.

The houses in this area were all small, one story homes with simple front porches. Each was painted a distinct shade of earth tone. Just as I had imagined, they were wonderful quaint little cottages like I dreamed Marvin and I would own and start a life together within. Occasionally, I passed one with a second story. I hadn't made it far when the houses became sparser.

"Yes, alone," I heard the familiar voice in my head.

Normally, I would have ran or looked for cover at the sound of the ratty haired Dweller. Today however, if he was near, he could have me. I would not be stopping or running from the danger. The Dweller was like a dog with a bone. He wanted me and I knew in my gut, eventually he would find a way to capture me. Besides, without Marvin… The tears once again began to flow down my cheek with the realization… What was the purpose?

"She's just standing there," I heard him tell someone in my mind.

"Get her then," I heard another male voice.

"Wait for me!" I heard in my head a whine from a jubilant female voice.

The female voice was the jolt that brought my careless jaunt into pity, back to reality. I didn't know if I knew the eerie voice, but it sent shivers through my spine. I had accepted my fate with the ratty haired guy. However, I knew I needed to run from the familiar but unfamiliar voice. I turned to look around in every direction, but still could not see anyone through my tears.

Suddenly frightened, I began to run in a panic. I could hear the foot steps of someone running behind me and they were gaining. Slowing to look over my shoulder wasn't an option. I felt overwhelming fear. I closed my eyes as a warm hand grabbed my arm and slowed my pace. I could hear the person beside me heavily breathing. When I looked with eyes full of tears, I was shocked to see that it was Marvin. I jerked my arm out of his hand and wrapped them both around my stomach, leaning over. I felt ill.

"Great," I heard in my head.

"What's wrong?" Marvin asked. "I saw you running."

As if he cared. His new liaison had started my day off badly. "I'm fine." I lied. "I just need a moment."

"A minute is all we need," I heard the female say and the ratty hair guy chuckle in return.

"You're shaking all over," Marvin stated in an alarmed but soft voice. "Did you see him again?" He placed his hand across my back to steady me.

I found his touch emotionally painful. I shrugged away. His presence and closeness were painful reminders of how much I needed him. How safe and comfortable I once was wrapped in his arms, before Tiffany. I could not control warm tears that started rolling down my cheeks, nor the sound of my hyperventilating. This was too much.

"What is he doing," I heard Dustin saying in his head.

I couldn't see Dustin approaching, but I knew he was. "Elizabeth, what happened?" Dustin asked walking up from behind me. He bent his knees to look me directly in the face and started wiping away my tears with his hands.

"Look who joined the party?" She questioned in my head.

"Interesting, isn't it?" The ratty hair guy replied to her.

Marvin lowered his hand from my back and I noticed his muscles tighten under his shirt. Was I wrong? He appeared genuinely sickened by the sight of Dustin comforting me. A hint of how he once felt about me. Dustin seemed oblivious to him even standing there. I caught a glance of the old

Marvin longingly looking at me. I had the urge to ask Marvin not to go, but he had already turned his back and walked away with his fists balled up.

"Come here," Dustin said as he pulled me towards him, placing his arm around my shoulder.

"Tell me," Dustin demanded almost as if he were my big brother wanting to sort out whatever was wrong in my world.

"Marvin is dating Tiffany!" I stated in a broken voice as my heart accelerated. Marvin must have heard me, his steps faltered for a moment.

"Good for him," Dustin replied gaining my attention.

I pulled away from him and stopped. "What?"

"With him out of the game, I don't need to worry about him wanting you back," Dustin replied with a happy grin.

"Isn't that sweet," the girl whined in a voice of disgust.

Sweet? My tears slowed. I could not believe what he had just said to me. Anger bubbled up from my gut and I no longer wanted Dustin's presence.

"Follow my lead," Dustin whispered to me. "Marvin, wait up!"

I tried to keep my feet firmly planted on the ground. However, Dustin's strong grip on my wrist allowed him to pull me along. Didn't he feel my reluctance to follow him?

"I love a good chase!" The ratty haired guy said in my head.

Marvin simply stopped, turned, and watched the two of us as we closed in on him. "Were taking the day off," Dustin firmly stated when we were standing before Marvin.

Marvin slightly nodded at Dustin returning, "Well, three's a crowd."

"Good point," Dustin replied as he seemed to be gloating. "I couldn't pick a better day for the two of us to play hooky!"

"Hmm," Marvin hummed as his fists were once again clenched. He simply glared at Dustin. He began to briskly walk through the quaint neighborhood.

Dustin pulled me along with a smirk plastered on his face. I watched him peer at Marvin as his mind said, "Play along!"

"I was just out for a run," Marvin returned as if he too could hear Dustin. "I think I'll finish."

Before I could interject Dustin asked, "Maybe we could join you on your way back to the Keeper Complex?"

"Do what you want," Marvin icily stated. "However, I have plans."

"You don't have to worry about that," Dustin retorted in his mind.

Dustin pulled me along until I was freely jogging with them. In silence we all three ran and then made our way into the lobby of the Keeper Complex.

"There you are!" Tiffany's sticky sweet voice echoed. "Where did you go?" She strutted over and began to cozy up to Marvin. With a pouty lip, she complained, "You disappeared."

"Just taking my morning run," Marvin retorted seeming to force a smile onto his face.

I didn't know Marvin normally took a morning run. That even made me feel worse. I thought I knew him.

"All is forgiven then," Tiffany said in her obnoxious fly catching, syrupy voice as she tapped his nose.

"You should run now," Dustin's mind stated.

"To class?" Marvin sarcastically asked back.

"Anywhere you want," Tiffany stated clearly putting on a show for both Dustin and my benefit standing as close to Marvin as she could.

"Please take her anywhere but here!" Dustin said in my thoughts.

I once again watched as Tiffany left with my Marvin. I was hollow and empty. No amount of time was ever going to mend this. I glanced at Dustin who was patiently waiting for me to gain my composure and thoughts. Even though he was here propping me and my emotions up, I knew in my heart I was never meant to be with him.

Tilly

My skateboard sailed down the cement walk allowing me to suck in the fresh air my mind needed. Being at odds with Trevor left me feeling restless. I wasn't sure how to handle the man who was once Trevor the boy. The truth was, our paths were no longer parallel. I didn't want to face the fact that we were going in different directions. He had found his voice and became a strong, independent man over the last few months leaving me powerless to wind him around my finger anymore. It was bound to eventually happen and it had. Tonight had been a perfect example…

"Tilly," Eddie hummed as I crawled through the window onto Trevor's cot of a bed.

"Hey," I replied.

"What are you doing here?" Trevor questioned as he turned from completing his homework.

"Am I not welcome?" I returned.

Trevor gave me a don't be silly look and explained, "I just thought you would be out with Andy."

It wasn't Andy I desired to take a moonlit stroll with. Trevor probably already knew this though. Anthony was out there tonight and I was trapped in the jail that was Keeper House. "I can't go out anywhere!" I exclaimed.

"Why not?" Eddie piped up clearly interested. As much as he liked gossip, he should have been a girl.

"Why hasn't the ladder been fixed?" I pointedly asked as I glanced between the two of them.

"Don't look at me," Eddie replied with a small shrug. Then he pointed at Trevor.

"I'm not fixing the rope," Trevor matter of fact said with a tone that rang with finality.

"And why not?" I demanded.

"We heard Elizabeth crying again," Eddie said as he cracked his knuckles.

"Have you been getting love notes?" Trevor questioned before I could comment about Elizabeth.

"Is this about Harry?" I asked in return.

Trevor's lack of answer screamed it was.

"As far as guys go, Harry is harmless," I said as I rolled my eyes. "A little annoying, but harmless."

"What was Elizabeth upset about tonight?" Eddie threw out looking concerned.

"Marvin," I replied shaking my head. Eddie had a one track mind.

"Then you're not getting notes," Trevor threw out.

"My getting notes or not isn't your concern," I pointedly told him.

Trevor glared at me. The protective, jealous fool really did believe that Harry was leaving me notes. He also thought Harry was a threat. With a heavy sigh, I eased the tension and his nerves, "Elizabeth is the one getting notes."

"That is only because Harry doesn't know which bed is yours," Trevor adamantly disagreed.

"What do Harry and the love notes have to do with fixing the ladder?" I questioned.

"He thinks Harry has been using the ladder to get into your room," Eddie spilled.

"Where would you get a crazy idea like that?" I retorted. Eddie's hand was circling his ear as if to say crazy.

"Elizabeth," Trevor said catching me off guard.

"You're buying into her paranoia?" I questioned. This was unbelievable!

"I assume she did tell you she thought the ladder was giving someone access to your room," Trevor surmised.

"Not exactly," I replied. "She's just paranoid about the windows in general."

"See? If you want to talk about paranoia," Eddie interjected. "How about Trevor and darkness being all around. Dark souls are walking amongst us."

"Can it," Trevor turned and spouted to Eddie.

"So what did Marvin do now?" Eddie asked to change the subject under Trevor's glare.

"I want you to fix the rope for the ladder," I demanded ignoring Eddie. "No way," Trevor said with the same tone of finality. "I'm not fixing it."

"How do you propose I get in after curfew?" I threw out. "The ladder only connects our rooms."

"I don't," Trevor snapped. "Be like everyone else. Follow the rules."

"Dude," Eddie mumbled with as much shock across his face as I felt.

Had Trevor gone wacko on me or what? I stared at him and couldn't help but remark, "What are you, my new warden?"

"Don't be so dramatic," Trevor said as he handed me a stick of gum from his desk. "This isn't a prison."

"I suppose you will be following the rules when you go out for midnight basketball," I retorted knowing this would back him into a corner as I unwrapped the gum. "According to Eddie, it is your new past-time."

"You're right," Trevor agreed. "I'll need to play during the day from now on."

That jab hadn't gone the way I had planned. I thought it would help me wind him around my pinkie. Where had Trevor's sense of adventure gone? He was sounding a lot like a square.

"Tilly," Trevor called. "I really don't want to argue with you."

"Then don't," I countered and blew a big, calming pink bubble. How could he do this to me?

"Oh, a lover's quarrel," Eddie said under his breath.

"I can't and won't fix the ladder," Trevor sighed. "Can you please just leave it this time?"

"Why can't you fix the ladder?" I returned.

"Darkness all around," Eddie hummed.

"Wait," I said as I held up my hand. "This has to do..."

"Your overall goal is to be able to sneak in?" Trevor questioned interrupting me.

I nodded while shaking my head. Of course that was my overall goal. Hello!

"Eddie and I will work out another way," Trevor said. "Would that make you happy?"

I reluctantly agreed. Finding myself powerless to convince Trevor to simply fix the ladder was insulting. He reiterated, as I left to crawl down to my own window, that he wouldn't be fixing the ladder. It would only hang down to my window for now. I guess in the end, another way to sneak in and out would suit my needs. However, Trevor putting his foot down was just hard to swallow.

Eddie was obnoxious and bothersome as well tonight. All he wanted was for me to dish the dirt on what Marvin had done. He was a gossip queen.

The thing neither of them knew was that it wasn't sneaking out to see a boy tonight that I needed the ladder so desperately for. I had Marvin in my cross hairs. Just when Elizabeth was starting to sleep peacefully, Marvin hit her hard. Tonight, she once again cried herself to sleep. What was he doing with Tiffany? Why would he parade his new relationship in front of Elizabeth? I would give him one chance to explain himself before... Guess it was a good thing we were technically dead!

I sucked up what sense of pride I had left with my remaining daylight. I then made my way to see Scott at the Administration Complex. I don't understand how my father could think he was the perfect man for me. He was super boring. The only thing interesting about asking for his help was irritating Sadie. They were dating, but she had every reason to see me as a threat. It might take a little time, but I could have him if I really wanted him.

I worked enough magic to get a very long rope from his engineering department. Painful was the only word capable of describing having to ask Scott for help. Easy was convincing the other young guy in the office to help me. He was putty in my hands. I simply was a goddess. The only draw back... I owed the stranger. I would remind myself tomorrow at my lunch date with the new young man how useful the rope was when tied onto the end of the rope ladder.

Rhett's shack of a house was dark. I banged on the door like it was on fire. I saw the light in the kitchen flick on. I banged harder and louder. Even though, technically, we were dead, I was going to wake up anyone still living.

The door opened to a sleepy looking Rhett, "Tilly? Is something wrong?"

"Rhett, where is he?" I shouted feeling raw anger kicking in and coursing through my veins.

Rhett rubbed his eyes and intently and sleepily peered at me saying, "Marvin isn't home."

"Right! At this time of night?" I retorted. He was upstairs sleeping. I knew it. He was just too much of a coward to face the music. "Don't try and hide him from me. I am going to hang him up by his ears! What he did today..."

"Believe me or not. He went out with a group of friends," Rhett replied trying to calm me. "What did he do?"

"Like you don't know he is dating Tiffany," I sarcastically replied.

"Tiffany?" Rhett questioned with a look of shock and disbelief.

As I much as I caught him off guard, I was taken back by the fact it appeared he didn't know. "Wait. You didn't know?" I questioned.

Rhett shook his head, "Honestly, no."

The gall of him to spend his time with the demon in curls. "She's awful!" I began. "How could he! And to flaunt her in front of Elizabeth."

"Oh," Rhett replied. I watched his stance change from shock to understanding.

"You know something you're not telling me," I surmised.

"Yes, I know to stay our of Marvin's love life," Rhett replied. "It would be healthy for you to stay out of Elizabeth's."

"I disagree," I stated. No way would I let him sidetrack me. I was going to make Marvin pay if he couldn't give me… "Elizabeth is my best friend. I won't stand by and let someone hurt her." Silence fell between us and I asked, "Do you know where Marvin went?"

"Not really," Rhett hem-hawed. "What are you going to do when you find him? You're not going to do something rash, are you?"

"I'm going to give him an opportunity to explain his actions to begin with," I stated placing my hands on my hips.

A moment of alarm flashed to and from Rhett's face. "He's not going to talk with you about Elizabeth."

"Do you know why? There has to be a real reason behind the break up. There has to be a reason behind him dating Tiffany," I added. "Otherwise, he is not who I thought he was and Elizabeth is truly better off without him."

He stood stone faced and then asked, "What does she believe?"

I sighed as I stared Rhett down. What was his game? Why should I tell him? Maybe I could fish about and make some sense out of this whole situation. "She believes that Marvin is her soul mate."

"Don't say that in public," Rhett warned.

I knew this was serious to say since you could only declare soul mates once. However, it was how Elizabeth truly felt. That was, "Until seeing him with Tiffany today, she thought if she could just see him, talk to him she could…"

"Stop!" Rhett demanded. "Is she not dating Dustin? She ran right into his arms from Marvin's."

"So you think that too," I said under my breath. I didn't even know where to begin with that one. Yes and no. I threw my hands up and said, "She has always had this weirdo attraction to Dustin. She even used to sniff him."

He looked at me odd saying, "Sniffing?" Then he waved his hands never mind saying, "Exactly. And don't forget Dustin dated Tiffany."

"I know," I said. "That's why I don't trust him. Anyone who would date Tiffany." I shook my head in disgust. "I just don't understand the attraction." When I looked back at Rhett he had a smirk. "But! The attraction is only an attraction!"

"Right," Rhett sarcastically said to me.

"No really," I disagreed. "His is just filling her time. She longs to be with Marvin."

"And you know this how?" Rhett questioned. When I didn't answer, he concluded, "Because she tells you." A moment of silence fell between us before he asked, "Are actions not better indicators as to how someone feels?"

"Actions?" I questioned appalled. "Like her crying herself to sleep nightly over Marvin. Nightmares, talking in her sleep. Wearing Marvin's T-shirt and sweats every night to bed because in her words, "It's all I have left of him." Those are actions of someone who is heart broke. The persona she puts on with Dustin is a show for all to see. If Marvin makes her cry one more time. I'll pay him back!"

"Boy that sounded like your mother," Rhett said under his breath.

"What did you just say?" I didn't give him a chance to answer. "I thought you actually were cool, that you really cared about us. Why did I even bother to talk to you about this? You've been a bachelor your whole life. You wouldn't know love if it slapped you in the face!"

He shouted at me as I walked away, "You have no idea about me!"

He was wrong about that. Rhett was the head rat and Marvin was a mole.

CHAPTER TWELVE

Elizabeth

Someone was knocking at my door. I peered at my dreadful and ghastly appearance in Tilly's mirror. The stress of realizing Marvin and I were never to be was unbearable. I had tossed and turned all night. I guess I must have slept, even though I didn't feel as if I had. I had deep circles and even they looked great compared to my blotchy skin. It was Saturday and my appearance wouldn't leave a hint of my restlessly sleeping in. It definitely wasn't beauty sleep.

The doorknob turned with Destiny sticking her head in.

"What?" I snapped at her.

She let the door swing open and I could see she was carrying a huge, plain, white box. She held it out saying, "This came for you."

I reluctantly grabbed the box and tossed it on my bed. I turned to look at her attempting to read me with big eyes. "Anything else?" I sharply asked.

"A thank you would have been nice," Destiny mumbled.

I took a deep breath, she was right. I shouldn't take out my frustration on her. She turned to walk away as I called after her, "Sorry..."

She was out the door and gone. I pushed my door shut and sat down on my bed looking at the box. A simple white envelope was attached. I pulled it off and opened it finding a simple note scribbled in Marvin's handwriting.

I'm sorry for yesterday. I gave you the wrong idea. Marvin

I removed the lid to find a dozen long stem roses. They were gorgeous. I thought my heart was going to skip a beat. The moment was brief though as confusion set in. Was he not dating Tiffany? I sat on my bed recalling the images of the two of them that had been running through my dreams. It was her that hung on him. His hands were actually tucked into his jean pockets the whole time. He was nervously jingling their contents. Not to mention, I had seen a hint of anger at Dustin consoling me. Was I wrong then or wrong now?

I jumped up and began tossing clothes out of my closet. I picked a comfy blue T-shirt and a pair of faded blue jeans and dressed as fast as possible. With my hair combed into a ponytail and my teeth brushed, I left Keeper House to begin the trek down into Spring Park.

Today was Saturday. I knew Marvin should be playing basketball with his friends. I longed to see him. I had made so many stupid choices. If he would only give me an opportunity to make it up to him, I would.

There he was, dribbling. His muscle shirt was sculpted to his lean athletic body. He glided across the court, around his friends, and easily made basket after basket. Marvin was insanely attractive.

It was Jessie who happened to see me perched on the bleachers drooling over Marvin's physic. He caught Marvin's attention. With one glance my way he hung his head and slowly walked over to the fence. I practically floated down to greet him. I don't remember my feet hitting the risers on my descent.

"Marvin, thank you," I said with tears in my eyes. "Do you have time to talk?"

"Not really," Marvin hesitated appearing confused. "We're in the middle of a game."

"I'll wait," I threw out.

"You can't wait," Marvin disagreed.

"Then you have no choice but to let me say what I have come to say," I stated backing him into a corner.

"Are you in or out?" Jessie yelled from further out on the court.

Marvin sighed and turned saying, "Guess I'm out." He jogged around the fence and I met him at the end.

The flood gates opened and I spouted with tears in my eyes, "Marvin, I knew it deep down, our breakup was all wrong."

"Elizabeth," Marvin said biting his lip.

"You were always right," I said pointing to my heart as he had done before. "We complete each other."

"Elizabeth," Marvin called.

"I have been heart broke about loosing you," I frantically stated as I looked at my wringing hands. "I tried to push you away in my mind, to deny how right we are for each other. My life is nothing without you! I thought I lost you and then you sent me the note and the gorgeous long stem roses. We can't live this life without each other!"

"Elizabeth!" Marvin stated irritated. "What are you talking about? I didn't send you a note or flowers."

"Yes you did," I disagreed. Digging in my pocket, I pulled the note out and rattled it around. "It's right here."

Marvin shook his head no and the magnitude of the situation hit me. If he hadn't sent this, then he didn't want to get back together with me. I gasped and instantly, panic overtook me. He had sent this note to someone else.

Marvin steadied my shaking hand and looked at the note. Instantly, he appeared extremely angry as he asked, "This came to you with flowers?"

I nodded without looking at him. "Long stem roses. I thought it was so romantic."

"I didn't send them to you," Marvin once again said. "I didn't actually send flowers to anyone."

"You don't have to cover up for my sake," I said while breathing deeply.

"They just got delivered to me by mistake." I paused as I felt the urge to simply run. I looked up trying to convince myself out loud, "It's okay. It has to be."

Marvin's fists were balled up and he still appeared extremely angry. It was Jessie who broke our uncomfortable silence calling from behind the fence nearest to us, "We need you back in or we'll owe them."

"Okay," Marvin sighed. "I'm really sorry about this."

I shook my head and stepped around him. There was nothing for either of us to say. I slowly made my way back towards the hill leading out of Spring Park. I would crawl back into my bed and stay there once I returned to my room.

As I walked across the bridge in a daze, Tiffany was leaned up against the railing. She gave me a devilish grin saying, "Did you enjoy your hopeful morning?"

This made me stop dead in my tracks. "What did you say?" I questioned.

"You're certainly appealing," Tiffany cackled. "Oversized T-shirt, boring hair... The jeans are a step towards cleaning up your trashy look."

"You sent me the roses?" I questioned ignoring the comment about how I looked.

"I sure enjoyed the show," Tiffany cackled. "Marvin didn't know what to do with you. That is, other than break your heart again."

"Why?" I asked as a tear rolled down my face.

"I told you long ago that you should have chosen better friends," Tiffany said.

"This isn't a prank," I sobbed. "This is real."

"The best lessons are the ones that hurt the most," Tiffany returned as she moved to shove me backwards. "But don't worry, your lesson isn't complete yet. You will pay for stealing my Dustin." While walking away, she said over her shoulder, "Tell Tilly I'm no longer playing."

Tilly was serious about Anthony, so I was baffled that she went out with some new guy. However, I was glad she was off on a lunch date. I couldn't and wouldn't be able to tell Tilly about this. The thought of Tilly scheming and getting revenge for Tiffany pulling such a cruel joke scared me, much less getting even for Tiffany threatening me. No way would I tell anyone about this. I had humbled myself and humiliated myself in front of Marvin. How could I ever hold my head up again?

Elizabeth

Destiny was busily using the ticket machine to find the perfect Real Life for us to view. I didn't understand why they just didn't call them movies. Long ago I had promised her we would attend the Hall of Babies together. Tonight was the time to pay up.

Tilly had been gone all day with revolving men. The unnamed guy she met for lunch was a bust. However, it wasn't long after her arrival back at our room till Trevor showed up. Then, they were off to make plans for Harmony. She pretended to be a little ill to ditch Trevor for tonight. Her nights were now reserved for Anthony. The problem was, Trevor was going to catch some real life with Ruthanne tonight. I needed to find a way to tag along so that I could keep an eye on him to ensure he wouldn't check in on Tilly and realize she wasn't home.

Trevor didn't much care for Anthony. I assumed it was because Tilly was head over hills crazy for him. Trevor and Tilly defied all reasoning. They both dated others, but deep down they really cared for each other. Not to mention, they were destined to be together as ruled by the Council.

"How about romance?" Destiny asked interrupting my thoughts while still using the screen to flip through the endless selections.

"No," I said while shaking my head. Was she oblivious or just heartless? No way did I want to see a romance.

Destiny sighed saying, "Maybe action or..."

"Comedy," I interrupted.

Destiny smiled agreeing, "Sure... a comedy would be great." With a shrug she added, "A little cheering up."

Nothing could cheer me up. Life didn't exist without Marvin. My selection was more about Trevor and Ruthanne choosing to watch a comedy tonight. Being in the same room with them for a vantage point was important. If I weren't here, I would still be hibernating in my bed. I had agreed to this night out because it wasn't like I had anything else to do.

"Okay," Destiny said as she grabbed the blue tickets which printed out of the machine.

I grabbed the slender, blue ticket she was holding out for me reading, Sebastian Bloom April Fools Day 2003.

Destiny was leaning on the ticket machine ignoring the guy behind us who was impatiently cracking his knuckles while waiting for Destiny to move. She was oblivious to his impatience and rolling eyes as she peered at the boy standing at the next ticket machine. With a deep sigh Destiny leaned over and tapped him on the shoulder. He looked over at her and smiled as she told him, "Your date is looking for you at the concession stand."

"Huh," He hummed in return with a look of confusion.

"She told you to meet her at the concession stand, not the kiosk machine," Destiny stated.

"How would you know that?" He asked now clearly annoyed.

"A birdie told me," Destiny stated with that nosy neighbor attitude. She then stepped towards me mumbling, "Let's go."

I followed her across the lobby of the massive theater lobby. As we passed the long lines at the concession stand, I could smell the popcorn and hot dogs. Destiny let out another sigh, abruptly stopped, and scanned the long waiting lines. In a flash, she headed off towards the center line. I could see her telling something to Shannon who appeared completely annoyed with Destiny who simply smiled back at her before walking back towards me.

"What was that about?" I questioned.

"Her boyfriend," Destiny answered. She must have read the confusion on my face. "The guy at the kiosk machine."

"Oh," I replied. It was no wonder Shannon was giving her dirty looks.

"I never get thanked for my deeds, do I?" Destiny replied.

Deeds? Snooping and carelessly making others aware of your snooping wasn't doing a good deed. Destiny was always sticking her nose in where it didn't necessarily belong. I followed her lead as we entered a dimly lit hallway as we fought the pushing line to the ticket taker. When I caught her attention I asked, "Do you overhear Shannon tell him where to meet her?"

"You're questioning my intentions too?" Destiny asked as the ticket taker handed her back half of her blue ticket. I watched as she took her ticket stub and shoved it in her pocket.

"I'm not trying to pick on you," I responded as I handed my ticket to the brown suited tall man.

"Comedy, door twelve," he responded with a look saying he was bored to tears.

"Thank you," I replied taking my ticket stub from him.

"Yeah, yeah," he hummed as he waved me on.

Destiny was unusually quiet as we walked down the dark hall with floor lighting. "Why does it matter how I knew?" Destiny questioned in a mutter to herself.

We walked under a sign labeled theater twelve as I decided to tackle the problem she didn't see. I followed her down the lighted pathway. I tapped her on the shoulder and pointed to the row which was a few rows behind Trevor and Ruthanne. "Let's sit down this row."

Destiny nodded still being overly quiet.

As we sat, I decided it was now or never. Maybe she had never had anyone tell her how annoying her meddling was. "Destiny," I said gaining her attention as she removed her headphone and placed it in her lap. "I think others view your insights as…" I hesitated trying to find the right word.

"Nosy," Destiny answered as she rolled her eyes and crossed her arms across her chest. "I've heard others say it."

"If you know that is what others think," I began, "Then why do you insist on..."

"When I have something to tell someone... When I know something, I have to tell them or I can't get it out of my mind. I have an uncanny way of knowing things about others. That's all," Destiny flatly answered.

"You just know things?" I repeated.

"Yeah," Destiny replied as she turned on her individual television. Large screens at the front of the room weren't used for real life. Real life movies were straight from the Earth Plane. They were looks into the lives of real people and their dramas as they happened.

"Tell me the oddest thing you just know," I threw out.

"That's easy, the true princess," Destiny adamantly responded.

"What did you just say?" I questioned feeling caught off guard. How had she pulled Leo's nickname for me out of thin air? Much to my dismay, he had now simply shortened it to princess.

"You wouldn't believe me if I told you," Destiny hummed.

"You don't know that until you tell me about it," I returned.

"It's a fairy tale that centers on a stolen stone that the Keepers and Dwellers fight over," Destiny said as she nervously looked around. When her eye caught mine she said, "I'm going to get a drink and popcorn. Do you want any?"

"No, I'm fine," I replied as I watched her fidget and quickly rise up from her seat. In a flash she was off. It was if she was running from the conversation.

I retrieved my headset from the arm of my chair and began to unroll the cord plugging it into the chair. I then turned on my individual television which hung on the back of the chair before me. I turned it on and listened to ads play over and over while watching Trevor peer at Ruthanne. She was busily chatting and he appeared to be hanging on every word.

Suddenly, I felt a rock hard, cold hand on my shoulder. I tried to turn around to see who was behind me but felt the strong hand holding me to my seat. With my free hand I pulled off the headset covering my ears. The room was surprisingly noisy as everyone around me was watching, listening to, and laughing at their own real life. Whoever it was behind me, leaned up and whispered in my ear, "Hello."

I cringed recognizing the familiar voice in my ear. I instantly grabbed the man's arm beside me. Startled, the stranger turned to look at me. I pointed to the unwanted hand on my shoulder. He then turned to give the young man the hand belonged to a let go look. He then took off his headset asking the young man behind me, "Is there a problem?"

"No," the ratty haired boy responded as his hand let go of my shoulder. I turned and my fear was realized. The ratty, black haired pale Dweller was seated directly behind me. From under his black derby hat, he was smiling his crooked grin with one corner of his mouth turning up and one turning down. "Just getting an old friend's attention."

The man beside me frowned mumbling, "Kids." He placed his headset back on and went back to ignoring us.

I stood up and scooted past all the legs of those seated to make my way to the aisle. I concentrated on the legs and feet I was passing. I was too scared to peer into his eyes. I knew Trevor was seated a couple rows down. Once free from my row, I turned and ran straight into the ratty haired guy. How did he move around so fast to get between myself and Trevor?

He stood taunting me with a devilish grin as I heard in my head, "He won't be helping you tonight."

My only hope was the lobby. I backed away from him as he cautiously took subtle steps matching my pace.

"She is making this easy!" I heard in my mind. "Backing right into the blind spot."

As I felt the rear wall hit my back, I looked up to see the back of the last chair we passed. His perception was correct. Even if everyone in the room wasn't enthralled with their personal viewing television, they couldn't see me.

I took a deep breath and looked up to confront him knowing I was in serious trouble. Those dark, black, lifeless eyes which burned through me were making my legs shake. My body wanted nothing more than to step to him as he extended his hands for mine. For a fleeting moment, chills ran up my spine. My unwillingness to give into the sensation of stepping towards him passed. My legs became suddenly heavy. His stare intensified and I knew I was no longer able to walk.

Instinctively, I closed my eyes and inhaled a deep breath remembering that with each breath my life force would return to normal. The problem was how close he was now standing to me. On one hand, he smelled enticing. On the other he left me with a feeling of pure evil and hopelessness. Maybe, I was simply destined to be lost in the dark.

"Don't fight it," I heard him taunt in my head.

It took all my self control as I willed my hand to my shirt collar. I could feel the cold metal of my locket with the ends of my fingers. This wasn't the first time I was forced to use my locket to escape him. I rubbed the locket and thought of my room and inaudibly mumbled to myself, "Keeper House."

I could barely feel his grimy hand touching my bare arm when suddenly I fell to the floor of my room with a sudden thump. Instantly, I grabbed my arm where he had touched it. I sat up gasping for breath as I laid my burnt arm across the edge of my bed. Another long, red, blister was present. I was overwhelmed with pain. I clutched my arm to my chest and crawled to the trash can feeling absolutely sick. I bit my lip to hold back my screams.

My heart was rapidly beating and I simply couldn't breathe. Then, the room began to spin...

Trevor

I was startled awake by hands shaking me. Elizabeth was standing in our room at my bedside with her finger over her mouth whispering, "Shh."

I sat up and instantly grabbed a shirt off the floor and pulled it over my head while asking, "What are you doing here?" I looked over at the clock mumbling, "What time is it?"

"Around 4:30," Elizabeth answered.

"4:30," I repeated as I pushed back the covers irritated. It was Sunday and I wanted to sleep in. Besides, how in the world did she crawl through my window without my noticing? "What's wrong? Is something wrong with Tilly?"

Elizabeth stood shaking her head adamantly no saying, "She's in bed. There is something wrong, but it's not like you think."

I leaned over and flipped the lamp light on. In the light, I instantly noticed the red burn on Elizabeth's arm. I hopped up and grabbed her hand asking, "Where did you get this?" Elizabeth pulled her arm free with a small wince. I watched as she protected the burned arm. I was fully aware of the possible source of her injury.

My partner in the Underground was Mark Spirs. During the day, he was a member of the council guard and often rode the lift to the black arch with those who are sentenced to go through it. He told me story after story about those sentenced and sent over to the Dwellers through the black arch. They were incredible stories of how the elevator always waited for any confession that was burning in their mind. Then, it would rapidly spin pinning those riding to the side. When it stopped the lift door would open revealing a fuzzy existence beyond the lift. He claimed that usually this was when those sentenced would become nervous as Dweller hands appeared to pull them through while burning their bare skin upon touch. The guards were well aware of the hands ability to burn and often wore clothing to protect their arms and hands from being exposed. In addition, they always stayed back from the opening until those they were delivering were through. However, on occasion, they still received burns. Blisters were a job hazard, as Mark put it.

Elizabeth appeared nervous concerning my stare. She and I both knew the burn on her arm was from a Dweller. We also both knew the last burn she received wasn't from a curling iron as Tilly and her had claimed. She was still holding her arm as I asked, "Are you putting something on it?"

"The same sap as last time," Elizabeth sighed with a slight nod.

"Where did you get the sap?" I questioned knowing Mark had struggled to find something to sooth his last burn.

"Professor Zirak gave it to me last time," Elizabeth mindlessly answered. She paced nervously between the beds as if she were building up the nerve to tell me something. Finally, she spit out, "I'm being stalked by a ratty haired Dweller."

"The one that attacked you in the Humling town?" I asked.

"You know?" Elizabeth questioned in a low voice so as not to wake Eddie.

"Yeah," I answered as I ran my hand through my hair. Of course I knew about their adventure. Tilly had been forced into telling me. I had been a little peeved because they shouldn't have been there to begin with. The Humling dude was far more dangerous for Tilly than she would ever begin to see or admit.

"It was the same one," Elizabeth admitted as she shuffled her feet in apparent stress. "The problem is… I know I should have told Tilly long ago. I didn't realize how dangerous this all was until…"

"They attacked you," I said finishing her thought.

"Yeah," Elizabeth replied and then took a deep breath.

Everyday, it became more apparent to me that the common Dweller could be living in the next room and most Keepers wouldn't realize it. The perfect world we lived in was, for the most part, oblivious to Dwellers and the danger they represented. Elizabeth was perceptive. "What makes you think you are being stalked?" I asked. "Have you seen him inside the dome?"

Elizabeth let out a huge sigh before beginning, "He did this." She pointed to the red blistered burn. "Last night his hand did this to me in the dome."

As far as I knew, the only place to get such a burn was the black arch. I had already pondered her last burn episode and couldn't fathom how she had purposely or accidentally approached the black arch. Making me feel crazed was the thought that somehow Tilly might have been with her. I couldn't bare the thought of Tilly being in such serious danger. Even if I could only admire her from afar, a world without Tilly wouldn't be a world I could live in. I cringed inside as I asked, "Where were you?"

"Catching real life in the Hall of Babies," Elizabeth answered trying not to look me in the eye.

"I didn't see you there last night," I stated to her wandering eye. I had assumed she was with Tilly last night.

"I went with Destiny," Elizabeth stated.

"Destiny," I repeated. I couldn't imagine sitting that close to someone who smelled so bad. "Did she see him?"

"I don't think so," Elizabeth replied. "She went for popcorn."

"Well, you certainly weren't looking for trouble watching real life." However, it didn't add up. How had he burned her? There were rare but known cases of Dwellers in the world of the Humlings. However, I hadn't read anything about them burning Keepers. "How did he burn you?"

"You don't see the places where his fingers grabbed my arm?" Elizabeth asked pointing to the marks clearly showing each pronounced imprint.

"He just grabbed you?" I asked feeling a little baffled.

Elizabeth once again lowered her arm and looked away.

"There's more, isn't there?" I questioned.

"Not really," Elizabeth hummed as she began to fidget again while shuffling her feet.

"Right," I sarcastically said.

Elizabeth seemed to be searching for something to say to me as her mouth spilled, "I wasn't able to move."

Tilly had already told me about the effect Dwellers had on Elizabeth. There was sure to be more to the story, however Elizabeth wasn't ready to share. If I hadn't lost track, this was multiple encounters. I had to ask to establish if this was true, "Have you seen him regularly in the dome?"

"Three times now," Elizabeth replied.

"Where?" I asked.

"Once in the Ghost Complex, once in Keeper Complex, and last night in the Hall of Babies," Elizabeth replied.

"What were you doing each time?" Trevor asked.

"Looking for the ghost Rhett wanted us to find, using the lift to go up to my office, and watching some real life," Elizabeth automatically answered.

"Does Tilly know about your run-ins with him?" I asked and began to hold my breath dreading what she was going to tell me. It was obvious that Tilly knew more than she was telling me. If I didn't know, how was I going to protect her?

"He wrote a message on Tilly's mirror in our room at some point during the night," Elizabeth replied as I saw the first hint of fright creep across her face.

"What did he write?" I inquired as I jumped up.

"I'm not giving up," Elizabeth said as she pulled my chair from under my desk to sit down.

Instantly, I felt relieved. "I can set your worried mind at ease," I began. It was more likely that this was truly a message meant for Tilly. This was Harry's doing. "Do you remember Harry, Ruthanne's brother?"

Elizabeth nodded answering, "Yeah."

"He has been sort of stalking Tilly," I told her. My warning to him had obviously fallen on deaf ears. "Stalkers leave notes."

"What?" Elizabeth asked.

"He has a history," I explained. He had crossed the line this time by being in her room at night while she was sleeping. I would need to have a more serious talk with Harry, one without Ruthanne around.

Tilly never saw any male as dangerous, a lesson you would have thought she would have learned on the Earth Plane after marrying the Dweller who tried to drown her. With Harry, she had once more bit off more than she could chew. She just didn't realize it yet.

During his life on the Earth Plane, Harry relentlessly stalked his college girlfriend causing her all kinds of trouble. Once returning to Home, he continued to stalk her in her Humling town. It got so out of hand that he went before the Council who ruled he couldn't leave the dome. Ever! This was a small detail that he often ignored according to Ruthanne. Her family secret was one that I would love to repeat if it weren't for not wanting to betray Ruthanne.

Now Harry had a new target, my Tilly. I was in the middle with no clear way to protect Tilly without upsetting Ruthanne. Eddie was right. I had chick problems.

Elizabeth looked terribly disappointed at my conclusion.

"How did he get in?" I asked.

"The rope," Elizabeth answered. "Tilly got a rope and has been tying it onto the ladder."

"I told her...," I began and stopped mid sentence. Tilly had always fascinated me with her independence and strength. Until I understood how many dangers were around us, I never saw her unstoppable spirit as something less than desirable. I felt as if my knowledge of the Underground was slowly driving a wedge between us.

"You really believe it was simply Harry?" Elizabeth asked.

"I have already warned Harry to leave Tilly alone," I admitted.

"Tilly would love that," Elizabeth said with a huff.

"That's why we aren't going to tell her," I added.

"I guess it's a good thing I erased the message," Elizabeth shrugged. She stood and shuffled her feet back and forth seeming deep in thought. "May I ask you something?"

"There's more?" I asked feeling my head spin.

"Destiny started to tell me about a fairy tale," Elizabeth began. "Do you know anything about the true princess?"

"True princess," I repeated. "Never heard of it."

"Would you be willing to do a little digging?" Elizabeth pointedly asked.

All things with Elizabeth seemed baffling. "Sure," I reluctantly answered knowing when Elizabeth asked for help there was usually a reason.

CHAPTER THIRTEEN

Trevor

The group was finishing their basketball game as I walked up to the court in Spring Park. I hadn't joined my fellow spies last night. Instead, I took Ruthanne to catch some real life. A night without thinking about the Underground was peaceful. That is, until Elizabeth woke me. As she left, I knew it was vital to bounce some of this off my partner.

"What are you doing here?" Mark asked as he wiped the back of his neck with a towel. Then he proceeded to wipe his perpetually running nose.

"Couldn't sleep," I replied.

"Thoughts of your girl keeping you awake?" Mark asked with a chuckle.

"Not exactly," I retorted. "Have you ever heard of someone who can't physically move under the stare of a Dweller?"

"Are you asking in general, or do you know someone this has happened too?" Mark seriously returned.

"Just a theory I'm kicking about," I added with a shrug.

"You crawled out of a warm bed this early to ask me about a theory?" Mark asked staring me down.

Mark was a lot like me. He could read there was more meaning behind my inquiry or I wouldn't be asking.

"I believe that's the effect the Dweller guards hold over those they guard," Mark said off the top of his head. Then he shrugged a little adding, "I believe that is what I read."

"Read where?" I asked.

"The archives," Mark answered. "You need to spend some serious time studying."

The archives. The very place where I first learned Dwellers regularly walk amongst us. Between training, keeping up with Tilly and Ruthanne, and my Underground work... When would I happen upon more time to study?

"I can't blame you," Mark interjected. "If I had a girl, I would spend less time studying too."

"Do you know anything about the fairy tale of the true princess?" I threw out.

"Why?" Mark returned wiping his nose again.

"Someone I know asked me if I had ever heard about it," I answered.

"Man, your friends are weird," Mark said. "What is all of this about?"

"Nothing, really," I replied.

"Don't you and your friends have anything better to do than talk about girlish fairy tales?" Mark retorted with another smirk.

I had to agree. I ran with an eclectic crowd.

Elizabeth

Trouble was sure to find me when I made my presence known back at Keeper House. I could hear Tilly in my mind saying, "Throw caution to the wind." This was exactly what I was doing as I skipped the professor's brunch. My day's adventure was a secret. I followed the red carpeted pathway around the outside wall of the Hall of Records and secured myself a place amongst massive bookshelves to spy on the front desk.

Today was the day I would find myself. I knew deep down the key to getting Marvin back was my understanding who I was. My world was dull and heavy without him. Whatever was in my past was so awful it drove him away. I couldn't fix what I didn't know. My plan was simple. I intended to start with the long, twelve digit Keeper Identification Number which was printed on the second page of my blank chapter. In the restricted area, there had to be a list of Keepers and their numbers.

"Miss Cantrell," I heard a stern voice speak from behind me. "What are you doing here this time of morning and on a Sunday?" Mrs. Bradford inquired.

I took a deep calming breath as I turned to face her. Why not test the waters. "I want to look up who my Keeper is," I calmly stated.

"You don't know?" Mrs. Bradford said in return with a puzzled look on her face.

"Well, I want to contact them," I added hoping to cover my deceptive trail. "I need some advice on my future study choices, you know, some input!"

"Then go to the Hall of Babies and look them up in the directory of addresses," Mrs. Bradford stated as if my presence and idiocy was a nuisance.

"That's a great idea," I hummed as I moved away from Mrs. Bradford. I said over my shoulder to her surprised face, "Thanks!"

Trevor

Tilly was out with Andy. Elizabeth was in the professor's office getting raked over the coals for missing brunch when I used the ladder to gain access into their room. I needed a sample of the sap Elizabeth was using to doctor her burnt arm. Not only was I curious about it, but reproducing the sap could help the council guards recover from serious burns the hands beyond the black arch often caused. If only I had answers for the questions burning in my mind. If the professor had some unique knowledge for treating Dweller burns, why had he not shared?

My acquisition of the sap sample went smoothly. I had just dropped it off in the Underground's lab for analysis and hoped to soon have answers. The poor guys in the lab were practically working inside a closet, so I left to give the guy on shift room.

As I strolled out into the busy main cavern of the Underground, I knew I needed to face it. Mark was right about my urgent need to study in the archives. Since he was a couple training classes ahead of me, he was also ahead of me in studying. This actually fit his personality and public persona. Mark was a nice enough strong guy, but most probably viewed him as a nerd or bookworm. He and his perpetual runny nose were perfect for the Underground since no one would suspect him.

Today, I intended to put any notion of Tilly, Ruthanne, Elizabeth, Harmony, or training aside. I walked past three dark offices. One was Mr. Bradford's office with the radio receivers waiting for his ears. The other two were a mystery to me. I had never seen anyone seated in them. Beyond them was a narrow hallway with a low ceiling that led to the archives room. Bending over to walk down the hallway and not hit my head, I had to wonder why no one had carved out more head room.

Once in the Archives room, I noticed a familiar head buried in a book at the nearest table. I went over and pulled out a chair asking, "Do you not believe in sleep?"

"I believe my partner has been holding out on me," Mark hummed in response with a serious look on his face.

I sat down understanding Mark had found the answers to my not so sly questions earlier this morning. His face looked shocked as well as elated at his discovery.

"I knew if you were asking," Mark continued with a knowing look. "There had to be more to it."

"What did you find?" I questioned.

Mark looked all around to see if anyone was in ear shot before leaning over to whisper, "The true princess has to do with the Gateway Stone," Mark stated.

"The what?" I asked in response.

"The Gateway Stone," Mark whispered again. "The stone which powers the black arch."

He fiddled with the stack of books before him pulling out a volume that appeared ancient with a faded cover. He flipped through the pages apparently looking for a passage. I watched with curiosity until his finger tapped the book signaling he had found what he wanted. He slid it over to me, "Read this description."

With the book in front of me I read...

The origin of the Gateway Stone is unknown. The stone efficiently moves people or goods between planes of existence. It is generally powered by the energy drawn from those holding, touching, or wearing the stone. Misuse of the gateway stone is subject to those who are in possession of it.

The stone is a blue sapphire and has been the focus of national rejoicing and crisis. It is primarily used by the Council of Keepers to access the Black Arch portal into the plane of the Dwellers. The most noted crisis was the use of minute shavings of the gateway stone to power travel by locket. Speculation exists that a locket was taken into the Dweller Plane allowing dark souls to harness the Gateway Stone's energy to travel at will. Using the Gateway Stone for travel by locket was discontinued to counterweight the ripple effects of The Event.

"I had no idea how the black arch worked," I said aloud. "Dwellers use stone shaving in their lockets to enter through the arches?"

"They don't teach that in training," Mark said as if understanding my comment.

"When did you learn about the Gateway Stone?" I questioned.

"When I entered the guard," Mark answered. "However, my true understanding of it came from studying books here in the Underground. The Gateway Stone is referred to in many different texts. Each holds different information about it, according to the books context."

"What else do you know about it?" I questioned.

"When we, the Keepers, started using the Gateway Stone as a portal key for the black arch, we started growing old as a people. Everyone before its use, stopped aging at thirty."

"Huh," I sighed.

"Okay, so the stone allows the arch to work," I hummed as Mark went back to the book before him. Once again he pushed another volume in front of me.

This volume was clearly different than the other. The pages weren't typed but hand written. I put my hand across the page to hold my place as I peeked at the cover. Just as I thought. This was a book from the Dweller collection. They were always handwritten and whatever was written was usually dreadful.

The True Princess and the Snake

A day will come when the princess will appear,
The bridge between light and dark.
Away from her destiny many will try to steer
The journey she will unknowingly embark.

Unlike all who came before,
No memories of her troubled past exists.
Many resources into her will pour,
No history of her life can be seen through the mist.

As her place in peace at home grows longer,
The snake waits in the land of strife.
The sworn guard's loyalty grows stronger,
Protection at all cost becomes his way of life.

The bridge between childhood and adulthood will be the test.
Will strength and courage prevail?
The destiny of home on her shoulders will rest,
Will she turn coward and fail?

If life shall be as it was meant,
Earth plane will host as good and evil spar.
No hope exists that the snake will repent,
It lies silently in the grass watching from afar.

Resolved to battle,
The snake waits to betray if given the chance.
It is the new heir in waiting ready to take the saddle.
Be warned that the snake and darkness share romance.

The sacrifice of the true princess would be grave,
Darkness would replace the day.
There is no Hope to save,
Darkness would come out to play.

"How did you know where to find this?" I questioned.

"I have been slowly reading the dark works to get perspective of my enemies," Mark answered. "I have been methodically checking them out in order. The only volume I skipped was the one the archive historian said no one ever looks at because it was filled with fairy tales for Dweller children."

"Are there Dweller children?" I questioned out loud recalling Elizabeth asking about children.

"Guess so," Mark responded deep in thought. "After you asking, I remembered this book which I skipped. Then, I couldn't sleep."

"You had to look," I said understanding. "You are indeed a resourceful knowledgeable spy."

"Do you believe this is some kind of prophecy clues hidden in a child's book?" Mark questioned.

"I don't know," I returned.

"This reminds me of Keeper Warrior. Man, you need to level with me," Mark demanded. "I'm too smart for you to convince me that you came up with this on your own."

The file in my mind on Elizabeth was starting to make sense.

"There you are," the lab technician said from the doorway of the archives room. "I was beginning to conclude that you had left."

Mark stared right through me as I squirmed and inquired, "What did you find?"

"The base of the product is a simple white jelly," the lab tech began. With a confused look upon my face he further added, "It's antibiotic cream. However, the interesting part is the high ratio of ginger mixed into the product. It's a ginger cream."

"Ginger?" Mark questioned.

"Yeah," the lab tech answered. "Looks like someone took regular antibiotic cream and mixed it with ginger in a ratio of half and half."

Mark looked at me strangely and began, "Why..."

"Hold on," the lab tech interrupted. "That's not what is interesting. The ginger quality has traces of being in pure dark form. It was grown in the land of the Dwellers."

"It's a Dweller's healing cream?" Mark questioned to the lab techs nod.

"Yes, stop by and fill out the paperwork so I can process my findings," the lab tech said to me.

Unhappily, I shook my head in agreement and sighed. I hadn't dreamed the sap would be of Dweller origin. Now, having to explain the sap, I was going to drag Elizabeth right into the middle of all this. I couldn't tap dance around it any longer. We all had bigger problems though. The sap was given to her by Professor Zirak.

"Trevor, we are partners... Tell me what is going on," Mark demanded. "You're keeping something from me."

"Give me a day to sort this out," I answered.

"No," Mark adamantly stated. "You and I together can give the lab tech a day, but you need to level with me."

CHAPTER FOURTEEN

Elizabeth

Crying wouldn't do any good. I was laboriously trudging my way through my new punishment for skipping brunch yesterday. The theory I concocted about Professor Zirak's punishments not being able to get any worse was idiotic. Professor Presnell even allowed me to miss class today. She was elated with my punishment as well as the possibility of getting rid of me for the day.

I could hear Professor Presnell huffing and spouting, "It's time someone taught Miss Cantrell a thing or two about respect."

"I couldn't agree more," Mr. Brassbuckle stated flashing his pearly grin at the star-struck professor.

She smiled back over the rim of her huge, red glasses continuing, "I can see you are just the man for the job."

Watching the professor bat her eyes at Mr. Brassbuckle was stomach churning. Her gray hair looked pale in comparison to the slight shade of pink her skin was turning as she slightly blushed.

"I have another student I would happily give you," Professor Presnell coyly stated.

"Miss Bradford wasn't involved," Professor Zirak stated interrupting their stare.

"She's always involved," Professor Presnell disagreed rolling her eyes.

In a flash, Mr. Brassbuckle reached for Professor Presnell's hand. He clearly did not want to lose her attention. In an old, southern gentleman fashion he kissed the top of her chubby hand. Still bent over he tilted his head upward and offered, "Until next time."

What a nightmare. The thought of Mr. Brassbuckle and Professor Presnell together was a terrifying thought.

To my dismay, Mr. Brassbuckle placed me into a windowless filing office which housed floor to ceiling stacks of papers to be filed. One thing was certain, I had enough paper to file to last me a lifetime. I figured that was pretty much his point. Their jest was that if I never left this room, I couldn't get into trouble.

It didn't take me long to realize I couldn't make a dent in the stacks. The more I filed, the more that seemed to appear in the never ending in-basket which set on the edge of the desk. It would get so full that I would be forced to move the stack. As soon as I did, more would appear. I no longer was attempting to read anything further than the eight digit number scrolled across the top of each paper.

The strange machine was exactly like the machine Professor Presnell used on the first day to record our test scores. The only difference I could see was the keypad attached to the front in which I typed in the eight digit number. As I placed each paper into the machine, it was slowly sucked in and then simply disappeared into thin air. It was an extremely slow process with my needing to type each number individually into the keypad.

My stomach was growling as I rhythmically typed in a number without thinking about it. When I hit the last digit, the light bulb went on in my head. The digits were my number, the one listed in my chapter in the Hall of Records. I did a double take and couldn't believe my eyes. I was peering at a report from an unknown Keeper, actually from my Keeper, for an Elizabeth Kaswell.

I stood holding the paper in my hands. They began to shake. There could be no doubt, Elizabeth Kaswell was me. I looked at the date and time file stamped across the top of the page. It couldn't be a simple coincidence that the file date was the date I arrived at the hospital. The report said simply, re-entered.

The machine behind me began to loudly beep while awaiting the paper. I entered a ninth digit into the key pad and it beeped again displaying a message, entry too long.

I placed the paper on my desk and thumbed through the pile of remaining papers in the stack. All were file marked from the day of my re-entry. Nearly at the bottom of the stack of files was the familiar number scrolled across another paper. The name was Elizabeth Cantrell and the status was once again re-entered. I placed it next to the first paper. The time file stamped on both were seconds apart.

Who could deny this proof? I folded the papers together and shoved them into my pocket. I would have ran straight to Marvin before. I was sure his soul had to be experiencing the same ache as mine. I simply wasn't ready to give up on Marvin. His heart was missing its other half, as mine was. I only had a handful of those in my life who truly cared about me. The two most important were Tilly and Marvin. I couldn't let Marvin go and now I had the proof in my hands.

Like a robot, I worked all afternoon while thinking about my proving what I already knew to be true. I was Elizabeth Kaswell. Taking Mrs. Bradford's advice, I went to the Hall of Babies after work and stood in line waiting for the lady behind the desk to help me access the directory of addresses. Without the name of my Keeper, I was certain I wouldn't get information about them. However, I was armed with a new truth and decided to look up my own address. It was so obvious it pained me.

"May I help you?" The lady inquired.

"Yes," I said and smiled. "I need the address for one Elizabeth Can… Sorry, Elizabeth Kaswell."

"Elizabeth Kaswell," she repeated as she typed the name into the computer before her. "She doesn't have an address. Hold on, let me dig a little further." She hit button after button, viewing screen after screen. "It seems she went to the Earth plane with her mother."

"Her mother?" I questioned.

"One Christy Kaswell," she answered watching me. "She hasn't returned yet from the Earth Plane."

"And Elizabeth?" I asked.

"It's strange," she mumbled as she once again was peering at her computer.

"Strange?" I repeated.

"I show she has re-entered, but I don't have an address," she said with a confused look on her face. "She's required to list an address with us."

"Is everyone required to do that?" I asked.

"We do have rules and laws. Yes, Humlings are required to do this," she answered peering at me like it was a dumb question.

"Humlings?" I repeated.

"Um… Yes, Miss Kaswell being a Humling, she is required to file her address," she responded to my shock.

I didn't know whether to be relieved or upset.

"Anything else?" She asked.

"No," I replied forcing another smile across my face. "Thank you."

"You're welcome." She yelled past me, "Next!"

I shuffled away from the desk dumbfounded with the new information. Just when I began to believe I was a Dweller, I now discovered I was a Humling. My family existed somewhere out there and my gut comprehended why they were unable to visit me. Kaswell was a Humling name. My Humling family wouldn't be allowed in the dome. That would answer the mystery as to why I re-entered in the hospital. Maybe this explained why my name been changed. All of this new knowledge led to yet another unanswered question. How in the world did I end up with the Keepers? Hmm… I really ought to allocate some time researching if it was common for a Keeper to have Humling parents. Not to mention, it still didn't answer why the Dweller was stalking me and leaving the journal entries. The plot certainly thickened.

However, I had learned some new very valuable information. Christy Kaswell was my mother's name. I opened the locket while I shuffled down the hall. My family stared up at me. I had assumed they didn't care, but now I realized they were simply still on the Earth Plane.

Trevor

Deep in my soul, I still hoped Elizabeth was a Humling since she returned through the hospital. I wanted someone to explain away all the little things which didn't add up. Someone who could let me go back to a time when I lived in bliss, unaware of the danger Elizabeth posed if she were indeed a Dweller. Mark helped me search for Elizabeth's chapter and we found it to be empty. Mark informed me what he believed that meant. Ghost and Dweller time wasn't recorded in chapters. I hung onto my last ray of hope that I wasn't right. Somehow, she was Humling and had spent time in the ghost world. Rationally, my fear was becoming realized. It was more likely that we did have a Dweller living amongst us, and she was my friend.

"Crash!" I heard Eddie greet.

I turned and Elizabeth was making her way through the rehearsal room door with my Tilly. They were happily chit-chatting. The problem with all of my discoveries was I didn't see or feel that Elizabeth was a threat. How could I be so wrong?

Tilly split off and headed towards George and Jay on the stage carrying strange looking attire for them. Tonight was a Harmony special dress re-hearsal that Rhett insisted we have. Tilly seemed to take his meddling in stride with no idea as to why Rhett was so concerned about her welfare. Se-crets swirled in my world like a tornado. Each player was adept at keeping their own secrets, leaving me forced into silence.

"Bro, where have you been?" Eddie asked as he plopped down in the chair beside me. "Have you seen what Tilly picked out for us to wear?"

"Don't complain," Elizabeth said as she shook some type of clothing in her hand at us. "Yours can't be as bad as my wearing practically nothing on stage."

She settled into the chair next to Eddie who glanced over at her grinning like a sheepish cat. I recognized that if Elizabeth was a Dweller, Eddie was no match for her and had no idea how much he needed my protection. However, I couldn't stop him from being smitten. "Where's Kim?" I asked trying to steer his attention away.

His eyes darted to mine leaving no doubt he wished I hadn't brought up Kim.

"She went with her Mom to purchase uniforms for her sister," Eddie explained.

"She's not coming to practice then?" I questioned.

Eddie appeared to be biting his lip while looking at me with exasperated eyes. "No, she won't be along," Eddie returned giving me a hush up look.

"That's a shame," I hummed. "With all the time you've been spending with her, what will you do with a night off?"

"Bro," Eddie said and then shook his head. "Harsh bro!"

He clearly wasn't happy with me. He wanted to use the time tonight to court Elizabeth. However, I now understood what a dangerous action this might be. His fingers quit taping the arm of his chair. He got up and marched off angrily without saying a word. He could be mad at me, it was for his best. His being angry would pass. We were family after all.

"You certainly chased him off," Elizabeth stated. "He appears to be a tad bit angry."

"Sorry," I replied.

"Nah, it's okay," Elizabeth said. "I have a feeling he's more into me than I am into him."

"What did Brassbuckle dole out today?" I asked.

"Only an endless amount of paperwork to file," Elizabeth huffed.

"That bad?" I reacted.

"Worse than bad," Elizabeth answered. "What was Tilly's Earth Plane husband's name?"

"Why would you want to know that?" I shot back.

Elizabeth shrugged.

"Something to do with the filing?" I asked.

"I was just curious," she sighed. "I've never heard Tilly say."

"Heath Lund," I answered watching for any hint of recognition in her body language and eye expressions.

"When someone is a ghost," Elizabeth began. "Is their time, spent as a ghost, recorded?"

"No it's not," I answered continuing to watch for any hint as to why the fifty questions. "Time is also not recorded for Dwellers."

The look on her face said it all. I had hit a nerve. She wasn't going to admit her thoughts to me, maybe not even to herself. However, deep down she left me no room to conclude otherwise. I also knew exactly who else was aware. Marvin.

Did Marvin, a committed member of our world, dump Elizabeth out of patriotism? Had he discovered who she was and backed off? If I discovered Tilly was a Dweller, which she isn't, I'm not sure I could walk away from her. Marvin, apparently, didn't care for Elizabeth as much as I did Tilly. Did he love the Keeper world and Ghostie world more? I had so many questions as a spy. My hat was off to Marvin if he walked away from love to keep his world safe. I couldn't do it. I couldn't walk away from Tilly or Ruthanne. I realized as I pondered, I had a flaw. I loved too deeply and I was loyal to the women in my life to the point I would die for them. Marvin was a walker in my eyes. Even if Elizabeth was undeniably a Dweller, I wouldn't give up on her either. She was my friend after all.

Elizabeth

I milled around the rehearsal room door waiting for Tilly, Rhett, and Trevor to get engrossed in Harmony. When they were busy looking at the black cased electronic song holders, I quickly made my way through the rehearsal room door into the small hallway. Ahead of me were the familiar black curtains which lead to Grand Hall and the right door onto stage. I could hear Tiffany's group practicing their choruses. However, I wasn't interested in them. Nor was I interested in the hallway to the right which lead behind the stage to another entrance to Grand Hall and the left door onto stage.

I fumbled with the curtain against the wall to my left, revealing the concealed door which led to the props room. I had avoided the lift for days since I melted down on Leo. I owed him an apology. Once I stepped under the door frame and the curtain brushed my back, I found the familiar musty, earthy smelling storage room. It was complete with a series of lockers standing side by side and a series of musical instruments piled in cases almost to the ceiling. Once I lifted the second curtain revealing the larger props, my nose was delighted with the smell of gingerbread coming from Leo's small apartment.

I again felt the curtain brush my back as it swooshed closed behind me. The sectioned off storage areas in this room hadn't changed much. They still contained an array of furniture, costumes, and artificial plants. In the back of the room I found the free standing, wooden, painted scene of a castle with a huge flower garden, a lake, and a small door painted amongst flowering vines. The faded brass door knob which was attached to the child size door was cold to the touch, just as I remembered. I took a deep breath as I gave the door a good knock.

When no one answered, I could only hope Leo wasn't ignoring me. With my back to the wall, I slid down until I was sitting on the floor. I leaned my head back against the wall. All I wanted was to apologize. I thought we were friends, why was he going to make me apologize to him in front of everyone? Of course, I had embarrassed him in public, so wasn't that fair? Hmm… It would be fair, but I wasn't leaving without saying what I came to say. I listened at the tiny door and I could hear him humming away inside. The door squeaked as I shoved it open and stuck my head in.

"Princess!" Leo exclaimed as he turned to see me. He said this with such reverence, almost as if he saw me as some kind of royalty. His smile disappeared in response to my annoyed stare. Leo began to stammer, "Oh… Sorry…"

I held up my hand to stop him as I crawled through the door into the miniature loft apartment. I asked, "Why didn't you answer the door?" Before he could answer, I continued, "Could you not hear my knocking? You knew it was me, didn't you?"

Leo in a panic lost grip on a hot pan of gingerbread cookies. He adamantly disagreed, "No, no, no! You don't understand!" I watched as he forgot that his second hand had no baker's mitt on. Instantly Leo yelled, "Crap!" The tray of gingerbread cookies slammed to the counter as he placed his burning fingers into his mouth and then turned to run cool water over them.

"Leo?" I called in concern realizing I never meant for him to burn his hand. The white painted ceiling fell just short of my being able to stand up, forcing me to move towards him hunched over.

He turned to peer at me, "You don't understand. I can't open the door!"

"You can't open the door?" I repeated feeling confused. Who couldn't open their front door?

"You won't like me anymore if you knew why!" Leo exclaimed.

"You're a prisoner, aren't you?" I assumed out loud.

Leo's large eyes closed with the unspoken truth not needing to be spoken.

I sat down before the mini breakfast bar in his homey kitchen. I spied the second entrance which was directly across from the door I entered, remembering it led to the lift. I pointed to the lift door questioning, "You can only use that door?"

"Yes," Leo said as he sat on a stool opposite of me. "However, I can only go into the lift. Not beyond."

"What did you do?" I asked in wonderment.

"I was carrying out my master's plan!" Leo exclaimed. "My only regret is getting caught." With another huff he added, "Now you know how I failed you princess. I will understand if you can't look upon me."

I peered up at the white painted ceiling with the exposed pipes which ran across this miniature version of a loft apartment. Although I doubted he knew it, he had called me princess again. It was so ingrained, he did so without thought. "Can you tell me why you call me princess?" I questioned.

"That's simple," Leo stated. "Because you are a princess."

"I still don't understand," I stated.

"Not only do I know you are a princess," Leo said. "I believe you are the true princess." He gave me a knowing look rolling his eyes. The realization hit him that I really didn't understand. He added, "The one I spend all my time writing about."

"Writing?" I repeated totally confused.

Leo walked around the breakfast bar which opened to the dining room and living area. He stood before his dining table and the only vacant chair. He pointed around the table at the other five chairs which were covered in notebooks and various stacks of papers. The accumulation of stacks overflowed from the chairs to the floor. As he strolled around the table towards the china cabinet, he began, "All of this is the writing I have done on the subject of the true princess." I watched him open the china cabinet which stored no dishes. Instead, more stacks of notebooks, papers, and office supplies loomed. "Your not remembering only proves my point as to you being the true princess."

"Then explain the true princess to me," I stated seating myself in the floor.

Leo walked back over to the counter and offered me a piece of fresh gingerbread.

"Thank you," I said as I graciously took it.

Leo circled the breakfast bar and sat back on his stool. "Let me give you the brief overall fairy tale version." He broke off a piece of gingerbread himself and took a small bite. "The true princess will arrive having no remembrance of the power she holds as the bridge between light and dark.

"The gray," I said as my thoughts slipped out.

"You are more light than gray," Leo seriously stated about my assumption. "The true princess will find her place amongst the royals while those around her will do anything to protect her and keep her from her destiny. The power to separate the light and dark rests in her hands. Her greatest enemy waits to unravel her world and will do anything to keep her from her destiny. If the enemy prevails, darkness will overtake all."

"You are right about my having enemies and I don't understand why," I began. "However, you dreaming up my having some unknown power... That is crazy!"

"You do," Leo hummed in response and shoved another cookie in his mouth.

"You really believe that?" I asked as I pointed to the mess of papers. "And have been writing about it."

"All of those," Leo said with a full mouth. "My life's work!"

"You still haven't explained what you did," I said off the top of my head.

A buzzer ding began to fill the air. Leo let out a sigh, "Sorry, Harmony must be over." He hopped off his chair. "I'll have lots of people to move."

"Guess I'll go," I stated.

"Probably a good idea," Leo said as he reached for the tiny doorknob. He turned to point at the opposite door saying, "Make sure and leave through that door."

"I will," I assured Leo as he disappeared out into the lift. The smell of the gingerbread delighted me. I helped myself to several more cookies before making my way hunched over to the door.

CHAPTER FIFTEEN

Marvin

A loud thud, thud, thud on the door woke me from a sound nap in the recliner. As I often dreamed since loosing Elizabeth, I was holding her in my arms and my world was right. Back to reality, I hurriedly shuffled down the hallway, swung the door open, and coldly answered, "What do you want?"

"I need to talk to you," Trevor replied while peering around to see if anyone was watching him.

"Trevor, go home," I unhappily stated. I wasn't interested in talking with him. I gave the door a push to close it as I turned to walk back to my chair. Maybe Elizabeth would once again visit me in my dreams.

I could hear the door creak back open and feel Trevor pursuing me inside. In disgust, I turned into the kitchen as he said to my back, "I know Marvin!"

Whatever he thought he knew paled in comparison to the real truth. "I doubt it," I said under my breath flipping on the coffee maker. Coffee kept me up at night and from dreaming of Elizabeth.

He continued to trail me, stopping under the door frame of the bright yellow kitchen. "I know Elizabeth is a Dweller!" Trevor loudly spit out.

Every muscle in my body instantly tensed up. The stairs behind us creaked as I spun around catching Rhett's eye. As I focused on Trevor's face, I tried to remain calm and cool by asking, "What would make you say that?"

Trevor tossed a book onto the round table saying, "This would!"

Rhett brushed past Trevor picking up the book. Appearing stunned he asked, "Where did you get this?"

Trevor stood silent as I traipsed over to inspect the book. "You didn't answer me. Why would you conclude that Elizabeth is a Dweller?"

"This book confirms a royal Dweller guard has the power to render the person they are guarding immobile," Trevor responded. "Does that sound familiar?"

"Tilly must have mentioned Elizabeth's reaction?" I said fishing.

"She did," Trevor simply answered appearing distressed.

"How did you get a guide to becoming a Dweller guard?" Rhett pointedly asked.

Trevor appeared to be ordering his words. When he noticed Rhett was still staring at him anticipating an answer, he said, "Maybe the truth will set me free. The book came from the archives."

"Archives?" I questioned.

"How did you get access to them?" Rhett seriously questioned Trevor.

My head swiveled to peer between Rhett and Trevor. What was I missing?

Trevor stared Rhett down, looking him directly in the eye spouting, "Does it matter how I got it?"

"You're silent but deadly," Rhett sighed as a smile crossed his face. "I never saw you coming. I do have to add that you and Miss Bradford make the perfect pair."

"I'm glad you mentioned Tilly," Trevor sighed. "She is the reason I am here." He pulled out a chair and sat down at the round table. Then he continued, "I must ensure Tilly is safe."

"You believe Elizabeth is harmful to Tilly?" I asked feeling annoyed. What could be more stupid?

"Of course not," Trevor corrected me. "Elizabeth would never harm a fly. Those, who are chasing her, would."

"You're under the assumption that someone is chasing her?" Rhett seriously inquired.

"She does," Trevor replied. "As a matter of fact she says a Dweller is stalking her."

"At least, she finally has a healthy fear," I said under my breath as I plopped down in the chair across from Trevor.

"He scares the devil out of her," Trevor added. As if taunting me he added, "Always showing up."

No matter how many times I repeated to myself that this was best, someone always found a way to make me doubt my decision. She should turn to me for protection and understanding. "Elizabeth confided in you?" I questioned.

"Look, you left her," Trevor icily returned. "She has no one to confide in. Yes, she told me that."

I stood up and clenched my fists. Trevor had no understanding about what I had done for Elizabeth. His taunting me was too much. I couldn't take more. Nor could I explain it to him.

"What did she say about him showing up?" Rhett interjected.

"She's seen him inside the dome and beyond it," Trevor stated eyeing Rhett's and my demeanor.

I peered at Rhett and couldn't help but pace. My mind kept chanting over and over, "You made the right decision." Trying to convince my heart, "You love her enough to let her go. It is what is best for her."

"I assume you both knew about Elizabeth," Trevor prodded.

"You can't tell Tilly," Rhett sternly stated to Trevor since the gig was obviously up.

"You don't think I know this?" Trevor retorted with a tormented face. "All I need is to protect her."

Rhett stared Trevor down summing him up. All of a sudden he asked, "Do you have some grand plan for her safety?"

"I had to confirm what I concluded was the truth," Trevor sighed. Appearing dejected he added, "My whole life has revolved around watching over Tilly. He looked directly at Rhett asking, "Were you not concerned about the Dweller harming Tilly?"

"Of course," Rhett quickly answered. "There isn't much I can do."

"I'm not settling for that!" Trevor shot back.

"Settling?" Rhett repeated clearly offended. "Don't spout off when you don't have the full picture."

I tried to make a keep your mouth shut look at Rhett as Trevor challenged, "Enlighten me."

Rhett appeared slightly flushed and tongue tied, much to my relief. I couldn't comprehend why Trevor was so easily crawling under Rhett's skin.

"Of course," Trevor taunted. "Not going to say a thing?"

"I have to trust..." Rhett paused. "To put my faith in what I believe. What I know."

"And what is that?" Trevor again returned.

"Why did you come here?" I interrupted pouring myself a cup of coffee to hide my face and the fear in my eyes concerning Elizabeth.

"To try to make sense of it all," Trevor said. "Since you knew, why didn't you attempt to do anything about it?"

"Who says we're not doing what is best?" I challenged.

"Best for whom?" Trevor spit out. "Elizabeth or Tilly?"

"What is best for everyone concerned," I answered.

Trevor looked exasperated at our not leveling with him. He stood and I assumed he was heading for the door. I rounded the table, fully intending to get between him and the exit. I demanded, "You aren't going to tell anyone."

"Or what?" Trevor challenged.

"Think about it," Rhett interjected.

Trevor tuned to stare at Rhett before saying, "I have thought about it. None of this will matter to Tilly since she sees Elizabeth as her best friend."

"They are best friends," Rhett reiterated.

"She will only rebel against the establishment where Elizabeth in concerned," Trevor said under his breath.

"What do you expect Tilly to do if she believed Elizabeth was in trouble?" Rhett threw out.

"I can tell you," I stated. "Tilly would fling herself at the Dweller as a distraction to help Elizabeth."

"The tickling," Trevor surmised appearing disgusted and pained at the same time.

"The best defense is an offense," Rhett stated. "Can't you trust us to leave it at that?"

"Do I have a choice?" Trevor stated.

Everyone had a choice and sometimes the choices weren't pretty or easy.

Trevor

I exited the mess Rhett and Marvin called a home and headed for the Underground headquarters. It wasn't my night to come in, but I had to report this. It pained me to betray Elizabeth. Mark and I weren't able to enter the Underground after hours on any other evening than Wednesday since only on Wednesday night was the locker room attended. I entered through the Ghost Complex and this was the only locker portal they chose to give me access to. Belle was the locker portal's Keeper and only worked days with the exception of Wednesday evening. Thus my problem, it wasn't Wednesday.

On any other night of the week, I could meet a handler at the outside basketball court located in the park. A group played every night except Monday. What would be strange about guys playing basketball in the middle of the night? I guess I was the only one who had thought this could be viewed as odd behavior. They all thought it was inconspicuous. It did allow all of us to pass messages along to the handler. However, tonight was Monday and no one would be there.

Tonight I would need another path into the Underground since I wasn't privy to information about the whereabouts of the locker portal on any given Monday. Mr. Bradford made the comment that he never used the locker portals, leaving me to conclude the filing cabinet which set in his office at the Underground was his own private portal. I couldn't go to the Bradford's house. Mrs. Bradford would assume I was reneging on our deal for her to be kind to Tilly.

My plan led me here, to use the filing cabinet portal in Mr. Bradford's office. As you would expect with any Complex Administrator, his office was large with impressive wooden furniture. The light from the hallway shining through the massive windows revealed the far wall was filled with a row of tall filing cabinets all made from the same light furniture wood. I moved to close all the blinds leaving one cracked enough to leave a dim light shining. Moving towards the filing cabinets, I began to pull open the top cabinet drawer from each one. As I went down the row and was satisfied that each was a filing cabinet, I let them shut.

Since I couldn't move any of the four drawers of the last filing cabinet, I understood the average Joe would assume they were locked. However, in my mind, I had found the key to getting into the Underground. I ran my hands over every inch of the filing cabinet, but found no magic button to push. Frustrated I turned back towards Mr. Bradford's desk and strutted over to sit in his chair. I had to think like Mr. Bradford. I leaned back in his plush, comfortable chair pondering where he would hide the key to the entrance. Somewhere that no one would suspect?

My eyes were drawn to the wall across from the desk which was filled with photos of his family. I stood, rounded the desk, and began to move and feel each individual picture. Coming up short, I leaned against the wall. That's when I caught a glimpse of something I recognized setting on the bookcase behind the desk.

I remembered the day our art teacher, Mrs. Bergus gave us an assignment to create clay vases for our mothers. I intently worked for hours sculpting what my fourth grade mind believed to be perfect. Even though my mother loved it and it is still displayed in the china cabinet, I now realize how off center and badly shaped it is.

Tilly insisted on creating something different altogether. She and Mrs. Bergus were like oil and water. The more specific Mrs. Bergus made her assignments, the more Tilly wouldn't follow the instructions. Even as a child, Tilly was head strong. She insisted the bottom of her vase should be carved to allow for a hidden compartment. She thought her mother would place her jewels in it. Mrs. Bradford didn't like it and openly told her so. Tilly assumed for all these years that her mother threw it out.

Lucky for me, I was the only person alive who knew the secret that vase held. Who else would mess with Mr. Bradford's kid's art project? I walked over and gently picked the vase up. Turning it over, the silver key stared up at me. "Thank you Tilly!" I hummed. With the key in hand, I slid the key into the top of the filing cabinet. One complete door swung open revealing a perfectly good locker portal underneath. I placed the key back into the vase and set it back in its place on the shelf.

I stepped into the locker. As soon as the door closed on the filing cabinet, the familiar feeling of air swirling around me like a tornado and the shaking began. When it ceased, I pushed open the door and stepped out into Mr. Bradford's office in the Underground.

"What in the devil are you dong here?" Mr. Bradford said jumping up from his office desk. "Why in the world are you using my private transport?"

"I can explain," I replied.

"You're absolutely right," Mr. Bradford began. "You're going to explain in great detail!"

Before I could respond, the filing cabinet was shaking as if it were being beat up from the inside. Just as suddenly, it stopped with its door flinging open. Rhett and Marvin seemed to fall out of thin air.

"You let them tail you?" Mr. Bradford spewed at me.

"You!" Rhett spewed at Mr. Bradford.

Rhett stood with his arms folded across his chest. It was apparent he shared Mr. Bradford's disgust.

"You followed me!" I yelled at them.

"We knew you would lead us straight to whomever you intended to tell," Rhett answered.

"Whatever he intends to tell me is none of your business," Mr. Bradford spewed at the two of them.

"That's where you are mistaken," Marvin stated as he stepped forward challenging Mr. Bradford.

"You're not in control here," Mr. Bradford warned. "I wouldn't take a step closer."

Rhett grabbed Marvin's arm to stop him as he asked, "Where are we?"

Mr. Bradford appeared as if every bone in his body was angered by this question. "Now you're here, you're in," Mr. Bradford mumbled shaking his head in disgust. "No choice." He sat down on the side of his desk and spewed at me, "They trailed you. Why don't you do the honor of explaining?"

"You are in the Underground," I stated. "Our spy network!"

"What do you mean once we're here, were in?" Rhett asked looking about.

"You won't be allowed to leave until you have pledged your oath of loyalty and silence," Mr. Bradford angrily stated.

"You can't stop us from leaving if we choose," Rhett disagreed.

Suddenly, Rhett pulled out a card from his pocket which resembled a destination card. As suddenly as the card was in his hand, a door magically appeared in the wall beside the filing cabinet. Before Marvin could react, Rhett had swiped his card in the door lock. I watched as the door swung open revealing a huge office. It wasn't an exit as Rhett believed.

Mr. Bradford stepped forward stating, "Shall we..." You could see Mr. Bradford's reaction caught Rhett off guard. Mr. Bradford smiled and pulled an identical card from his pocket taunting, "I have one too."

"Mr...?" Mr. Bradford hesitated searching for a name while peering at Marvin.

"Lagedge," Marvin returned.

"Great," Mr. Bradford smiled as if he had the upper hand. "Mr. Lagedge." He turned to peer at me,"Trevor you better come along too."

I trailed the group through the door and found myself standing in a massive, plush office. Mr. Bradford's Administration office paled in comparison to this magnificent office. Before me was a comfortable seating area which reminded me of someone's personal living room. Next to it was the longest desk I had ever seen. Before it four chairs pranced. Three of the walls were covered in massive book cases with a variety of volumes shelved. The fourth wall was a continuous line of tall, slender, and somewhat familiar windows.

Rhett and Mr. Bradford moved towards some type of red button next to the only other door in the room. Mr. Bradford held out his hand letting Rhett push it. Both were staring each other down with tension that could be cut with a knife.

"What's all that about?" I asked Marvin who was standing next to me watching them as well.

"Your guess is as good as mine," Marvin replied.

Mr. Bradford and Rhett moved in unison to the seating area. Instead of sitting on the couch together, they each took a chair next to each other. Marvin's eyes flickered to mine as he sighed. I followed him and we sat down on the couch together to wait for whoever was going to respond to the button which had been pushed.

The silence was deafening. If there had been crickets chirping, it was silent enough to hear them.

Then, the door swung open and Mr. Solliday entered the door. Now, I knew exactly where I was. I was in Mr. Solliday's personal office in his home. I was seated in Dogwood House. No wonder the tall and slender windows seemed familiar. There wasn't a child alive who hadn't spent time daydreaming outside the fence surrounding Dogwood House.

"Oh dear," Mr. Solliday sighed as he came through the door and spied the four of us. He moved to sit in the lone chair left in the seating area. "To what do I owe this pleasure?"

"I'll start," I said before anyone else could answer. "I needed to file a report at the Underground tonight."

"You should have given the report to the handler," Mr. Bradford reprimanded.

Mr. Solliday held up his hand to silence Mr. Bradford. Then he patiently said, "Let the boy speak his mind."

"There is no handler on Monday and it wasn't my day to come in," I defended myself. "I figured Mr. Bradford had his own port to the Underground. I used it."

"We followed Trevor to Bradford's office and watched him use the portal," Rhett interjected.

"Then we tried the portal for ourselves," Marvin added with a sly grin. "We had our reason."

"It blows my mind that you let them tail you," Mr. Bradford again reprimanded. "What a rookie move!"

"May I ask why you felt the need to follow Mr. Stillholm?" Mr. Solliday asked Rhett and Marvin.

"He knows," Rhett simply answered.

"You know too?" I questioned Mr. Solliday totally in shock.

"What were you going to file tonight?" Mr. Bradford spit out, clearly annoyed, before Mr. Solliday could answer.

"This seems to have really crawled under your skin," Mr. Solliday retorted to Mr. Bradford.

"It has!" Mr. Bradford stated. "We have gone to great lengths not to be discovered. We have protocols."

"I take it you have never had a surprise visit before," I stated and watched Mr. Bradford shake his head no.

"Why didn't you come to the house?" Mr. Bradford pointedly asked.

I began to answer, "I thought Mrs. Bradford would think..."

"Point taken," Mr. Bradford interrupted me. I was sure he had second thoughts about airing his dirty laundry.

Mr. Solliday was watching the odd exchange with a raised eyebrow. "Is everything okay at home?" He asked Mr. Bradford.

"Yeah," Mr. Bradford said wanting to bury the subject considering who was in the room. "Again, just spit out whatever undercover facts you have acquired."

"Elizabeth is a Dweller!" I sadly stated.

"Oh that," Mr. Bradford said in a dismissive tone. "I wondered how long it would take you to figure that out."

"You've known all along?" I returned with a shocked look on my face.

"What are the two of you involved in?" Rhett interrupted dismissing my astonishment.

"I could ask the same of the two of you," Mr. Bradford stated.

"Gentleman," Mr. Solliday began. "One day, this was bound to come to a head between the two of you." He pointed between Rhett and Mr. Bradford. "Since the two of you were two of the smartest trainees to ever pass though,

I recruited both of you out of the same training class. It has been a tight rope walk ever since. The two of you understandably have a high disregard for each other." His attention then turned to Marvin and me as he pointed between the two of us, "However, I didn't expect the two of you..." With a heavy sigh he continued, "Thomas and Mr. Stillholm are part of the Underground."

"Actually, I lead it," Mr. Bradford interjected craving to one up Rhett.

"Yes," Mr. Solliday said. "The Underground is a secret network which tracks Dweller movements."

"Why?" Rhett asked peering directly at Mr. Solliday.

"You know why," Mr. Solliday sharply answered Rhett obviously shutting him up.

The way Marvin was peering at Rhett left me to believe he too was confused by what was transpiring.

"And they are?" Mr. Bradford asked pointing to Rhett and Marvin.

"Simply knowledgeable," Mr. Solliday answered.

Rhett visibly smirked at this comment with an air of confidence returning. Mr. Bradford didn't buy the explanation. You could tell by the way he folded his arms across his chest.

"This Underground network tracks Elizabeth?" Marvin questioned.

"Of course we do," Mr. Bradford stated in a defying manner.

"How long have you known?" I asked Mr. Bradford.

He chuckled a little. "Since the moment she was born," Mr. Bradford answered. "Don't look so shocked, Rhett did too."

"Wait," I responded. "You knew her before her memory loss?"

"Memory loss…," Mr. Bradford repeated slowly with another chuckle. "It's all a big charade."

"Like she's acting?" I returned.

"She's not," Marvin strongly threw out in her defense.

"I've gone round and round with Albert about this," Mr. Bradford countered.

"You've known that long too?" I questioned Rhett.

"I grew up with Christy, her mother," Rhett answered.

"If you deem it as a charade," I began. "And all of you know, why haven't you confronted her about her memory loss if it's a game?"

"I have requested that no one approach her about this," Mr. Solliday stated.

"Why?" I automatically questioned.

"Christy was my daughter," Mr. Solliday stated. "Elizabeth is my granddaughter."

"That can't be," I returned.

"Christy, Solliday's daughter, married Walter," Rhett interjected.

"Walter was a Dweller," Mr. Bradford summed it up cutting in.

"Wow," was all I could muster to say as I turned to eye Solliday. "Why would you trust your daughter to a Dweller?"

"Walter wasn't any Dweller," Mr. Bradford interjected.

"No he wasn't," Mr. Solliday agreed. "Mr. Stillholm, in the beginning I never believed I could trust him. However, he was the man my daughter was in love with. When she began tossing around the term soul mate, I told him he must prove himself before I would trust him or allow them to declare themselves soul mates publicly."

"How was he to prove himself?" Marvin asked before I could.

"Let's just say he went on missions," Mr. Bradford answered.

"Walter never said a thing to me about the Underground," Rhett said clearly irritated with Mr. Bradford.

"Any task he took on he completed directly for me," Mr. Solliday said. "They were missions that were to dangerous for the regular members of the Underground."

"The missions into the world of the Dwellers," Rhett questioned.

"Indeed," Mr. Solliday agreed and then appeared temporarily lost in his own thoughts.

"He was a great source of intelligence," Mr. Bradford interjected. "People freely confided in him. Dwellers and Keepers alike trusted and liked him."

"Walter had a way of making everyone around him at ease," Rhett stated.

"We all trusted him despite what he was," Mr. Solliday stated.

"Eventually, Walter started singing like a canary," Mr. Bradford stated shaking his head. "He was trading deep Venema family Dweller secrets in exchange for safety from his dark family who were tracking him like blood hounds."

"Then my granddaughters were born and I understood if they were ever found, they would be tracked as well," Mr. Solliday admitted.

"So you tried to hide them?" Marvin asked.

"Amongst the Humlings," Mr. Solliday stated.

"Which, I said was a mistake since Walter didn't complete his most important mission," Mr. Bradford said in a complaining tone to Mr. Solliday.

"What was his mission?" I asked.

"Individual missions are private between myself and the party asked to complete them," Mr. Solliday said giving Mr. Bradford a dirty look.

I peered at Rhett who seemed to take the dirty look to heart. However, behind his eyes was a deep understanding. He knew what the mission was.

"Why do you talk about him in past tense?" Marvin asked.

The three of them looked at each other before Mr. Solliday answered, "The Dwellers came for him and took him home into their world. We weren't able to protect him."

"He hasn't tried to return?" Marvin inquired.

Again, the three of them exchanged a look. "He's gone from us forever. The Dwellers sentenced him to live eternally one life after another on the Earth Plane."

"How do they enforce that?" I questioned.

"They have their own version of the Black Arch," Mr. Bradford responded.

"Then Elizabeth isn't crazy," I said in astonishment. "There are two black arches, one here and one there."

"She asked you about it too, didn't she?" Marvin said to the dismay of those watching our exchange.

"I've told you, she's acting," Mr. Bradford hummed.

"And your daughter?" I asked wondering if Christy suffered the same fate.

"She and Elizabeth went deep into hiding," Rhett answered for Mr. Solliday.

"What about the other girl, Elizabeth's sister?" Marvin intently asked.

This time none of them looked at each other as if they were all attempting not to make eye contact. "Christina was darker than her father," Mr. Solliday admitted. We should have sent her to them from the beginning. The reason Walter was captured was due to Christina... My granddaughter's betrayal."

"How old was she?" Marvin threw out.

"Eleven," Mr. Solliday answered with a tone of sadness.

"How did Elizabeth end up here?" I asked.

"Before Elizabeth went to the Earth Plane, she wrote time and time again always asking to become a Keeper," Mr. Solliday said with a grin. "It was as if she knew she belonged in the world of the Keepers. I always assumed Christy encouraged her."

"Your promise," Rhett said seeming to understand more than the rest of us.

"Promise?" Marvin repeated.

"I promised Christy that when the time was right for Elizabeth, I would train her to become a Keeper," Mr. Solliday explained for our benefit. "More importantly, I promised to keep her safe for a lifetime."

"She left a Humling," Marvin surmised. "That's why she awoke in the Hospital."

Rhett's eyes flashed to Mr. Solliday's as Marvin sighed shutting his eyes. After a deep breath he asked, "There's more?"

"Then Elizabeth arrived here," Mr. Bradford smugly stated. "She is every bit as cunning as her father."

"Cunning?" I questioned in disbelief. "Elizabeth is naïve, gullible, trusting…"

"Is she?" Mr. Bradford interrupted.

"Get real," Marvin said under his breath. "Elizabeth is full of light."

"She's capable of being a spy, a keeper of secrets, unlike you Mr. Lagedge," Mr. Bradford said with a smug grin. "Elizabeth embraced her father's spy position for that last mission."

"The mission?" I once again questioned.

"Again, we will not disclose any mission's purpose to anyone other than the person whom the mission was assigned," Mr. Solliday said giving Mr. Bradford another dirty look.

"The night in the park," Marvin mumbled peering at Rhett. "You knew."

I had no idea what they were referring too as I watched Rhett nod his head yes.

"I assume you have a plan to watch and protect Elizabeth then," I threw out.

"Elizabeth is well watched," Mr. Solliday stated.

"You are aware a Dweller is stalking her?" I returned.

"There are many Dwellers in her world," Mr. Bradford spouted. "She is one and probably heads their spy network here."

The shock on Marvin's face matched the shock I felt. We both had more to worry about than just the one lone stalker.

"Besides, she's being kept busy," Mr. Bradford added. "With all that extra weekly work we have assigned, there is no doubt she will crack soon. If Zirak can't break her, Brassbuckle will."

"They know?" I asked feeling flabbergasted.

"Zirak believes she's a Humling," Mr. Bradford began. "Brassbuckle is in intelligence… Don't you see the connection?" Giving me a scrutinizing look he added, "Yes, Brassbuckle knows." Then a grin crossed his face. "He also enjoys sparing with Mathilda."

"Tilly," I instantly corrected feeling my skin beginning to boil. How could he have knowledge that someone was deliberately picking on Tilly and not care? Was he not supposed to be her father? Besides, he failed to mention Tilly's safety. Shouldn't he be more concerned about her, his daughter? I couldn't help but pointedly ask, "Is someone watching Tilly?"

"When she is with Elizabeth, she is watched," Mr. Bradford responded.

"What about when she is not with Elizabeth?" I pointedly asked.

"Come on Trevor," Mr. Bradford responded. "She's in no more danger than the rest of us."

"I disagree," I countered. "If she is on their radar, then she needs protection too."

"Your time would be better spent worrying about what Elizabeth pretends not to know," Mr. Bradford stated while shaking his head at me.

"Give it a rest," Marvin said. "Elizabeth isn't a threat to anyone."

"She comprehends and has more knowledge about herself than she lets on," Mr. Bradford taunted.

Mr. Solliday held up his hand to hush all of us, "We need to decide where we go from here."

"Trevor and I return to the Underground," Mr. Bradford began and then pointed to Rhett and Marvin. "They can crawl back into whatever hole they came from."

"Thomas, you do understand your own protocols," Mr. Solliday interjected.

"No," Mr. Bradford instantly said with a look of horror on his face. "Not them."

"Rhett, Mr. Lagedge, I must inform the two of you…"

Mr. Bradford let out a huge angry exhale.

"You are the newest members of the Underground," Mr. Solliday continued not smiling while ignoring Mr. Bradford's huffing.

"I'm not working for him," Rhett stated while gesturing towards Mr. Bradford. "He is a henpecked nincompoop!"

"You do realize I might be as unhappy about this as you are," Mr. Bradford retorted. "Long ago you showed your true colors. You desert those around you!"

"Don't go there!" Rhett retorted as he jumped to his feet.

"Or what?" Mr. Bradford spewed back at him as he matched Rhett's angry stance.

"You both are right," Mr. Solliday stated in disgust with their outbursts as he stood to his feet to get between them. He held up his hands to both of them as he said to Rhett, "You will work directly for me."

"I don't want him ever stepping foot in the Underground," Mr. Bradford spewed as he angrily began to pace behind the chairs.

"You don't have to worry about that," Rhett stated as he plopped back down in his chair. "If I ever see you again, it will be much too soon."

Mr. Solliday gave Rhett another stern look. Then he turned to look at Marvin. "Mr. Lagedge, you will be assigned like any other member of the Underground."

"You have a new partner Trevor," Mr. Bradford said in a taunting voice from behind my chair. "You were responsible for them tailing you. You can be responsible for Mr. Lagedge. Any assignment I give you, drag him along."

"And Mark?" I asked in response.

"He will remain your primary partner," Mr. Bradford stated. "You need him much worse than he needs you."

"What if I don't want to be a member?" Marvin stated.

"Man," I huffed. "I tried that one too."

"It is done," Mr. Solliday said in a tone of finality.

CHAPTER SIXTEEN

Elizabeth

Professor Kegley put us through the longest day by subjecting us to Mrs. Bradford teaching our class. Naturally, Tiffany was the teacher's pet and she flaunted it all morning. I was relieved to go file for Mr. Brassbuckle, although I still hadn't made any progress. I could swear there were elves causing my stacks of paper to grow. There were more papers stacked today than yesterday. Considering my punishment wouldn't be deemed complete until every last paper was filed, this torture of a job was sure to last me a lifetime.

Finally, I made my way back to the Hall of Records to finish out my work day filing books on the massive shelves. I worked hard to finish earlier than expected. I needed a few free moments to do a little research. I wanted to view the chapters on both Christy Kaswell and Heath Lund. I already discovered they were in the restricted section. For once, I had a plan. Taking Tilly's advice, I was throwing all caution to the wind. Without Marvin, there was nothing left to do but figure out who I was and what happened to my family.

I walked up to Carmen and circled to the back of the desk. There, I claimed the cart holding the chapters to be filed in the restricted section.

Carmen huffed while never looking up from her book, "What do you want?"

"I thought I might file these," I said as I gestured towards the chapters on the cart.

"In the restricted section?" Carmen asked as she put her book down.

"I just thought I would do you a favor," I hem-hawed. "I'm finished with mine and have a little free time."

"I don't know," Carmen hummed.

"It won't hurt my feelings if you tell me no," I baited her understanding she wouldn't do any favors for me. "I would love the time off. Perhaps you would let me leave early?"

She peered at her watch and looked up with a sticky sweet grin saying, "You still owe me almost an hour."

"So, I'll file," I said with a fake sigh.

"Don't tell anyone," Carmen warned pointing her long skinny finger towards me in a threatening manner.

I pushed the cart past her and then rolled my eyes. Little did she know I wouldn't be telling anyone.

I made my way to the shelf which housed the chapter for Christy Kaswell. I simply stared at it imagining what I would learn. I was on the verge of discovering myself, if it would open for me. With the chapter in my hand, I ran my fingers over the glossy, white cover. It had nothing on it except the black printed name, Christy Jo Kaswell. I was surprised as the chapter seemed to fall open in my hands. The invisible lock which was to be in place wasn't. I found the first page was dedicated only to a blank, black line with the word Keeper printed underneath. As with my chapter, the Keeper's name was missing. The next page was the same with one black line containing a long number, with the words Keeper Identification Number printed underneath. I turned the page finding it blank with nothing to read. The next page and the page after that were all the same. The whole chapter was empty. Incredible! Another dead end.

I shoved the chapter back on the shelf and filed a few books on my way to find the name Heath Lund. This chapter was the polar opposite of the last one. The cover was dull and black with a hard to read gray printed name, Heath Lund. The chapter had no apparent lock like Keeper chapters. I flipped through its pages and it too was empty. I leaned against the book case. How in the world could this one be empty as well? My world just seemed to get heavier and heavier. Both chapters were, sadly, blank just like mine.

Tilly

I was steamed at the gall of Tiffany. She wrangled her way into convincing the Professor she should have a private showing of her Harmony performance tonight. Sunday was quickly closing in and my group needed to practice for Sunday's Harmony performance. My nemesis enjoyed informing me that we were kicked out of both Grand hall and the rehearsal room tonight. I should have pulled a few more strands of hair from her head to get even. However, I was temporarily practicing self control.

I might not have cared if it weren't for the fact I told Anthony I wouldn't be seeing him tonight. He made plans to go into The City with Gary to see Wyatt. They were probably at food row eating all kinds of stuff which Emma would disapprove of. How they could be from the same family baffled me. I could go join them, but I had the feeling Anthony was looking forward to a guy night. Actually, this didn't bother me. Usually it would if a guy found anything other than me as important. I couldn't help but smile with the realization that, even though he was going to guy night, he would think about me a dozen times in every minute. My gut understood I was his world and it felt surprisingly good. I found pleasure in my new place as his girlfriend.

Sauntering toward the basketball court in Spring Park, all I could hear was the dribbling of a ball. Eddie told me Trevor was at his new favorite pasttime, basketball. Since the two of them had always been close, Eddie seemed to feel betrayed by Trevor's sudden lack of interest in skateboarding which Eddie's whole life revolved around. However, it was fabulous for Eddie's love life. Kim was newbie, but becoming a permanent part of Eddie's skateboarding group. She also seemed to be falling hard for Eddie. Go figure! He appeared to be the only person inside the dome she didn't stutter around.

As I stared through the chain link fence, Trevor was intently playing with a group of strangers. That is, other than Marvin. When Trevor caught glimpse of me he smiled, waved, and then passed the ball to another guy. Actually… Wasn't he the nerdy guy Trevor was hanging out with on the day he skipped class?

"Hey," Trevor greeted me while breathing heavily. "I thought you would be going out."

"Nah," I said noticing how manly Trevor appeared in his sweat soaked shirt. "Eddie let me know you were playing ball."

"Was he with Kim?" Trevor asked.

"No," I replied.

"She came by on her board," Trevor said. "She's been practicing a new trick and wanted my opinion before she showed Eddie." He let out a chuckle. "When she gets lost in thoughts of Eddie she doesn't stutter."

"They are going to make a cute couple," I added to his obvious thoughts.

"When he sees it," Trevor hummed with a frown.

I understood what he was alluding too. Eddie had an unhealthy attraction to Elizabeth. However, Elizabeth wasn't at all interested in Eddie.

"Do you just want to hang out?" Trevor asked.

Before I could answer, nerdy guy alluded, "This must be the infamous Mathilda Bradford. I've heard so much about you."

"Who hasn't?" I retorted as I flashed him my best flirtatious grin.

"Tilly, this is Mark," Trevor said as he introduced us looking genuinely nervous. "Mark, this is Tilly."

"It's nice to meet you," Mark stated as he gave me a small gentleman's bow.

As a giggle escaped me, Marvin broke in saying,"Be nice."

"Like you should talk," I returned feeling agitated the square still believed he should inform me about how to act.

A gentle breeze blew towards me and I caught a whiff of Marvin. Did he no longer bathe? "Marvin you stink," I stated with my thoughts falling out of my mouth.

"He's been eating ginger hoping to increase his strength," Trevor mindlessly replied.

"Ginger to increase your strength?" I repeated shaking my head. "That is crazy!" Elizabeth and the square really were the perfect pair, except for the part of him breaking her heart into a million pieces. Why was I even standing in his presence? I turned to stare down Trevor adding, "Are you making Marvin your new best friend?"

"Who are you telling Trevor who he can and can't be friends with," Marvin quickly retorted before Trevor could answer. "I think he should only answer to Ruthanne."

"You're scum!" I threw out at Marvin feeling my blood boiling. He was out of line with the last comment.

"Whoa," Mark loudly muttered with big eyes while wiping his apparent runny nose. He didn't see my comment coming.

"I suppose you believe that because I broke up with Elizabeth?" Marvin returned.

"You're no better than the dirt on the bottom of my shoes," I calmly replied suddenly wanting to slap Marvin in Elizabeth's defense.

Trevor grabbed me by the arm and began to pull me away. "Trevor Stillholm, you let go of me!" I demanded. I struggled to get my arm free which really wasn't going to happen. Trevor pulled me out of ear shot of Marvin and the rest of the guys. As I wiggled and struggled, I had to wonder when Trevor had gotten so strong.

"Can it," Trevor demanded as he released my arm.

"What is up with you lately?" I asked. "How dare you man handle me!"

Trevor's hand brushed lightly and tenderly down my arm as he intently peered into my eyes. "I'm sorry. I had to pull you away."

He appeared genuinely sorry, but I wasn't about to let him off the hook that easily. I had to figure out a way to get Trevor wrapped back around my finger where he belonged. No way was I losing my touch.

Then Trevor casually added, "I like Marvin. He's a cool guy."

"You don't care about what he did to Elizabeth, our friend?" I returned.

"She's moved on," Trevor stated defending his position. "Is she not dating Dustin?"

"You know she is," I replied. "You also know how much she wants Marvin back."

"I gave her advice concerning just that," Trevor said. "I told her you can't have your cake and eat it too."

In a huff, I turned to walk away. I didn't have to put up with Trevor's drivel.

Trevor caught my hand saying in a begging voice, "Tilly." I turned too peered at him as he begged, "Come on, and don't be upset with me."

"She's my best friend," I replied in exasperation. "Hanging out with him is downright a betrayal."

"Can't I be friends with both of them?" Trevor asked in a pleading voice.

"I don't know," I replied. "Can you really be a good friend to both?" My hands flew to my hips. "Would you drop hanging out with Marvin if I asked you too? Would you do that for me?"

"Tilly, do you really want to pick my friends?" Trevor asked intently peering at me. Again his hand gently brushed my arm. "You already know that you are the most important person to me." Trevor sighed and then let go of my hand. "I don't want to argue with you."

"Then don't," I shot back. I took a deep breath to re-center myself. The truth of the matter was, since I had a free night, I needed Trevor's help. "I have something important for you to help me with. That is, if you can leave your new best friend."

Trevor stood silent. I had put him in his place, I felt satisfied. With a little work, Marvin would be out where he belonged.

"What is going on?" Trevor asked in an attempt to break the silence.

"It's your other friend," I replied. "We need to assist Elizabeth with her huge work load."

"Work load?" Trevor asked appearing caught off guard.

"Mr. Brassbuckle told her she would be through with her punishment when she filed all the papers in the filing office," I reiterated. "Did you realize that the papers never stop appearing to be filed?"

"What do you have planned?" Trevor asked appearing slightly afraid of my answer.

"The plan is to gather as many filing machines as we can," I began.

"Yes," Trevor said.

"And have a filing party," I finished.

"Divide and conquer," Trevor replied giving me a relieved but knowing look.

"Not only would it help Elizabeth, but it would stick it to Mr. Brassbuckle," I said with a smile as I saw the look of shock on Mr. Brassbuckle's face in my mind.

"Brassbuckle…" Mark interrupted from behind me. "Is he the guy with the flashy grin from the Keeper Complex?"

"The one and only," I replied as I rolled my eyes.

"Count me in," Mark threw out wiping his runny nose on his towel. "I had a run in with him just the other day."

Trevor appeared very unhappy about Mark's offer of help.

"I'll round up some of the guys," Mark added. "Most have had run-ins with him and would love the opportunity to…" He stopped and looked directly at me, "As you put it, stick it to him." He gave me a big wink from behind those nerdy glasses before jogging back to the fully watching group of guys who were using the moment to drink water from their bottles.

"Your plan is in motion!" Trevor said with a smirk and shake of his head.

Just when I thought I lost control of him, he fell right back into line!

Elizabeth

I walked down the hall towards my appointed room of doom. I had been so glad to leave here yesterday, and now really didn't want to come back so early to view all the work which awaited me. Finding a note on my night stand from Tilly, I couldn't understand why she hadn't slept in her bed. Why did she want to meet at my filing room? We didn't need to instigate any new punishments or repercussions from Mr. Brassbuckle.

I stopped dead in my tracks when Mr. Brassbuckle's office door suddenly opened. I let out a sigh and closed my eyes thinking, oh crap! Opening them, Tiffany strutted out closing the door behind her. As she passed me, she leaned over saying, "Guess you didn't know about the cameras?"

"Cameras?" I questioned turning to peer at her.

"Carmen and I imagined we would catch Tilly," Tiffany hummed. "The night lady had a little trouble awhile back with someone getting into the restricted section at the Hall of Records."

"You assumed it was Tilly?" I questioned knowing it was Dustin and I.

"Guess I was wrong," Tiffany hummed in an arrogant manner. "I couldn't be happier to view you helping yourself to restricted chapters."

"Prove it," I said calling her bluff.

"Don't worry, I already have," Tiffany stated happy with herself. After Tiffany cackled she peered intently at me. "What were you looking for?"

I didn't dignify her question with a response.

"I'll figure it out," Tiffany spewed as she pointed her finger in my face. "I won't stop until I have ruined you!"

"Get in line," I mumbled to myself.

"I used the tape in the best way possible," Tiffany taunted with pure venom spewing. "Mrs. Bradford wouldn't do today."

"You didn't," I said through my teeth.

"It just fell right into Mr. Brassbuckle's hand," Tiffany said as she walked backwards obviously appreciating my look of anger. With a happy little wave, she flashed that last devilish smile.

I had to give it to Tiffany, she was crafty. The thought to give the tape to Mr. Brassbuckle to get me into more trouble was genius. Her spite was a result of her jealousy over Dustin, but she really didn't have anything to feel that way over. I was never convinced that Dustin was into her and I wasn't really all that into Dustin, no matter how it all appeared. However, it was apparent she was out for blood. My blood.

Since I definitely didn't need to run into Mr. Brassbuckle, I tip toed past his office. I began to breathe deeply to try to calm my unsteady breath and rapidly beating heart. He was sure to hang me out to dry and demand an explanation. Professor Zirak wasn't going to be able to use a called in favor to get me out of this one. I could only hope Mr. Brassbuckle didn't say anything to Mrs. Bradford. They would all gang up on me. I had better quickly come up with a believable and good story.

I backed all the way to my filing office door, turned the knob, and backed in to ensure I was not seen. Once the door was shut, I turned to see a room full of people staring at me. Then I saw what they had done. The papers were all filed.

"What have you done?" I asked Tilly in shock.

"You're welcome," Tilly stated as she ran her finger down the bare wall which couldn't be seen before due to the stack of papers waiting to be filed.

"It took us most of the night," a young man stated grinning.

"Of course," I replied scanning the room in astonishment. "It's amazing!"

"Great," one young man said while slapping his hands together. Then he pretended to dribble a basketball across the floor and pitch it in one of the many filing machines as he added, "I'm gonna bounce."

"I'm with you," another stated with a yawn.

"Who are all these guys?" I whispered to Tilly.

"Prospective dates?" Tilly shot back with a devilish grin.

"You didn't promise them all dates, did you?" I asked.

"No," Tilly said with a grin. "These are the guys Trevor has been playing basketball with."

"We're night owls," one young man stated as if it was the explanation as to why they had stayed up all night to help.

"Until next time," the young man said to Tilly.

"She easily ran her hand down his chest, holding his gaze, as she answered, "Of course."

A young man with huge black rimmed glasses standing next to Trevor said under his breath as he wiped his running nose, "Oh, please!"
Trevor slightly shook his head at the young man.

"Oh," Tilly hummed catching the stream of guys before they left. "Could you each take one of the machines and return them for me."

She handed each one a machine as they passed through the door. They happily carried them off as she gave each one their own individual flirtatious grin. Tilly knew how to work her magic on men.

"You did all of this?" I questioned. "How did you do all of this in such a small time frame?"

"There were more of us," runny nose guy said as he stepped around the desk. "Most of our girlfriends went home hours ago to catch some beauty sleep."

"It was way more fun when they left," Tilly said flashing him that same flirtatious grin.

He seemed to ignore Tilly's flirting and extended his hand introducing himself, "I'm Mark."

"Elizabeth," I replied as I shook his hand.

"Nice to meet you," Mark politely responded with a look of fascination across his face.

"Thank you," I said feeling nervous under his stare. "It's nice to meet you too."

"Oh boy," I heard Tilly huff. Then she muttered, "I lost one to her again!"

Tilly must believe runny nosed Mark was into me. He kind of pulled a Marvin by ignoring Tilly's obvious flirting and paying attention to me. He wasn't scoring any points in her book.

Trevor was still patiently filing papers which were still appearing in the in basket. "If you're ready to get Brassbuckle, we'll leave."

"Brassbuckle?" I questioned almost in a whine.

"Yeah," Tilly replied watching me. "That's the plan. To show him you've filed everything. You know, to get you out of trouble."

"I see," I sighed.

"Is there a problem?" Trevor seriously questioned reading the nervousness across my face.

Before I could come up with a response, Mark turned to Trevor asking, "You think he's in yet?"

"He's here," I replied knowing Tiffany had just seen him to spill the beans about me. "I guess I'm definitely going to get Mr. Brassbuckle."

Trevor turned off the machine with a smile. "Great, I'm going to get some breakfast."

"Where are we going?" Tilly asked.

"I was going to grab something at Keeper House before class," Trevor replied.

"How about eggs and toast?" Mark threw out. "My kitchen is always open. I usually cook for my two room mates."

"Room mates?" Tilly repeated.

"When are all of you going to sleep?" I questioned.

"I'll find a quiet place," Tilly reassured me with a devious grin which made Trevor give her a disapproving look.

"Sleep?" Mark returned with a grin and chuckle. "Who needs sleep?"

"Thank you for this," I said as they moved in sync towards the door.

"You're welcome," Tilly stated.

"Divide and conquer," Trevor added with a grin.

"Get going," Tilly urged as she glanced at my continually filling basket.

With a sigh I exited the filing room after I gave them enough time for them to disappear. I trudged slowly to Mr. Brassbuckle's door wondering how I was going to explain my nosing around in the restricted section. Not to mention, my magical ability to file all those papers so quickly.

I knocked on the door and heard him respond, "Come in."

Unhappily, I opened the door to see Mr. Brassbuckle flash me that slimy grin. "Good morning Miss Cantrell. To what do I owe this honor?"

"You told me when all the papers were filed, my job would be complete. Correct?" I asked.

"Of course," Mr. Brassbuckle agreed.

"I've caught up the filing," I said and waited for the gauntlet to fall.

He stood asking as a moment of shock flashed across his face, "You filed everything?"

"Except for the new stuff currently coming into the in-basket," I replied shaking my head yes.

"Let's have a look," Mr. Brassbuckle said as he rounded his desk no longer smiling.

"Okay," I mindlessly responded as I exited the office a step ahead of him.

Mr. Brassbuckle hurried past me and made a bee-line straight for my filing office. I was on his heels as he flung open my door and stopped dead in his tracks. He shook his head a moment and then entered my office. He turned a full circle, looking at all the bare walls which were once unseen behind the stacks of papers which extended form the floor to the ceiling. When he turned to me, he looked at me very suspiciously and asked, "How did you file all of this so quickly?"

As if a bell had gone off in my head, I suddenly knew telling the truth was the best answer. Something borrowed from Trevor. I explained, "Divide and conquer!"

"Divide and conquer," Mr. Brassbuckle repeated under his breath with a huff.

"My job is complete?" I inquired.

Since Mr. Brassbuckle was cunning and smart, I stood waiting for some type of backlash. He just stood staring at me. I could only assume he was waiting for me to spill the beans about how I had completed this. However, my lips were sealed because I wouldn't get my friends into trouble.

"I suppose your job is done," Mr. Brassbuckle eventually stated. As if he suddenly remembered Tiffany, the grin reappeared across his face. "Miss Cantrell, do you have anything else to tell me?"

No way was I about to admit something unless I had too. I slowly shook my head and answered, "No."

"Good morning," Dustin interrupted as he wandered into the filing office behind me.

I turned to grin at him. Never had I been more thankful for an interruption. Dustin unknowingly had an uncanny way of appearing at the right time.

Mr. Brassbuckle stood as still as a statue with his fake grin glancing between the two of us. "Then you had better head to class. I wouldn't want to be the cause of your being late."

Stunned it took me a few moments to return, "Thank you."

"May I walk you to class?" Dustin inquired as he offered his arm to me.

"That would be great," I replied under the stare of a confused Mr. Brassbuckle.

CHAPTER SEVENTEEN

Elizabeth

Everyone would say I was crazy. I could hear them gossip about this being just another get Marvin back scheme, but tonight I would follow Rhett in hopes of figuring out what work Marvin and him were completing together. Rhett's words about their work project just kept replaying in my head. The more I contemplated the comment, the more something didn't add up. Marvin worked for the Administration Complex doing who knows what. Rhett worked for the Ghost Complex as a ghost hunter. What could they be working on together? Curiosity was killing me.

Tonight was a perfect opportunity to trail Rhett. Tilly and the gang left early to take a late afternoon nap before Harmony. They should be waking and all they would have on their minds was Harmony. Unfortunately, I would be skipping choir practice tonight. Tilly was certain to worry about my whereabouts and probably not be happy about my missing practice.

The Ghost Complex evening cheer and wager were complete. The bet was dry cleaning. The day shift lost last time and they longed to reclaim this prize. The crowd was disbursing from the Elephant Room with the night shift going to work and the day shift leaving. I watched Rhett bid goodbye to his ghost hunting group and disappear back into his office. When his office went dark and he did not exit, I began to wonder why he was sitting in the darkened room.

I made my over to his windows and knelt down low to view in the bottom of the windows where the blinds left a tiny gap. Not seeing any sign of Rhett or movement, I had to wonder… Where had he gone? I leaned against the wall, trying not to draw unwanted attention to myself. When I was sure no one was looking, I knocked on his door to no response. I could feel my heart rapidly beating as I turned the door handle and waited for a response from inside. As the silence prevailed, I quickly made my way into his dark office and closed the door behind me.

The office was pitch black and I couldn't see anything. I leaned against the door and waited for my eyes to adjust. The seconds seemed like hours. Realizing I still couldn't completely see, the realization hit me that it would be necessary to turn on the light. I reluctantly did. I squinted under the bright light as I scanned the room and let out the breath I had been holding. Finding no Rhett, I noticed the door in the corner of the office was slightly ajar. I made my way to it and slowly pulled it open enough to peek in. A dirty closet holding Rhett's winter coats and gear greeted me. I pushed all the coats on the rod to one side, hoping to see a door hidden behind. I shook my head thinking I was getting super paranoid. Why would Rhett have a hidden door in his coat closet?

Then it hit me, Rhett wasn't in here and it couldn't be more obvious. Of course, this coat closet had to be more than it seemed. Just like the small closet of an office that Jacob used for Mrs. VanCues. I methodically moved around the small room intently looking at every inch. Coming up empty handed, I felt sure there was something I was missing.

After walking and scanning the entire office, I was at a loss. Disappointed, I thought about leaving. What popped into my mind was the fact Rhett disappeared in the dark. Instantly, I strutted over and flipped the light switch back off. Then I made my way back around the room seeing if I could discover if anything had changed. When I came to the coat closet door and opened it, I couldn't help but see shimmering rays coming from one single hole in the floorboard. I got down on my knees and stared with one eye down through the hole. A private portal was underneath this floor. I put my finger through the hole and pulled on the board. Several floor boards lifted with ease in one piece reminding me of how a cellar or crawl space door is sometimes opened.

A ghost portal appeared. I scanned the damp wall. No key pad was visible leaving me to assume this portal was wired to take you to a certain destination. Rhett was hiding a secret.

Curiosity prevailed! I had come too far to hold back now. I grabbed one of Rhett's winter coats and let my hand run down the cold, damp walls to steady myself as the cool breeze coming off the water shower hit me. With a deep breath, I inhaled the fresh air and stepped off the third step. The ice cold, invisible water shower hit my skin and its bone chilling cold left me shivering. The sound of the water hitting the rocks below was deafening. Feeling frozen, I hurried down the remaining three steps and out the door at the bottom to escape the chill.

As I peered around, I was standing in a large reception room of some kind. It was shaped like a huge stop sign, or octagon, with a stage being the focal point of the room. To one side of the stage, I could view a full kitchen. To the other, I could view an open storage room for tables and chairs. The other walls each had a single, double door. The room was filled with long banquet tables. Strangers were seated at the tables and happily talking amongst themselves.

As always, I felt astonished as my feet rested on the invisible ground which was a foot above the regular Earth Plane ground. I skipped around a couple times enjoying the feeling of floating on air. That was something I had always wanted to do, but couldn't when in the presence of Tilly and Rhett's crew.

"Just got your ghost legs?" A bystander questioned.

Instantly, I stopped twirling and wiggled my feet. As I looked up, an average looking lady with a kind smile was watching me. I wasn't about to tell her I wasn't a ghost. I returned the smile, "I guess you could say that."

"Welcome," she said as she held out her hand. "I'm Lucy Johnson."

"I'm Elizabeth," I greeted her.

"This must be your first meeting?" Mrs. Johnson inquired.

"Yes," I stated. "Mrs. Johnson…"

"Miss," she corrected me. "I never married." With a shrug she added, "Just call me Lucy."

"Sure," I replied as I smiled at her. "Where am I?"

"Your first ghost society meeting," Lucy stated.

"What?" I questioned.

"Hang with me tonight," Lucy stated in a motherly protective way as she gestured for us to walk together.

I accompanied her across the room as she explained, "You are automatically a part of the ghost society upon your Earth Plane death. Most don't realize we exist until they make a conscious decision not to enter the light."

If I had been drinking anything, I would have choked. Contrary to popular belief, ghosts knew they weren't going into the light. Everything they taught us on this subject had been wrong.

She reached over to rub my back saying, "I know. That decision is always a hard one since the light of Home looks so warm and inviting. Don't worry, now that you've made the decision, it will begin to fade."

I shook my head in agreement simply not sure what to say for a moment. "You don't worry about what you might be missing in the light?"

"Never," Lucy quickly answered. "I'm happy here. You will be too. Now, you just have to worry about those hunters."

"Hunters?" I questioned.

"Yeah," Lucy said with a small wave of her hand. "They are annoying. It's one of the topics during our meetings almost weekly."

"So you meet every week?" I questioned.

"Wednesday evenings," Lucy returned. "Like clockwork!"

We stopped at a table with an odd crew sitting at it.

"Got your photo?" A young man with spiked hair wearing a studded collar around his neck asked.

"Of course," Lucy stated like his question offended her.

"Who'd ya hit?" A young lady with purple hair asked.

"Hit?" I questioned.

"The hour is almost up," a middle aged man stated. By his appearance, he was obviously the more conservative person at the table.

"Every Wednesday night has a theme," Lucy said. "Tonight we are in the midst of a scavenger hunt for who can get the best photo of themselves with someone famous."

"So you haunt the Earth Plane and get a photo with someone famous," I repeated to clarify.

"Of course," the young man with spiked hair replied. "We're ghosts."

"You're stereotyping yourself," the middle aged man countered.

"Let me introduce you," Lucy stated. She pointed at me. "This is Elizabeth." Then she pointed across the table first to the middle aged man. "This is Arthur."

"Hello," Arthur greeted me.

"Madeline," Lucy stated as she pointed to the purple haired girl.

"Yeah, she's mad alright," the spike haired young man interjected.

Madeline hit him on the arm as Lucy said, "The two of you stop."

"I'm spike," the young man spoke up before Lucy could introduce him.

"You just have to be called Spike," Arthur said with a tone of annoyance. "Kids." He then looked at me saying, "Welcome and it is very nice to make your acquaintance."

Madeline rolled her eyes as she stood and leaned across saying, "Don't listen to stuffy and silly. Nice to meet you."

"Stuffy?" Arthur repeated.

"I'm not the one with purple hair," Spike retorted.

A gavel on the podium banged loudly from behind me. I sat down in the chair next to Lucy as a woman in pigtails began to speak, "The contest time is officially over. Please make your way back to enter your photos if you haven't already done so. Judging will begin in five minutes."

When I turned back around, I caught a glimpse of Rhett sitting with his back to me talking with an old gentleman. They weren't sitting at a long banquet table like everyone else. They were seated at a small round table shoved into the back of the room.

"Who are they?" I asked as I pointed towards the small table.

"That's Royce and his son Rhett," Arthur seriously stated.

Lucy glared at him as if he had said too much.

"What?" Arthur questioned. "Everyone eventually figures it out."

"Yes, but we usually don't tell someone so new," Lucy reprimanded.

"Figure what out?" I asked.

"Rhett is not a ghost," Madeline leaned over and whispered. "Watch out for him. He's one of those hunters."

"He is," I asked attempting to appear alarmed.

"He'll get into your head," Lucy warned.

"He'll get into your head," Spike mimicked causing himself to get another slap on the shoulder.

"Hunters try to make you enter the light," Lucy stated. Giving me another motherly grin, she said in an assuring voice, "Just stay away from him until you get your ghost legs."

With that, they all chuckled.

Still peering at the two, I stated my mind, "He looks so old."

"Royce?" Arthur questioned.

"He is," Madeline stated as she peered at him over her shoulder.

"Royce started the ghost society," Arthur began. "He is one of the oldest recorded ghosts."

"Rhett never tries to talk him over," Madeline interjected.

"Or so the story goes," Spike added as if the subject really bored him. "He is the only ghost that Rhett can't catch. That's a laugh, since he never tries."

Rhett was famous in the world of the Keepers for always getting his ghost. The old ghost was reported to be the only one to ever stump him. Tilly thought the old man was crazy because he wanted to live a second life on the Earth Plane. His desire to do so, according the story, was due to his wife disappearing during the Event. He sneaked into baby row and forced his way back to the Earth Plane. Now, I was aware that Rhett wasn't trying to catch the old ghost. Not only wasn't he trying to catch him, the old ghost was his father. "Does anyone else ever visit him?" I questioned.

"Why would you ask that?" Lucy questioned in a serous tone.

"I just wondered if there were other hunters to watch out for," I stated hoping to cover my too obvious question.

"Hunters always wear a stuffy grey sweater," Madeline stated. "Unless they have that grey sweater, chances are they aren't a hunter."

"Don't worry," Lucy said giving me another motherly grin.

"The old guy who visits doesn't wear a sweater," Spike threw out.

Silence fell over the table. I was curious, but couldn't ask any more questions without being discovered. In my mind, I had a good idea of who the old man was. That ghost, Rhett's father, was rumored to have been Albert Solliday's best friend when he was a Keeper. Chances are Mr. Solliday was visiting him. The world of the Keepers was much more deceptive and insane than people realized.

The double doors beside our table burst open. Every head at our table turned. Instantly, I wanted to crawl under the table. Facing me were the ghosts from the hotel. The ghosts which iced Tilly for spouting off to Brian about crossing over into the light. Tilly and I had been forced into the hunt that day and I knew we weren't exactly their favorite. In addition, I knew they could blow my cover if they remembered me.

You could see the group scan the room looking for trouble. I casually asked, "Who are they?"

"Trouble," Lucy answered with one word.

"See the smallest," Madeline leaned as far across the table as she could. "Cute as a button with her fair hair, big bow, and dimples."

"But a thief," Arthur finished. "Be mindful of anything in your pockets."

They hit the nail on the head. She was an adorable ghost child, but I remembered her game. The day on the ghost hunt she was stealing spoons and giggling as those served soup would look for their missing spoon.

"The teenager standing next to her," Madeline took a quick glance pointing.

"His name is Brian," Lucy interjected.

"He thinks he is God's gift to girls and women in general," Madeline finished.

"Stay away from him as well," Arthur stated. "He has a temper when he is rejected."

"Don't forget the bride's crazy!" Spike loudly whispered.

"The story is her fiancé left her standing at the altar," Madeline began. "She went to their honeymoon suite and waited for him to change his mind."

"Only he knew she was batty," Spike stated shaking his head. "Not marrying material."

"He didn't come and she took her own life," Madeline continued. "She still haunts her honeymoon suite and is said to get very upset when anyone insists on staying overnight in it."

"Looney," Spike hummed as his finger circled his ear.

"And the tall young man?" I questioned.

Again, silence fell over the table. It was Arthur that eventually spoke up saying, "His name is Charles. Do not socialize with him!"

"No one does?" I questioned.

"Beyond their group of friends," Lucy began. "No. The ghost hunters would be safer to associate with than Charles."

"Yeah, they left the rest of the crazies at home tonight," Spike said under his breath.

"The rest?" I repeated.

"There's a ghost boy who died of some disease, a soldier who died in some long ago war, and an old guy who died when he fell off his horse," Madeline explained.

"Don't forget the quack," Spike added.

"The doctor who insists we aren't dead," Lucy explained. "He and his nurse keep attempting to patch us up and heal us." With another motherly grin she assured me, "They are pretty harmless."

"Just annoying," Spike said from down the table.

"They always come together?" I asked.

"Bullies in a pack," Madeline responded.

"The ghost child girl and Charles are always together," Arthur added. I must have had an odd look on my face because he added, "Rumor has it that they are brother and sister."

"Really?" I questioned.

"She has lived in the hotel a long time," Arthur began. "Everyone speculates she was waiting for Charles. When he arrived though, she didn't desire to go on. She enjoyed playing jokes too much."

"Now they work on those nightly ghost tours," Madeline stated with a look of disgust on her face.

"No self respecting ghost subjects themselves to Earth Plane ghost tours," Arthur huffed in disapproval.

"It's bad to work on a ghost tour?" I asked the obvious.

"Very," Lucy stated. "We're ghosts. We can make our presence known if we choose too. However, flaunting it night after night for the benefit of those on the Earth Plane isn't healthy."

"You'll become a laughing stock putting up with the looky loos!" Spike added. A serious expression crossed his face as he warned, "Keep your distance." Then he gave a shrug. "If they give you any problems, just let me know."

"Tough guy now, huh?" Madeline teased.

I watched the bully ghosts disburse throughout the room. Charles had prevented others form icing me when I went on the hunt with Tilly and Rhett's crew. He couldn't be all bad. I would figure out a way to meet him.

The gavel hit the podium again causing me to slightly jump. I peered over my shoulder to see the pig tailed lady grinning broadly. "We have tonight's winner!" She exclaimed as the crowd erupted into cheers. "Our photo tonight shows a unique perspective on the subject of Earth Plane fame. Although most of you haunted prestigious Humlings, this person chose a riskier target. One that could readily see him."

"A psychic," Arthur mumbled. "Who would stoop so low?"

That is when I noticed Spike grinning from the other end of the table.

"Give it up for Spike! His photo shows him with the dog of a famous Earth Plane president," the pony tailed lady exclaimed. "Bravery! Most of us wouldn't tackle an animal that can see us!"

The crowd erupted into cheers as the photo appeared on the screen at the front of the room.

"Dork," Madeline mumbled as she watched Spike going to the stage.

"What does he get?" I questioned.

"An honorary seat at the Ghost Council for the next week," Lucy stated.

"The Council?" I questioned.

"Our rule makers and enforcers," Arthur answered. "You have a lot to learn."

That I did. This new world I discovered was intriguing.

CHAPTER EIGHTEEN

Elizabeth

Tilly wasn't happy with my missing Harmony, but really, what did I have to contribute? I couldn't sing. She claimed she needed my support. I apologized to her, but my adventure into the world of the ghosts had been fascinating and I didn't regret it. I wanted to dive in and discover more about them.

The apparitions played group bingo last night while the Ghost Council met. Imagine my reaction watching ghosts playing such a normal game. Early last evening, I lost track of Rhett. I assumed he went to the Ghost Council meeting. In the end, the Ghost Council made a few announcements and then slowly the ghosts disappeared one by one. Wow!

Dog tired described how I felt this morning as I made my way across the Keeper Complex foyer. I saw Jessie approaching me with his head buried in papers. He was walking and reading in the Department of Keepers lobby. I called his name. He looked up, but didn't acknowledge me. I stepped squarely in his path. He tried to ignore me by stepping around me. I moved to the left with him, blocking his attempt. He then tried to maneuver around me to the right. Again, I moved to the right staying directly in-front of him.

"What do you want?" Jessie questioned annoyed.

"How are Marvin and Tiffany?" I threw out to him fishing for information I really didn't want to hear.

"Are you asking me if they are dating?" Jessie returned seeming to be totally perturbed.

The truth was I didn't know if I did or didn't believe they were dating. I wanted to know, yet I didn't want to know. The thought of them together was heart shattering.

When Jessie noticed my lack of an answer, he said, "You really didn't know him very well to think he would date Tiffany. Yes, I know all about your getting upset and running away at the Keeper Complex. He was just there to do a job for the Department of Administration."

"When I saw him with Tiffany?" I mindlessly asked.

"He was shocked," Jessie stated. "No, he was more hurt at the fact you thought he would start to date Tiffany."

That was crushing and again my silence loomed.

"Marvin claims he understands why you took up with Dustin," Jessie threw out.

"What does that mean?" I questioned feeling annoyed by his tone. Why would Marvin, if he loved me, understand my taking up with Dustin?

"Yeah," Jessie said in a snotty voice. "He claims you don't remember. Your memory fog… Did you lay it on too thick? Or did he figure out your attraction to Dustin. He was a little slower than the rest of us figuring it out."

"You know, don't you?" I questioned.

Jessie hesitated appearing as if he were crawling out of his comfortable skin. "I don't understand why you would believe it was okay to hang with Dustin after he attacked you. There is just one logical explanation. It wasn't an attack."

"It's not what it seemed," I threw out.

"If you were an active participant…," Jessie said with his demeanor changing. "I don't want to hear because I would have to tell Marvin. I don't want to have to shatter what is left of your image with him. You so easily threw away what you knew the two of you had." With a now visibly red face, he spewed, "You gave up so easily and ran straight into your attacker's arms."

"No," I disagreed. "Marvin broke up with me!"

"He had his reasons and they all revolve around you," Jessie countered. "I would dump you if I caught wind you had a thing for Dustin. A man has his pride!"

"You have yours," I retorted. "However, you are wrong about Marvin. He threw us away."

"You don't have any idea how much he loves you," Jessie said in an angry tone. "What he would be willing to give up, what he would be willing to do for you!"

"I don't understand," I said shaking my head. "Just what has he done other than break my heart?"

"You are dense!" Jessie spewed in an angry tone. "He has unconditionally forgiven you for Dustin. I haven't. I think Marvin could do better than you. I spit on Dustin the night of the attack and you let me do it. You let Marvin believe you were innocent. Marvin is a man of integrity. You were lucky to date him."

I stood dumfounded as how to respond as Jessie turned and walked away. As I began to take a few steps towards the lift to my office, I heard, "Harsh!"

Destiny was leaning against the wall and I had to assume she heard the entire exchange. "Why were you eavesdropping?" I asked feeling irritated.

She pointed around. As I followed her hand gesture, I could see others peering at me. "Who could miss your exchange?"

"Great!" I mumbled as I continued to walk on wanting to escape her pressure.

"What if I could help you?" Destiny stated from behind me as she left her spot on the wall trailing me.

I stopped to wait for her to catch up. I rudely asked, "What do you want?"

"I'll assume by the tone in your voice you don't care if I am aware of someone who equally wants to get even with Tiffany," Destiny threw out shrugging her shoulders. "Never mind."

Against my better judgment, I asked, "What are you talking about?"

"If you want to know," Destiny replied. "Meet me at the ice cream shop instead of going to Harmony."

"Tilly will be very unhappy about my missing Harmony again," I said off the top of my head.

"It's up to you," Destiny hummed. "If you do decide to come tonight, let me tell you what the price of my helping you will be…"

"So it all boils down to what's in this for you?" I shot back interrupting her.

Destiny for the first time flashed me a sheepish grin as she shuffled her feet. "I want a date with Eddie."

"Eddie?" I repeated in a questioning voice.

"He is so handsome," Destiny stated in a giggly voice like that of a giddy school girl.

I could simply count this option out. No way would I be able to convince Eddie to go on a date with stinky Destiny. She could dream on.

Trevor

My thoughts drifted to early morning when I witnessed Leo, the lift operator, give Elizabeth another bag of gingerbread cookies. Something about him wasn't kosher. How did he know Elizabeth needed ginger? To hear the lift midget called her princess was equally odd. Shocked, I stared at him. Did he have knowledge of the Dweller story of the true princess? Questions burned in my mind all day leaving me to slip out of work early.

I went straight to the archives in the Underground and began to research any information about Leo. Finding nothing, I ran my suspicions by Mark when I caught up with him. Tonight, he was working in the Council Hall at the Administration Complex. Minutes ago, I walked down the hall catching

Mark's attention.

"What are you doing here?" Mark asked as he pulled me off to one side.

"Leo, the lift operator in Keeper House, can't be what he seems," I began to explain in a whisper.

"What makes you say that?" Mark asked looking around as if my topic of conversation made him nervous.

"What do you know about him?" I asked.

He motioned for me to follow him and once inside the Council Court Room he asked, "What tipped you off?"

"He gives Elizabeth gingerbread everyday," I answered. "Not to mention, he called her princess today."

He walked over and sat down in the chair behind the defendant's desk. As I made my way over to join him in the adjoining chair he began, "You know about the event?"

"Of course," I responded.

"You are aware of the rumor that a Dweller was captured?" Mark asked.

"No," I said out of shock. "Are you inferring they hid a Dweller in plain sight? Around trainees?"

"He's been rendered harmless," Mark stated as he pulled a tissue out of his pocket. "He is locked in that elevator."

"How do you know he never leaves the lift?" I asked.

"He doesn't," Mark said adamantly shaking his head while wiping his constantly running nose.

"Why didn't you confide in me as I have done in you?" I questioned feeling half-betrayed.

"Council guards are sworn to silence," Mark replied. "It's a council guard secret. However, he is monitored around the clock. Don't you see the big, hidden picture?"

"This is incredible," I said under my breath.

"We use him for intelligence," Mark said. "Dwellers tend to contact him."

All I could imagine were the Dwellers walking around in The Hall of Knowledge which was supposedly the safest place inside the dome. At least that's what parents thought. They blindly allowed their children to live there during training. I understood now why Mr. Bradford alluded to there being Dwellers interacting with Elizabeth.

"Dude," Eddie yelled catching up to me as Mark and I had stepped out of the council room. "Guess who I scored a date with?"

"Hopefully Kim," I replied feeling uneasy about what was going to come out of his mouth.

"Nope," Eddie said looking like the cat that ate the canary. "Elizabeth."

"What?" I asked in shock.

"Oh yeah," Eddie hummed in delight.

"Score," Mark chimed in. "She's cute."

"What's the catch?" I pointedly asked.

"Does there have to be a catch?" Eddie retorted while crossing his arms across his chest. "You don't think I'm cool enough to date Elizabeth?"

"Don't be drama queen," I stated.

"So there is a catch," Mark prodded.

Eddie turned serious, "I'm first going on a date with Destiny."

"Are you crazy?" I asked. "She…"

"Smells!" Eddie finished my thought. "I know. My nose burning will be worth it for a date with Elizabeth."

Mark simply chuckled under his tissue as he wiped his nose again.

"Why did Elizabeth bait you with a date with her in exchange for a date with Destiny?" I asked.

"I guess Destiny has been crushing on me," Eddie stated giving a small shiver of disgust. "I suppose Elizabeth is doing her a favor."

There was certainly more to this story. I couldn't help but wonder about his chick problems, "What about Kim?"

Eddie sighed while beginning, "Kim is amazing. She's a natural skater..."

"Unlike Elizabeth," I interrupted.

"It was a narly crash!" Eddie stated as we shared a rare moment of agreement about Elizabeth. Mark was staring at us waiting for the story as Eddie added, "Elizabeth only tried to ride once and she was a fish out of water."

"And Kim?" I again questioned.

Eddie smiled as he thought of her and continued, "Yeah, Kim's smart, funny... "

"Then what the problem?" I interrupted. "She's right for you!"

"I just have to know if there is anything with Elizabeth," Eddie seriously sighed.

"You are making a mistake!" I informed him. "You shouldn't risk what you have with Kim over a wild fantasy attraction. Elizabeth has never showed any interest in you."

"Marvin's history," Eddie stated. "I've waited for a chance and now I have one. I have to take it."

"You're creating problems for yourself," I warned.

"You're one to talk," Eddie shot back. "With all your chick problems."

"Sounds like trouble," Mark concurred.

Eddie and I were now descending the staircase at the Administration Complex in silence. It was written all over him. He wasn't happy about my reaction to his good news.

Dropping the conversation about the girls, I needed to re-focus on nailing down any final details for the Harmony performance. Tonight was the first full practice with our new keyboardist. New performance costumes were due to arrive tonight and handing them out was sure to be interesting. I couldn't imagine the choir members being extremely happy over the skimpy punk rock outfits. At least I now had something else other than Elizabeth to fill my thoughts for the evening.

Elizabeth

Coming into view was the familiar, small, natural rock building with the big plate glass windows. Huge painted ice cream cones on the glass announced this destination as the ice cream shop. The covered porch ran across the front with its hanging swing nestled between vine covered pillars. Marvin and I had spent many evenings here with him enjoying vanilla ice cream with peppermints mixed in. I always ate a scoop of double dutch chocolate. I couldn't face the super model blond that worked the counter and had purposely stayed clear of the shop. She wanted to date Marvin and I knew she would rub our breakup in my face.

"Thank you," Destiny said as I walked up to the covered porch of the ice cream shop to join her. "Eddie has already asked me on a date for Saturday night."

"I convinced him to ask you, but I'm not making any promises," I half heartedly warned. "You are on your own reeling him in." Then I hesitated as I replayed Eddie's cringe reaction in my mind. My suggestion of a date with Destiny was a mind boggler to him. It cost me.

"Understood," Destiny said as she turned to view the shop door as the bell above it dinged.

"You've got to be kidding," Janelle stated as she stepped through the door with an ice cream cone in her hand.

"I'm not," Destiny matter of fact replied.

"You want me to place my trust in Elizabeth?" Janelle asked as if the thought were crazy.

"I'm not untrustworthy!" I returned. "Besides, who says I can trust you."

"The two of you need to stop," Destiny stated. "If you put aside your past differences, you will see you both have a common dislike for Tiffany."

Janelle plopped down on the side of the porch letting her legs hang over. While she kicked her legs and feet back and fourth, she ate her ice cream. I understood she was seriously considering the situation, just as I was.

"Why haven't you said anything to anyone to embarrass me?" Janelle seriously asked. "You heard what Rodger said."

"It's not anyone's business," I replied understanding her reference to Rodger cheating with Tiffany. I also understood this was a test for me.

"I assume you told Tilly," Janelle threw out with a glance at me.

"I didn't," I replied. "I might have if you gave her grief over Harmony."

A devilish giggle escaped Janelle. Then she said, "Well, at least that's honest." Shaking her head, her face turned serious as she began, "I have a plan. With your help I can get my revenge at a bigger venue."

"A bigger venue?" I repeated.

"The Harmony performance," Janelle answered.

"Presnell will have your head," Destiny said under her breath suddenly appearing nervous.

"What are you planning?" I asked knowing anything which happened at the Harmony performance would be blamed on Tilly. No way would I let Janelle take Tilly down.

"It's more than in the planning stages," Janelle stated with a devious look upon her face. "Did you know Tiffany likes to keep a burn book?"

"Burn book?" I repeated. "What's that?"

"She writes all the nasty stuff she probably couldn't get away with saying to others," Janelle answered.

"You're creating a burn book about her in return," I surmised.

"Turn about is fair play," Janelle smirked. "Not a book, a tell-all video!"

"And you intend to show it at Harmony," I replied thinking out loud.

"Whoa," Destiny said under her breath clearly having second thoughts about bringing us together.

"I intended to show it in rehearsal," Janelle sighed. "Then I decided on the big enchilada, the Harmony performance itself! I want to figure out a way to get it played during the performance program."

"If you really desire to pull this off at the Harmony performance," I began. "Then, why did you quit Harmony?"

"I made a rash decision," Janelle answered. "I couldn't stand the thought of taking orders from Tilly." She shrugged a little adding, "Sorry, but that's honest. It keeps running through my head that if I do it at the Harmony performance, Tiffany would assume it was Tilly's work. That's not my intention."

"You want Tiffany to be aware that you're behind this, don't you?" I questioned big eyed.

"Absolutely," Janelle stated rising from the porch.

"What have you asked others to say on the video?" I asked.

"I would never put words in the mouths of others," Janelle stated. "I asked each one to tell me how they really feel about Tiffany."

"How many have you video taped?" I asked to get the full scope of the video.

"Let's just say... It's a long list," Janelle happily said in a dreamy state. "I have a lot of footage to work with."

"Most are fearful of Tiffany," I began. "How did you convince them to speak out against her?"

"That book of hers goes a long ways," Janelle seriously said.

"You've been showing others Tiffany's burn book..." I surmised drawing out my words.

"Only the portion written about them," Janelle stated. "Some of her followers were shocked to learn how she really saw them."

Showing the burn book was hurtful in itself. Janelle was taking no prisoners, considering no one in her quest to get revenge on Tiffany for stepping out with her boyfriend.

"What if I say at this point I don't intend to be involved?" I asked.

"I'll proceed without you," Janelle matter of fact stated. "You kept your mouth shut about Rodger..." Janelle stared at me. "If you aren't with me, keep your mouth shut about my plan. As long as you do, I'll consider no foul between us."

"Tiffany will assume it was Tilly who put the video together," I stated. "For that matter, so will Professor Presnell."

"No," Janelle disagreed. "I won't let that happen. Tiffany is going to know exactly who did this. She has shown no remorse for betraying me. When I confronted her in our dorm room, she actually told me every boyfriend I have ever had were her rejects. She claims they all dated me because she asked them too. Then, she would see them on the side. This is bigger than just Rodger!"

If anything Janelle said rang true, it was her last statement. I had no doubt Janelle desired, no needed, Tiffany to know it was her. The hurt was visible all over Janelle's face.

"You know she is out to ruin your whole life," Janelle stated.

"I know," I simply agreed.

"That's the part I don't understand," Janelle stated shaking her head. "How she can be so angry about you stealing Dustin, but not see she did the same thing to me. I'm supposed to be her best friend!"

"She's self centered," Destiny chimed in.

"I have to correct you," I stated. "I didn't steal Dustin."

"Elizabeth," Janelle said giving me a get real look.

That fact was beside the point. Tiffany was out for my blood and she wouldn't stop until she had it.

"Isn't it justice for all the pain she's caused others," Janelle reasoned.

That is when I noticed Janelle's stare go towards the road and a smile cross her face. I peered out and Mike was making his way towards us with a smile that was as broad as hers. She jumped off the edge of the porch saying, "We have a deal unless you tell me otherwise." She looked me directly in the eye, "Don't worry, I'll have the video ready. Your part is slipping the video in so it's played."

Janelle moved off and into Mike's arms. He leaned down and gave her a kiss which made my stomach churn. I tried to keep my focus on my own feet which were dangling over the edge of the porch.

"Did you know what she was planning?" I mumbled to Destiny.

"Not every detail," Destiny quietly said back to me. "Her aura simply screamed how angry she was with Tiffany."

"Your intuition?" I asked.

Destiny shook her head yes continuing, "Janelle was really into Rodger."

"How long have you known about Tiffany and Rodger?" I asked.

"Since the night Rodger cleaned out Trevor's room," Destiny said.

"You knew they were doing that?" I asked feeling my skin crawl.

"It was already done," Destiny said. "I saw Rodger as he was going to meet Tiffany. Both thoughts just came to me about him." She looked out at Mike and Janelle holding hands as they walked away. "She doesn't yet realize Mike is the one for her. It's going to work out for her in the end." She peered back at me smiling, "I could read that Janelle was actively looking for a partner for some type of scheme."

"And you thought of me? Why?" I asked.

"I also knew Tiffany would send you through the black arch if she could," Destiny stated. "I picked up on her laughing in her mind over the flowers, and over making you believe she was dating Marvin. She knew how hurtful this was to you."

I stared at my feet as I stated, "I didn't tell anyone."

Destiny quietly said as she placed her hand on my arm, "Marvin is in love with you, not her." After removing her arm she continued, "Since your motivation is so similar, the two of you make a perfect team."

"Are we going to end up together?" I asked.

"Huh," Destiny stated seeming to be caught off guard.

"Like Janelle, you know her and Mike will be together," I hem hawed. "Marvin and I… Do you see us together in the end?"

"Honestly, I don't know," Destiny stated. "I get vibes off some and don't get those same vibes off others. I only know he's in love with you and feels in his gut that he's doing the most loving thing possible." She paused to think. "The two of you don't make a lot of sense to me. I see this dark spot." She shrugged her shoulders. "I don't know."

Destiny, the nosy neighbor, was sure I was to partner with Janelle. On the other hand, she was as confused about my love life. Why did I listen to her crap anyway?

CHAPTER NINETEEN

Elizabeth

The office had been abuzz today because Mrs. VanCues' body was dying on the Earth Plane. The whole crew was waiting for the moment of her crossing to celebrate. Decorations had been pulled from every nook and cranny and took on a life of their own as they decorated the office. A massive sheet cake had arrived. Odd party hats appeared on all desks. Several ladies were working on making punch in a giant punch bowl. Everyone was eagerly awaiting the moment. If it weren't for the fact Mrs. VanCues was coming Home, this might be considered a strange custom for an office to do. In the end, her death wasn't sad, it was simply coming Home.

The one person, I wished were there to celebrate, was Marvin. He had a theory about a Keeper and a Humling being able to communicate telepathically when the Humling re-entered Home. I had always assumed this is why he thought I could hear others in my head. Marvin had picked Mrs. VanCues to work with to test this theory. She was psychic and he thought this bettered his odds that she would be able to hear him once she was in the Hospital. I knew he would barely be able to contain his excitement if he were here.

A bolt of thunder suddenly struck me. It dawned on me that he could still test this theory if he knew she were dying on the Earth Plane and coming Home today. After all, he intended to test his theory in the Humling re-entry Hospital. I peered around noticing no one was paying me any attention. They were all intently standing before the big screen watching Mrs. VanCues labor for every breath as she lay in the hospital bed on the Earth Plane. With an air of confidence, I strutted over to the lift, pushed the button, and made my way onto it without saying a word to anyone.

As the sliding door closed, I regretted not being able to tell Tilly were I was going. Tilly had been down in the dream portal all morning singing to Mrs. VanCues. She wasn't happy about my missing Harmony for a second night in a row. I don't know whether it was missing or the fact I wouldn't share with her where I had been. Keeping secrets from her wasn't easy, but necessary.

My partnership with Janelle was my secret. Tilly wouldn't understand and would insist Janelle was out to stab me in the back. It was possible she might do just that. The whole thing might be a scheme of Tiffany's. I was rolling the dice and could only hope they would land in my favor.

In deep consideration of the outcome, I made my way to Marvin's office. Standing before the door, I rested my hand on the door knob and took a big, deep breath. I knocked.

"Come in," Marvin's familiar voice responded.

I pushed open the door and entered finding Marvin sitting at a long table with his back to me. After inhaling a deep breath, I briskly walked across the room. I softly called, "Marvin."

I could see his shoulders suddenly tense as he turned to look over his shoulder. Immediately he turned his head from me and said, "Go away Elizabeth."

"I have something important to tell you," I stated as I pulled out the chair next to his.

He grabbed the chair barring me from sitting. "Elizabeth, you need to go." Marvin sighed deeply. "You keep showing up and I've moved on. What we had was good at the time, but it couldn't last forever. Nothing you say is going to change…"

"It not about us!" I interrupted. This was a mistake. Why did I come here when it was so clear he didn't want me in the same room with him? I took another deep breath to keep the tears at bay. "Never mind," I said feeling insulted and defeated. Tilly was correct. Actually, Destiny was too. The black hole she saw was the hole in my heart. We were through. Why should I care about his theory? I turned to take the walk of shame back across the room as he watched.

I heard him sigh as I stepped away from him. Within a moment he grabbed my arm stopping me. "Whatever you came to tell me must be important."

As I peered up at his face, I could see his annoyed and sad eyes peering at me. His finger brushed away a tear from my cheek. Then he pushed the wisps of hair which were loose behind my ear. Another deep sigh and he looked sorry, almost apologetic.

Feeling self-conscious, I said, "I came to inform you Mrs. VanCues will be coming home at some point today."

"The office must be ready to throw a huge serious party," Marvin stated while still watching me. "I'm sure her family will look forward to her returning as well as the staff being relieved. She was a handful."

"I wanted you to be able to test your theory," I stated.

"Thank you," Marvin said. "Thinking of me was extremely thoughtful."

"Thoughtful," I repeated in a small huff.

"Anything else?" Marvin questioned. He then pointed towards his work, "I've got work to do."

"Right," I said. "Work. Excuse my intrusion."

He followed me to the door saying, "Bye Elizabeth."

It was as if he had broken up with me all over again on this very spot. My emotions were still so raw. As I walked away, I took a deep breath. Then I forced myself to say in a pleasant controlled voice, "Bye!" Trudging away form what had been the best part of my life was hard on so many levels. Christmas never lasts I told myself. Marvin had been my Christmas. Now it was like New Years. He had moved on with his life and new resolutions. I felt forced to do the same like a two year old kicking and screaming. I wanted Christmas to last forever.

Elizabeth

I was sitting on the flat rock ledge, well above the tree line. This was the place where my hearts ache began. I clearly remembered Marvin and I, hand in hand, tip toeing past the houses that set on the ridge. We crawled over the steep edge and down onto the first ledge of the rambling rock formations. The ridge which ran the length of Spring Park was extremely high and steep in descent. Marvin held my hand as I climbed over the edge making me feel safe and secure. I knew back then he wouldn't let me fall. It was all just as I remembered. The stars and moon were incredible in the sky above me. However, I found it cold sitting by myself as a brisk breeze blew across my skin causing me goose bumps.

I had been so foolish that fateful night about giving into what my heart knew was right. Now, I was walking around dead, feeling empty, and longing for Marvin. If I could go back, I wouldn't change a thing. Each moment spent with him was worth all the soul crushing pain in my life now.

I picked up a rock beside me cursing my family secrets. Whatever was mysteriously shocking and disturbing about me had brought about all this heartache. I would cry, but there were no more tears left inside me. Channeling all my anger, loneliness, and loss into the rock, I hurled it over the edge. I could hear it striking the different rock ledges as it bounced down. With each crash, small pieces of it were sure to be breaking off, not unlike my fragmented life. When I couldn't hear it any longer, I figured it had found its resting place. If only in the chaos of my life, I could find solitude and peace somewhere.

Interrupting my thoughts were noises coming from a ledge below me. I crawled over to the edge and peered down. I couldn't believe who was staring up at me from a couple ledges down.

"What are you doing here?" I asked Marvin.

"Did you throw that rock at me?" Marvin asked standing up to stare at me.

"No," I replied. "I just tossed it over the edge. How would I know you were down there?"

Marvin's eyes peered up at me. For a moment they took my breath away. Tilly often caught me staring off into space during class and repeatedly asked what was distracting me. His deep brown eyes staring up at me were just as I remembered. I was guilty of daydreaming of them over an over again. I simply hadn't been able to confess to her that my inability to focus was my losing myself in their memory. My mind had been so preoccupied with thoughts of him.

"What in the world are you doing down there?" I again asked as Marvin looked away.

"Just having a quiet moment," Marvin returned as he peered out over the sprawling city contained within the dome.

He was down two levels and out on an island of a ledge. "Can you climb up?" I asked.

"Sure," Marvin stated in a tone which stated it was a silly question. He hopped over the gaping crevasse between ledges.

I cringed watching him jump. If he fell, I was certain my heart would stop beating. I hung onto the edge with white knuckles holding my breath as I watched him climb over the remaining two ledges. His muscular arms easily pulled him up with ease. Those same arms were meant to be wrapped around me.

"What are you doing out here?" Marvin questioned as he sat down next to me.

That was a very loaded question. No way would I tell him I ventured out here to feel close to him, to replay in my head the memory of when we first came here together. I wouldn't admit I missed the office party to wander aimlessly around visiting all of our special spots. I would rather face Tilly's wrath for missing Harmony. I wanted the opportunity to be alone and think of him. I was speechless.

"Star gazing?" Marvin asked under his breath with a disgruntled tone.

Stargazing. We had done that too atop Rhett's roof. I couldn't help recall how romantic the moment had been as my mind transported me back. I was standing on the crumbling sidewalk outside Rhett's front door watching Marvin, covered in dust and carrying a ladder, telling me of his plan for us to stargaze. It was the one and only night I tried to ride a skateboard. Very reluctantly, I made my way to the roof with my aching body and bruised legs from my fall. Every ounce of anxiety and fear melted away once we were reclined on the roof holding hands and watching the stars.

"I was about ready to walk back," Marvin said interrupting my thoughts as he pointed towards the last rock edge.

I followed Marvin's lead and stood to look over the ledge. Just as the stargazing had ended atop the roof, this unexpected moment of time with him was coming to an end. My mind was screaming to beg him to listen. I wanted to plead my case again. I had practiced what I would say to him every night as I lay in bed. Why couldn't I bring myself to tell him once again how right we were for each other? I had to find a way to move past this.

Placing my hands on the ledge, I began to consider crawling back up when I could suddenly feel Marvin standing very close to me. So close, I could feel his breath on the top of my head. He spun me around and we stared into each other's eyes. I closed my eyes and took a deep breath. I could feel the electric charge between us. I took another deep breath. My chest felt as if the electric charge had suddenly connected our two hearts. As I yearned for his lips to find mine, his hands found their way to my waist.

Interrupting my thoughts he said, "On the count of three. One. Two. Three."

I jumped in conjunction with him lifting me to sit on the edge of the upper ledge. He dropped his hands from my waist letting them rest on the rock beside me. For another moment he stood in front of me. Why had I wavered? Nothing else was certain in my life, only my deep desire for Marvin. Our hearts were one, not two. Whether he admitted it to himself or not, we were soulmates. He moved to pull himself up over the ledge beside me.

"Thank you," I told him as he held out his hand to pull me to my feet while using the other to dust himself off.

"It's getting late," Marvin said looking out as he shoved his hands into his pockets. I will walk you back." He paused and then mumbled as if convincing himself, "It's the right thing to do."

I disagreed, "I insist I can..."

"No way," Marvin replied to my unfinished thought. "We may not be dating anymore, but I won't leave you out here to walk back on your own."

He held out his hand for us to get started on our trek. I felt his hand rest slightly upon the small of my back. His touch felt warm, comfortable, and completely natural.

In silence we walked back through the yard and out onto the paved street leading back to the Hall of Knowledge. A strange look of regret, pain, and determined resign crossed Marvin's face.

"Could she hear you?" I asked breaking the awkward silence.

"Huh?" Marvin grunted back.

"Mrs. VanCues?" I explained.

"No," Marvin stated while jingling his pocket contents.

"Then your theory wasn't right," I sighed.

"You didn't let me finish," Marvin said shaking his head. "I didn't attempt to meet her today."

"You didn't go?" I half-questioned feeling irritated. "Why not?"

"It's not a theory I think is true anymore," Marvin sighed.

"Why not?" I retorted.

With a shrug, the silence overtook us again.

We walked in eerie silence along the path until I asked, "Then you don't think I hear my Keeper's thoughts?"

"What are you talking about?" Marvin seriously asked. "My theory had nothing to do with you."

My gut screamed he was being truthful about his original theory not concerning me. It also understood that Marvin didn't believe in this anymore because he knew I could hear Dwellers. I began to feel irritated again about him knowing more about me and not telling me. "Marvin, is the time in the Dweller world recorded anywhere?"

If he wasn't serious before, he was now. "Why would you ask something like that?"

"I was just curious," I retorted.

"You seem to always be intently probing into the workings of the Dwellers," Marvin stated as he nervously jingled whatever was in his pockets.

"Really?" I shot back. "Is it not possible that I was simply curious? If Humling and Keeper time is recorded while on the Earth Plane, I was just curious if Dweller time was."

"Dweller time is not recorded in any of our records," Marvin methodically answered. "As far as I'm aware."

"That makes sense," I said off the top of my mind.

"What has Tilly dragged you into?" Marvin questioned.

"This has nothing to do with Tilly," I replied firmly.

"Right," Marvin stated. "Level with me. I can always ask Tilly."

"Tilly knows nothing," I honestly said. Disapproval was spread across his face. "I was curious..."

"So?" Marvin prodded.

"I looked up Tilly's Earth Plane husband," I spit out. "You know the one who tried to drown her in the lake. The Dweller, Heath Lund."

Marvin sighed and stopped dead in his tracks with a look which screamed he knew exactly what this was about. "What would make you look up Tilly's Dweller husband?" Marvin said shaking his head. "Actually, what would make you look up a Dweller for any reason?"

"The Dweller had a chapter on the shelf," I replied.

"On which shelf," Marvin intently questioned.

"It was in the restricted section," I answered.

"Not that again," Marvin grumbled.

"I was filing for Carmen," I defended myself. "I only asked you because the chapter was blank."

"What were you thinking?" Marvin threw out clearly now angry. After a deep calming breath he continued, "I have something more important to talk about than Dwellers." Marvin paused as if whatever he was thinking simply inflamed his anger. "Where's Dustin tonight?"

"I don't know," I honestly replied. "I haven't seen him today."

As we reached the lawn of Keeper House, we quietly began to cross the lawn. Marvin appeared red faced and fuming. The arms length between us felt as if it were miles. There could not have been more distance between us.

I had to break the silence. I said, "Marvin."

"Don't try to explain," Marvin shot back. "I have no desire to hear about the other guy."

"You're one to talk," I retorted seeming to catch him off guard. "How could you go on even one date with Tiffany?"

"I guess that's the beauty of being free," Marvin stated. "We are free to date who we want."

"Exactly," I agreed in a huff.

"Have a good night," Marvin overly politely stated as he backed away from me. "One final piece of advice. Stay out of the restricted section before you get burned."

A good night? Who was he kidding? This had ended badly, almost as if he brought up Dustin to get out of the awkward goodbye scene. Then he reprimanded me. Well, both worked. The Marvin in my daydreaming was different than the Marvin I just snapped at.

CHAPTER TWENTY

Elizabeth

Keeper House was quiet due to everyone attending the final dress rehearsal for the upcoming Harmony performance. Arriving in my room, I couldn't miss the open windows. Without looking, I knew the familiar single brown envelope would be perched perfectly on my pillow. In simple black ink, Elizabeth Cantrell, would be neatly printed on the outside. I couldn't stop the Dweller that was leaving these for me. I plopped down on my bed, grabbed the envelope, and ripped it open.

Journal Entry #369

Watching from a distance exhausts me. She is simply my whole world.

Tonight our paths crossed. She and I were invited to the same party. Could it be any worse? I was introduced to her and I could feel the electricity between us. It appears she is drawn to me. Somewhere deep inside she feels the draw to me. I only wish she truly remembered. When she cordially held her hand out to shake mine, I could envision taking it. Pulling her too me and embracing crossed my mind. It was all I could do to put on my poker face. If I touched her, I would not be able to control myself. I crossed my arms tightly across my chest. I am certain she thought I was rude!

We sat across from each other. I believe I made her nervous. She dropped her napkin, ladled soup on her potatoes, and couldn't control her silverware. She blushed when she thought someone had seen.

Then my aunt finally got around as to why she invited me. She is black mailing me to force me to date her best friend's daughter. If I refuse to date her choice, she intends to let the Dwellers know about Bethany. I don't know if I should trust her. The risk of Bethany's exposure is forcing me to put my faith in my aunt. The girl she wishes for me to date is cruel to others and very self centered. I believe my aunt sees her fitting more into my world than Bethany. However, Bethany is already my whole world. Tiffany will never own my heart.

I gasped for air and suddenly felt as if I couldn't breathe. Suddenly, it became clear as to why the entries were being left for me. Dustin was the Dweller who had written all of these entries. I felt tears roll down my face with the realization that the girl he referred to at the dinner party was me. I was Bethany. The shock spread through my body with this confirmation of what deep down I already suspected.

My mind drifted back to the first evening when I became aware I couldn't trust Mrs. Farris, Dustin's aunt. She introduced me to Dustin with a devious smirk across her face. This memory brought back the butterflies in my stomach and sweaty hands as I stood in awe of the young man with spiky hair. The unique smell of Dustin had delighted my senses. However, he appeared frozen while watching me. I thought of him as rude, aloof, and tense. He was simply distancing himself from the me who knew him too well. All through dinner I had felt incredibly nervous in his presence. Then I heard his voice in my mind as he and Mrs. Farris appeared to be having a conversation. Mrs. Farris must be a Dweller as well.

Journal Entry #376

Tiffany is making me crazy wanting to spend every moment of the day with me. She is much more calculating and manipulative than most would ever know. My aunt was correct about one thing. Tiffany fits well into the darkness of my world almost better than the light of hers. Still, keeping up the appearance of liking her is weighing on me. Especially when I see Bethany watching us. It seems Bethany is oddly drawn to me and I hold on to the hope that she will one day remember me.

Most Keeper trainees are scared of Tiffany. Only one strong character named Tilly seems to stand up and challenge Tiffany on a regular basis. It seems she has been doing so since childhood. Who exactly does Bethany make friends with? Tilly. I am now walking a fine line in keeping my aunt happy and watching Bethany. Tiffany's venom at this point is less spewed at Bethany, but more directed towards Tilly. Tiffany vents her frustrations with those around her in what she calls a burn book. It is full of nasty, dark thoughts. It's a little childish. However, I believe this is how Tiffany vents her dark feelings. It allows her to control her impulses and remain in the light.

Sometimes, when I am close to Bethany, I wonder if she can hear me. She got into a mess with her friend. They actually lifted a chapter from the hall of records. She denied it, but I could swear she answered my unspoken thought. Next, I saw her with this guy name Marvin and my blood began to boil. Watching her with another male makes me feel as if I can't breathe. My heart races and feels as if it is going to explode and shatter into a million pieces. When introducing us, I again thought she giggled over an unspoken thought.

I remembered feeling envious of Tiffany when she put on a show with Dustin in front of me. Dustin's secret was behind him being cautious and avoiding me. The atmosphere of secrecy which surrounded him was necessary in his life. I had to wonder if Tiffany suspected Dustin's dark secret. I couldn't imagine him willingly entrusting her with it. Their relationship had always been difficult for me to get my head around. His public persona with her was of an adoring boyfriend. However, he was always making those sly comments in his head which always ended up in my head.

My pinning away after Dustin is what almost made me miss what Marvin and I had. Instinctively, I also knew Dustin disliked Marvin. How different to see things from Dustin's perspective.

Journal Entry – Final

Yes, now you know. This is about you. Elizabeth Marie Cantrell, Elizabeth Marie Kaswell, grand daughter of Albert Solliday. Bethany, grand daughter of Deward and Piper Venema. Which ever name you choose to use. All you, all the same. Your friend Dustin wasn't as smart as he thought. Imagine, accidently leaving his obsessive full journal about you for others to read. It's a great tool to use to blackmail you as well. Dustin authored all but this entry. Since he is to be punished as a traitor, he will regret visiting the place you once resided in the Humling world. You can always ask your young friends in Lakeland about the location. Your mother and their mother were best friends before the guard came looking for you. I'm sure they will have the address. Heed my warning, if you do not come and come by yourself, I will send the guard to pay your friends in Lakeland a visit. You have until Midnight. – The neighbor

I pulled the folder of journal entries from between my mattress and box springs and placed the last one on top of the stack. So many parallels existed in the lives of Dustin and me. We were uniquely suited for each other. We both had non-existent families. I had assumed Dustin's were Humling, but they were Dwellers. Unfortunately, just like mine. Dustin fully comprehended the difficulties I face. I owed it to him not to leave him hanging out there on his own.

I also knew my grandfather, Mr. Solliday, knew everything. Huh... all those times I was envious of Tilly for having parents who cared enough to show up when she was in trouble. Mr. Solliday was showing up for me, only I didn't know it. Tilly and I would have probably gotten into more trouble if he hadn't showed up all those times. He had to be a lonely man. His wife... The Dweller slave, Grace who was kidnapped during the event, had been so mistreated by the Venema family. Maybe Dustin had compassion on Mr. Solliday and never told him.

I hopped off my bed, tightened my pony tail, and knew what I had to do. I couldn't let Mrs. Farris or the Dwellers hurt Emma's family. No way would I risk getting my family of friends hurt either. I couldn't breathe a word of this to anyone. As I left my dorm room, possibly for the last time, I flipped off the light and didn't look back. I let my hand run down the wall of the girl's hall and onto the railing of the staircase.

"There you are," Destiny sighed as she stood at the bottom. "I've looked every where for you!"

"Destiny," I sighed. "I'm on my way..."

"I have something I've got to tell you," Destiny stated interrupting me mid sentence as she stomped up the stairs to stand before me.

"Can't it wait?" I asked.

"No, please let me get this off my chest," Destiny begged as she placed both her hands on my arm.

I plopped down on the step not sure I could take anymore surprises for the night.

"Elizabeth you are the true princess," Destiny spit out.

"What makes you say that?" I questioned understanding she was probably right.

"My intuition," Destiny returned looking away. "I already admitted to you that I have the gift of seeing. I know what is to come. Each generation has one person who sees. Long ago, the rare person who could see would assist the great leaders."

"Why did you hesitate to tell me this?" I questioned.

"Do you know what happens to those who have the gift of seeing?" Destiny asked in return.

"No," I replied.

"In history, the Dwellers seem to have a way of capturing those who have the gift," Destiny stated with a look of fear. "It's like the Dwellers know they are being talked about. Those who aren't captured go into hiding."

"That is why you play it off as being nosy," I surmised.

"You're the only one I have told about having the gift," Destiny sighed. "My gut resonated I was to trust you whole heartedly." She took a deep calming breath. "However, my mind screamed I shouldn't. I have tried to befriend you so I could set my mind at ease, so I could find out if you were trustworthy."

"I haven't told anyone," I said in an attempt to comfort her. "And I won't."

"The last to have the sight was Grace Solliday," Destiny stated. "Everyone knows what happened to her." Suddenly Destiny began to wring her hands, "I can't move on until I tell you that you are the true princess. I realized this when you asked me about Marvin." She took in another deep breath. "I think I only see the black hole because I'm not passing on to you what I should."

"Tell me about the true princess," I probed hoping not to let on that I knew a little about it from Leo.

"The Dwellers have it in written poem form," Destiny stated.

"Have you read the poem?" I asked.

"No," Destiny said shaking her head. "I only see the cover of the book."

"Sorry, go on," I said for interrupting her.

"The true princess centers on the stolen stone from the Hall of Babies. I'm not sure what the stone does, but it is of great importance to the Keepers. The Dwellers discovered this and stole part of it, or maybe all of it. I'm not sure on that detail." Destiny peered off for a moment before continuing, "Did you know that Keepers, Humlings, and Dwellers didn't grow old before the stone was stolen? At least no older than the age of thirty." Destiny threw out as if they were math facts. "When the stone is at rest in the Hall of Babies, the battles between Keepers and Dwellers can only be fought on the Earth Plane as God intended. Heaven is safe from the ongoing war."

"The stone is tied to the true princess because?" I asked.

"She is the only one who can retrieve it from the Dwellers," Destiny matter of fact replied.

"That's why they don't want you talking," I surmised.

Destiny cleared her throat and I followed her gaze to Eddie who was now standing at the bottom of the stairs. His appearance screamed he was nervous and topped with a little of, what was I thinking?

"Are you ready?" Eddie asked Destiny.

With a grin from ear to ear she said, "Of course." Then she turned saying to me, "Whatever may come, it's done now!"

"What's done?" Eddie asked.

"What is that smell?" Destiny asked as she wrinkled her nose.

Eddie appeared to be smirking as he said, "Vapor rub. Sorry, I have a touch of a cold."

I tried desperately to hold back a giggle and not let it escape me. I knew he didn't have a cold. He had rubbed the vapor rub all over himself so that he couldn't smell Destiny.

"Well then I had better take good care of you tonight," Destiny hummed.

As he grabbed her hand and they began to walk away, Eddie peered over his shoulder with a help me look. I gave him a wave figuring I would never be able to give him that date with me which I promised.

I rose from my place on the stairs hearing the front door of Keeper House slam shut. I made my way to the professor's door and knocked calling, "Excuse me Professor, may we talk?"

"Of course, my door is always open," Professor Zirak stated as he stood up from behind his desk.

I entered, closed the door behind me, and found a seat in one of his two chairs. Once seated, I saw an opportunity to ask him all kinds of questions that needed an answer, "How did I end up in your training class?"

He sighed, "If you are ready and open to discuss the assignment which has been eluding you, I will discuss with you what I know."

"Do you know I have more than one name?" I earnestly asked.

"I knew you probably had a different name as a Humling," Professor Zirak stated. "So... In a round about way, yes."

Sadly, he thought I was a Humling and didn't know the whole story. I asked, "How did you know I was a Humling?"

"I knew your Keeper," Professor Zirak replied. "One of my best students."

"Dustin?" I questioned to the astonished look on his face.

Professor Zirak sat back in his chair peering at me. "Dustin was indeed your Keeper and confided in me when he found out you were to become a Keeper," Professor Zirak stated. "I assured him no matter which department you were to train for, I would do my best to look after you for him. My job was easier when you tested and were to train in my department."

"So, you assigned me the extra work to help me catch up on all subjects everyone else automatically knew?" I concluded. He shook his head and my thoughts once again came out of my mouth, "And Tilly?"

"Well, keeping her busy kept her out of trouble didn't it?" Replied the professor with a chuckle.

He did have that right. "Do they often allow Humlings to become Keepers? I asked.

"Not usually," Professor Zirak stated.

My mind wandered to thoughts of Dustin. If the professor had information I was a Humling, how did he miss the obvious about Dustin? "Professor, you know that Dustin…?"

"Yes, he did recommend you for the program," interrupted the professor.

"Before?" I began to question. "Dustin and I…?"

"I do not get involved in matters of the heart. It's between the two of you," the professor once again interrupted. "I can tell you he is genuine, kind, and a true individual."

"Sir, can you tell me anything about my family?" Asked Elizabeth.

"I am sorry, I don't have any information about them," said Professor Zirak.

"You told me since all the books were empty, this should answer my question. I still don't understand," I complained.

"I understood without viewing your chapter that it would be empty. The locket around your neck is no ordinary locket. After that dreadful day long ago, you know… the event… they are now only given to Keepers who travel to and from the black arch. Although, I don't understand what business you would have in the black arch, I do understand your time in the black arch is not recorded in the Hall of Records," Professor Zirak explained.

I closed my eyes in shock. If I had been to the world of the Dwellers, it was likely to bring back the stone. "That must be why I have no memory," I said off the top of my head.

"I don't know why you seem to have no memory," Professor Zirak replied eyeing me intently.

In the last hour, my world had all fallen apart, and at the same time, into place. I needed to scoot before my friends started trickling in and I dismantled their world as well. My path tonight was for me alone.

Tilly

Here we were enjoying the grassy park outside the Administration Complex. As we sat on the grass, it felt amazing to run the greenery through my fingers. Anthony laid back to gaze at the stars. It felt natural as I lay back beside him.

"How was Harmony?" Anthony inquired.

"Elizabeth played hooky again," I complained.

"She's your best friend," Anthony countered. "I'm sure she has a reason."

"I have no idea what is going on with her," I sighed as I rolled over and placed my head on his chest. "She seems a million miles away."

Anthony fell silent as he stroked my hair. Unlike me, he was entirely comfortable. There had only been one other male which I felt this undeniable connection with. If there had ever been a first love, it was Trevor. Until now, Trevor was the only one I let my guard entirely down around. My heart fluttered when I was in Anthony's presence. However, I didn't know if he felt exactly the same about me. All those Humling girls he dated and probably cuddled up to annoyed me. I questioned him, "So, is this how you normally hold all your other girls?"

He half sat up and leaned on his elbows forcing me to sit up. He said, "Mathilda Bradford! Do you really presume I have ever held anyone but you like this?"

I couldn't look him in the eye as I began, "No... Yes... Well, maybe... I don't know!" I glanced back at him, "All those Humling girls..."

Anthony placed his finger on my lips to silence me as he said, "There has never been another girl like you for me."

"Well yeah! How many Keepers have you met?" I sarcastically challenged.

"Keepers or Humlings," Anthony said as he seriously looked at me. "There will never be anyone but you." He leaned over and pecked me on the lips. When he pulled back he said, "I'm in love with you Mathilda Bradford. Don't you know that?" When I didn't answer, he eventually let himself lay back appearing lost in his own thoughts. I once again laid my head back on his chest. He began to stroke my hair once more. Again he whispered, "I love you. I have known since the day we met."

"The day we met?" I questioned while my mind screamed that the time to run had passed. My plan about not getting attached had backfired. Now the sensation of being one was holding me firmly in place.

"I knew from the moment you challenged me to bungee jump," Anthony said still stroking my hair. "At that moment I grasped what I felt. I am in love with you."

How had this happened? I always convinced myself that love was a fairy tale since I feared the hurt that always came with attachment. With the exception of Trevor, anyone I ever allowed myself to get attached to had hurt me. I would run if it were anyone but Anthony. My heart knew whatever was to come, I couldn't bare to run from him. He didn't scare me. Taking a breath, I replied, "I love you too."

CHAPTER
TWENTY-ONE

Elizabeth

Climbing the creaky stairs of Lakeland Station, I felt the cool night air blowing off the lake and across my cheeks. As you would expect this late at night, all appeared calm in the sleepy shoreline town. The familiar farmers market was closed with each shack of a store neatly tidied up for the night. I sauntered along the pathway past many homes which were brightly lit. Inside, lighting spilled out their windows. Dogs and cats peered out the windows of many homes. I passed many with toys in the front yard waiting the next day's playtime.

After many heavy footsteps, the Tabures household came in sight. The small, fenced, white one story home was lit up like all the others. I entered the wooden gate and slowly shuffled up the cracked concrete sidewalk. The porch which rambled along the front was dark. Two small dogs startled me as they suddenly scampered around me with their tails wagging. I took a deep breath and knocked on the front door. The porch light came on and I could see Emma peeking out. Once she saw it was me, a huge smile crossed her face as she opened the door.

"Elizabeth, what are you doing here?" Emma asked as she moved to let me enter.

"I need to ask you something," I said.

"I don't want to talk about Tilly and Anthony," she huffed at me.

I could hear Anthony from somewhere in the back of the house, "Emma, who is it?"

"Not Tilly," she replied and rolled her eyes. "Thank goodness." She leaned forward adding, "What does he think? She should follow him home?"

He walked through the hallway door and plopped into a chair, "Hey, what are you doing here? It's a little late isn't it?"

"I really needed to ask you something," I repeated for him while ignoring Emma's sarcasm. I moved over toward their seating area.

"Tilly isn't mad at you, just disappointed," Anthony said off the top of his head. "Is that why you stopped by?"

"No," I replied. "I know she'll forgive me for missing practice tonight."

"How would you know she missed practice?" Emma asked Anthony. "I thought you were out with Gary." She shook her head in disappointment adding, "Your obsession with that girl is unhealthy."

"Her name is Tilly," Anthony corrected.

"Troubles more like it," Emma countered.

I plopped down on one of their floral chairs as both sets of eyes turned to me before Anthony inquired, "So what brings you here tonight? I'm sure it isn't to listen to us bicker."

"Where's Daniel?" I inquired.

"He's on a school trip," Emma stated.

I thought for a moment. No matter what came, Daniel would be spared. Now I needed to ensure Emma and Anthony were safe as well. I asked, "Did your mother have a friend named Christy?"

"Yes, but we haven't seen her in many years," Emma replied seating herself on the couch next to me.

"They went to the Earth Plane," Anthony said plopping his feet up on the coffee table.

"You say they?" I asked.

"Well yes, Aunt Cathy has two daughters, Beth and Crissy," Emma replied. "I don't remember them very well."

"We were all very little," Anthony interjected.

Where did they live?" I asked.

"Mountain Bluff in Shell Ridge," Anthony hesitated.

"Is that a suburb?" I asked.

"More like a few houses out in the sticks," Anthony stated with a smile on his face. "Or at least it used to be. We haven't been up there in awhile. It's a small, out of place, hole in the road," Anthony answered while stretching his arms and yawning. "Elizabeth, why are you asking?"

"You satisfied my curiosity," I told him as I sprung up and moved towards the door. "It's getting late." It all fit. When we first met Emma spoke of her mother's friend with the Keeper watch who happened to be my mother. I was Emma's friend as a small child. This was how I picked Lakeland on that first trip through the subway.

Anthony moved towards me seriously asking, "Do you think you know them?" When I hesitated to answer Anthony asked, "Is something wrong?"

"No," I said and shrugged trying to appear as if nothing was wrong.

"You are right, it's late," Anthony stated as he moved to grab the doorknob. "Do you want me to ride the subway and then walk you back?"

"Your getting caught in the dome wouldn't be healthy for either one of us," I answered.

"Why did you ask about Aunt Christy?" Emma asked from behind Anthony.

"It was something I read," I admitted. Hoping to quickly exit the door, I motioned for Anthony to pull the door open. I backed out the door saying, "Don't worry. I'll head right back home."

"You're going straight home," Anthony repeated to verify.

In a round about way, I was going home, my childhood home. I sighed reassuring Anthony, "Tonight, I'm going home."

Anthony stood on the porch and peered at me as I raced down their sidewalk. I could feel his stare on my back. He didn't totally buy what I was selling.

Elizabeth

There was a slight drizzle of rain in Shell Ridge when I arrived and faced wet terrain. Fighting the elements, I found the muddy mountain top road and located the home. The home was the only duplex on the lighted street and I felt drawn to the bright yellow exterior. Across the front of both residences ran big plate glass windows which gave no clues about what loomed behind them. The entrance to both residences faced a common hall which ran between the two. Now, standing before the door, my hands begin to sweat. I placed my hand on the door knob, took a deep breath, and opened the door to face my impending doom. The dark room openly exposed me to whoever or whatever was waiting in the shadows.

"Your father and sister, unnatural…," said Mrs. Farris in a cold calculating voice as she flipped on a small lamp at the desk which she casually sat before. "Your poor mother couldn't cope and escaped to the Earth Plane never to return. How amusing you have been, obsessively writing letters and waiting for the mail hoping someone would care."

"That's enough," Dustin screamed at Mrs. Farris in my mind as he stumbled out of the shadows. Not realizing I could hear him he peered at me, "Elizabeth doesn't listen to her!"

Dustin was visibly weak, covered in bruises, and appeared drained of all life.

"How romantic," said Mrs. Farris glaring at Dustin. "Her knight in shining armor... That is what you wish to be, isn't it?" An awkward silence fell and she continued, "Cat got your tongue. Your greatest desire is for her to remember you were in love with her from the very moment you laid eyes on her. You thought you had it all figured out when you convinced that old bat, Solliday, to let her be a Keeper. Then you dreamed that the two of you could live happily ever after in the world of the Keepers."

"Mary, you have said enough," bellowed a creepy voice I recognized within my head.

I began to panic as the young man with the ratty hair and black eyes came into view. My legs wanted nothing more to do than run. I stepped backwards as his strong arms caught me and wrapped very tightly around me in restraint. I was surprised when Dustin seemed not to be bothered by the sight, but greeted him, "Collin, so nice to see you again."

Collin nodded at Dustin and then stated, "Bethany, we have worked very long hours to find you. If we had only known you were with Dustin…"

I broke him off mid-sentence. "Yes, I'm sure he planned to return me himself soon."

"Really?" Collin questioned with an eyebrow lifted. "I thought our meeting tonight was due to a plan Mrs. Farris put together."

"I do have to compliment myself," started Mrs. Farris. "She was drawn here by the awful truth that is her true life, making my plan all the easier." She held up a Journal that visibly had pages missing. Dustin embarrassed, retreated and hanging his head knowing what I must have read.

"I must ask what part was your favorite?" Mrs. Farris taunted me. "Oh. Please tell me. The part about your dear old dad, the passages about your sister, or the passages about how Dustin deceived everyone." She looked at me in eerie silence. I was not going to answer. "Your favorite must be the consuming love he has for you." Mrs. Farris spewed.

"Yes Dustin, you really ought to know not to write down the dreadful details of life in our world," Collin stated as he moved his hands from around me and held my hair with one hand, pulling it straight up and making me stand on the toes of my feet. He began to thumb through the remains of the journal with his smile crookedly deepening. "Piper will be interested to see what an author you are."

I could not contain my need to protect him. I remembered the times Dustin had been there for me. "Stop!" I screamed.

Instantly, I wished I hadn't. Collins hand moved from the book to my face, holding it so tightly I felt as if the bones in my face were being crushed. "You must not scream at me or you will pay for it, princess or not," he growled.

His eyes, close to mine, looked more menacing than before and I was sure he meant what he said. I tried to nod and I knew he could feel it within his hand. He let go of my face. "You see Dustin, she just needs a strong hand," he stated clearly amused.

"So, did you figure out where I went and why I knew she was here?" Dustin asked.

"Oh yes, the book passed between Grace and Bethany did that," Collin replied smiling at me. "Bethany, you probably will take pleasure in visualizing what great care we gave Grace. Since she seemed to be more scared of those beyond the grounds than us, we tossed her out beyond the grounds. Never to be seen again."

"Collin, you didn't. She was an old lady." I heard Dustin state in my head.

"It was Tina's idea," Collin answered. She was so mad about being punished she sought revenge. She would have taken it out on you, but you weren't around."

I stared intently at Dustin who tried not to make eye contact with me. Suddenly I caught a brief glance of relief across his face.

"Collin, I can stop playing the part now." Dustin stated.

"What?" Replied Collin.

"All this trying to be nice. Trying to get her to trust me is simply wearing me out!" Dustin stated.

Collin chuckled, "Yes, you did get the harder of the two to guard. At least mine wants to be one of us."

"I don't know, I might beg to differ. But, as her guard," Dustin began as he trudged over to me trying not to stumble but look strong. "I will take her now."

Collin reluctantly let go and Dustin instinctively moved me back to the other side of the room. I could feel him leaning and placing some of his weight on me when Collin prompted, "What are you doing?"

Dustin held me by the hair the same as Collin, forcing me to stand on my tippy toes.

"Its not you Collin, its Mrs. Farris," Dustin said with a smile across his face. "Collin, did you know she threatened to harm Eliz... Bethany?"

Collin's glare was menacing as Mrs. Farris pleaded, "Only playing my part!"

While Collin's eyes were locked onto Mrs. Farris, I felt Dustin's hand grab mine and squeeze very tightly. I followed his eyes and could see Marvin, Trevor, and Anthony waiting outside the cracked front door. What in the world were they doing here? How did they know?

"When will the others be arriving to take us back?" Asked Dustin interrupting the thoughts in my head.

"Any time, I have called them," replied Collin in my head.

Dustin slightly nodded to the door as he moved forward to gain Collin's full attention. The front door violently swung open with Marvin, Trevor, and Anthony rushing the room. Collin was fast, but the three of them cornered Collin and pounced on him. Then it was blur with all of them wrestling on the floor. Before I knew it, Mrs. Farris bumped into me as Dustin was struggling to contain Mrs. Farris in his weakened state. All of a sudden Trevor landed at my feet with a big thud. As Mrs. Farris tripped over him, he and Dustin moved to restrain her.

My eyes were now glued on Marvin and Anthony as they struggled to get atop Collin who was unbelievably strong. It was Marvin who started belting Collin with solid punches to the face. Collin returned a few blows. However, with Anthony wrestling him as well, they were slowly over powering Collin. Then Marvin stepped back and centered himself for one last blow to Collin. When it hit Collin's face it made a crushing sound knocking Collin out.

In a flash it was over. Collin lay unconscious and instantly Marvin pulled a rope from somewhere and began to tie Collin up. As I spun around to peer at Mrs. Farris, Trevor had a rope which he was using to tie and restrain her.

Mrs. Farris began to spew, "Boys, you have just sealed your fate! They will track you down just like they track Elizabeth! Each one of you will be marked!" She watched the faces of those passing her and continued when

Dustin came by, "You are the worst of all, a traitor."

It appeared that no one paid any attention to her as we quickly exited the front door. However, none of us could deny the cold truth she spouted. After reading the journal I knew anyone attacking a guard was to be hunted down and dealt with. None of us were safe from their wrath. Dustin's fate was that of a traitor as Mrs. Farris had pointed out.

Dustin reached over and grabbed my hand with his, enter-locking our fingers. Before I knew it, we were holding hands as we ran through the slowing drizzle. This felt natural to me, but awkward because I could feel Marvin staring. We stopped running once under the shelter of the tree line. Then Tilly and Emma came into view. Before I knew it, both had their arms around me forcing Dustin to let go of my hand. The impact of their weight hitting me forced me back a few steps.

"You should have told us!" Screeched Tilly into my hair as she frantically hugged me. "I knew something was bothering you all week!"

"We came to help as soon as we understood you were in trouble," said Emma in a calmer voice.

I pulled away, looking at all of them, my friends, my family. I began to feel hot tears rolling down my face. I choked out, "How did you all know?"

"That starts with me," stated Tilly. "I found that folder which contained those entire journal entries which I always assumed were love notes." She watched me to see if I seemed mad and continued, "You know, I wasn't being nosy, the folder was in plain sight on your bed. I didn't know what to do after reading them."

"I found her stunned, sitting on her bed," stated Trevor. He was the only one I didn't expect to see. "My gut said we should go find Marvin."

"Tilly arrived at my door, quite honestly, a mess," Marvin started. "Nothing before ever seemed to bother her, but tonight I saw a different side. You know she never wears her feelings on her sleeves."

"Well, thank you," Tilly matter of fact stated.

Marvin did not acknowledge her and continued, "All she could get out was your name as she shoved the folder into my hands. They sat patiently and waited for me to read them."

"So everyone knows," stated Dustin with a sigh of relief.

"We knew who your friends in Lakeland were," Tilly started as Anthony moved behind her placing his hands around her waist.

"The subway adventure, you should have taken me on long ago," Trevor added with a grin.

"We decided to go visit and inquire what information they had concerning where your mother once lived." Tilly stated as Marvin glared at her. "Of course, I can't take credit for the idea. Marvin was hell bent on finding you."

"When we asked Emma what she had told you…" Marvin began.

"I knew if they were asking too, you were in some kind of trouble," interrupted Anthony with a sigh.

"And the three of them," Emma was pointing at Marvin, Tilly, and Trevor. "Were determined to go and rescue you."

"However, I wouldn't let Mathilda come without me," Anthony stated. He said her name like a parent who was upset with a child.

Trevor let out a huge disapproving sigh and rolled his eyes in disbelief over Anthony believing Tilly wasn't safe with him.

Tilly's reaction was surprising since she didn't even notice Trevor's glare. She sheepishly smiled at Anthony as he grinned down at her.

"Oh, stop it you two," Emma barked.

My eyes shot past them to Trevor. He appeared too pained to watch the two of them. Interrupting my thoughts was Mrs. Farris who was now screaming.

"We all need to split up," said Dustin's thoughts in an urgent manner.

"I agree," I answered without hesitation. The look on his face was one of shock. I had forgotten he didn't know I could hear his thoughts.

"Agree to what?" Asked Marvin who seemed a little puzzled.

"I will go with you," I informed Dustin.

He shook his head no and then responded in my head, "I am too weak. I won't be able to protect you." For a brief moment I stared into his eyes and I knew this to be true.

Marvin now had my arm and pulled me away from Dustin getting between us and loudly telling me, "You are not going to the Dwellers with him! I won't allow it." I could see him breathing deeply trying to catch his erratic breath.

Dustin held up his hand, "No, she won't be going with me. However, I do need someone… one of the girls to travel back to the dome with me to draw them away from her. They will assume she is with me."

I heard Tilly beginning to breathe unevenly and Anthony held her tightly trying to calm her. "It must be me," she stated with a strained voice as she looked at Emma.

We all knew this too be true. Emma would never succeed in accompanying Dustin. If they got caught, she would fall to pieces. Tilly would be better suited to handle the guards and better suited to assist the weak Dustin.

"No!" Trevor intently disagreed with horror and panic spread across his face.

Tilly leaned her head into Anthony's chest. He looked tortured at the thought of letting her go, but resigned to what would be her fate. He placed his arms around her. I felt guilty for giving Tilly a hard time over her growing obsession with him. Anyone watching could see they were meant to be together.

"Marvin, take her to Rhett's house," Dustin demanded.

"No, we will be going to Mr. Solliday," disagreed Marvin.

"He is not in tonight," growled Dustin. I could see his eyes turning black and cold like Collins and understood he was not making a request of Marvin, but a demand. I think Marvin could see the change of demeanor as he placed himself directly in-front of me to protect me. This seemed to annoy Dustin, who would never hurt me. He continued, "He goes out every Tuesday for the evening and won't return until morning."

"Why do you think they chose this evening?" Dustin stated to me in my thoughts.

"Of course, they chose this evening because he couldn't offer any protection for me," I stated for Marvin's benefit. "Dustin, do you think Rhett can help us?"

"Yes, he will be able to protect you." Dustin said in my head.

"Rhett can absolutely help us," Marvin muttered what Dustin appeared not to have answered.

"What about us?" Interrupted Emma.

"You should not go home this evening. If you do, they will follow you there. It will never be safe again. You must enter the dome as well," stated Dustin.

"Take Emma into the dome, are you mad?" Asked Anthony who was still holding Tilly very close.

"Man, if all you're worried about is your sister getting caught inside the dome..." Trevor growled no longer able to keep his composed manner. "It was you who insisted your sister be put into harms way because you were worried about Tilly's safety with me, which is a load of nonsense. I have always taken care of Tilly," Trevor said as he reached to pull Tilly away from Anthony. "How could you even consider letting Tilly go off with a Dweller?"

"Trevor stop!" Tilly demanded as she pulled her arm from his. "This choice isn't either of yours to make!"

"It's certainly not yours," Trevor disagreed.

"Why should we trust you?" Anthony questioned Dustin, but did not give him time to answer. "You are a Dweller."

"I trust him," said Tilly. "Because Elizabeth trusts him and she is my best friend." She could feel his stance tensing. She pulled away from him. Taking his hands into hers and looking directly into his eyes she spoke, "If I trust him, please trust me."

Anthony appeared defeated. He would do anything that Tilly felt strong about.

"Try that non sense on me and see if I cave," Trevor challenged.

"I agree with the plan," Marvin spoke up from in front of me.

"Of course you do," Trevor spouted. "It isn't Elizabeth in harms way anymore."

"Stop!" Tilly once again shouted. "We don't have time for this. You have to trust me too." Tilly held out her hand and placed it on Trevor's arm. They exchanged a long, deep glance into each others eyes. Their friendship went beyond the surface and all the way to their core. She trusted him, just as he trusted her in the end.

"If he gets you hurt...," Trevor stated stopping mid sentence. The unsaid threat was loud and clear for everyone in the group. He then peered around at all of us with agony and grief in his eyes, "I will spend the rest of my time in eternity making each of you pay as well."

Tilly placed her hand flatly on his chest in a calming manner as Anthony asked Dustin, "How do we get into the dome?"

"I thought you had that figured out by now," Trevor spewed.

"Trevor will take you," Dustin threw out adding to the tension. "Marvin and Elizabeth will use her locket to get back into the relative safety of the dome."

"Why don't we all use the locket?" Trevor threw out in desperation.

"Usually lockets don't have enough strength to carry a group our size," Dustin answered. "Anthony and Emma, the two of you will blend in with the other Humlings on the subway. Trevor, take Emma's hand and pretend the two of you are dating. I don't believe the guard will be able to spot you easily. Anthony, pretend they're strangers."

"Tilly, I will meet you in our spot," Anthony softly spoke to Tilly.

"I'll meet you at the door," Tilly said while nodding in acknowledgement.

"What door?" Trevor demanded to know.

"The hospital door," Tilly answered.

"We will find them, Geren." I heard an unfamiliar voice state in my mind.

My eyes instantly darted to Dustin's. He moved flinging Emma to Trevor, "Go now, they are coming." Dustin pulled Tilly next to him. I moved around Marvin to look at Dustin. He looked into my eyes and leaned over placing a kiss on my lips. I heard Marvin make a gagging sound, while Dustin told me, "Go, my love."

Marvin grabbed my hand and roughly pulled me further into the dark tree line. I wasn't sure if it was the kiss he was upset about or if I simply wasn't keeping up. I watched Emma, Trevor, and Anthony disappear down the street and heard Tilly, true to her nature, always resigned to see everything as one big adventure, say, "Lets go Dweller boy!" They disappeared in the opposite direction.

Then I saw Collin in the distance point towards me. I panicked and we ran deep into the woods until I felt I could no longer breathe. Everyone I held dear was in danger because I placed them there. Would it just be simpler to accept my fate? Maybe it wouldn't be so bad if Dustin were there. Then I looked at Marvin's bruised face. He took each of Collin's blows for me. He was as deeply in love with me as Dustin. I knew leaving would break him. Would it have served any purpose for all of them to have done what they did tonight if I gave up? I indeed could no longer breathe and my knees buckled as I fell to the ground.

"I could now hear Marvin, "Elizabeth! Oh no, wake up. " He was frantic with worry and had me wrapped on his lap in his arms as we sat on the wet forest floor. I could hear him and feel his hands gently shaking me. I wanted to stay wrapped in his arms. I never realized how safe he made me feel until now. Could I just stay and pretend my two worlds weren't colliding?

"I think the other ones escaped into the forest," stated Collin in my thoughts.

"I will go after Dustin and Bethany. Take Collin and go after the others,"

stated Geren in my head.

Instantly, I sat up startling Marvin. He jumped slightly as I almost hit him in the chin with my head. "We've got to go, they are coming." I fought the nausea in my stomach and fumbled with retrieving the locket from under my shirt. His eyes met mine for a brief moment before I closed them, rubbed my locket, and mumbled, "Rhett's home." The next moment we dropped onto the long wooden dark hall of Rhett's house.

"So that's how it feels," Marvin said from his place next to me as he got to his feet. I took his outstretched hand as he pulled me up. Then he appeared to be looking me over from head to toe. "You knew they were coming because you hear them, don't you?" I nodded somewhat ashamed of my gift. He smiled at me while softly pulling my face up to look at his, "I don't mind, remember?"

"What's going on?" Rhett asked as he descended the creaky staircase finding the two of us in what must have looked like a lover's embrace. Marvin dropped his hands as Rhett focused on me asking, "Miss Cantrell, what are you doing? Why are you here?" In that instant he looked from me to Marvin. "What happened to your face?" He stepped toward Marvin adding, "The two of you had better tell me what in the world is going on."

CHAPTER
TWENTY-TWO

Elizabeth

R hett and Marvin left me alone in the familiar eclectic decorated house. Rhett rattled on about it being a safe haven as he appeared to be checking all the windows. Whatever that meant. When they left, their plan was simple. They were going to retrieve the whole gang as they stepped from the subway into the Hospital. Rhett didn't think Trevor, Anthony, and Emma would have too many problems making their way to the Hospital. Collin had been the only one to see them and he had come after me instead of them. However, Dustin and Tilly were a different story.

Rhett appeared as deeply rattled about Tilly, just as Trevor had been. He paced while listening. His reaction, to the news of Tilly, was similar to when Tilly and I told him we thought Marvin was in trouble. He sprang into action and they quickly left. No longer able to sit, I made up my mind. I, too, was going to the Hospital. I couldn't sit still while my friends were being chased on the account of me.

As I stood before the marvelous, golden door in the foyer of the Hall of Knowledge I took a final, deep calming breath. The door would lead me to the hospital. I scanned my watch across the door unlocking it. I briskly entered the hall and peered at the simple, wooden door at the other end. I could only hope all of my friends had reached their freedom through that entrance.

The hospital was full. Every bench had Humlings and Keeper families awaiting their loved one. All were excited and happy with the belief they were completely safe as they sat glued to their spots. The center of the long hall held standing room only.

"It's busy tonight," I mumbled to myself.

"Earthquake," a bystander answered.

"Huh?" I responded.

"They all chose to come home at the same time," she again responded.

I smiled and nodded, now understanding. A mass exit had just taken place from the Earth Plane.

"Elizabeth!" Shouted the bald Mr. Farris over the crowd. "Mrs. Farris was just here and asked me to give this to you, if I saw you. " His hand was extended as he handed me a familiar, simple brown envelope with my name scrolled across the front in black ink.

"Thank you," I politely said as I turned to walk down the corridor to find an empty seat next to a wall. I looked back over my shoulder, he was gone. I sat and ripped open the envelope to find a scribbled note.

Bethany,

Dustin and your friend would like the pleasure of showing you what happens to those who betray us and stand in our way. Your friend will make a great slave and she will be made to bow down to you and the rest of your royal Venema family. We are only awaiting your arrival to continue on our journey home to the darkness. Come quickly my lost princess and bring any person with you that you deem slave material.

Collin

I gasped! Neither of them was going to appear through the simple, wooden door. My worst fear was realized. They had been captured. Since it was my responsibility to stop all of this, my shoulders suddenly felt heavy. I could only hope to negotiate myself for Tilly's release. The world of the Dwellers couldn't be all bad if Dustin were there.

From somewhere at the other end of the hall, it was Marvin who caught my attention. He was standing, watching me. A deep sadness overtook me with the realization Marvin and I would never be together. This was the dark circle Destiny saw in my future. It wasnt in the cards for us. I think he could read my face and feel my numbed heart. After all the heartache, I wasn't sure I had anything left to feel but regret. I would always wonder what might have been between us. The small, shared quaint house I dreamed of, our days and nights together, the children I was sure we would one day have… It would all be gone after this decision.

I pulled the locket from under my shirt, closed my eyes, rubbed it, and stated, "My guard, Dustin."

I briefly heard Marvin yelling, "No, Elizabeth!"

With a thud, I found myself in the shadows on a rock layered floor of a cellar. Quietly, I stood and watched for a moment. Dustin was curled up on the floor, writhing in pain. Tilly was quietly sitting beside him holding onto his arm which I was certain was broken. Tilly appeared unusually pale. Then she turned and I could see the bruise across her face. Someone had hit her very hard to leave that mark.

I peered at Collin standing over Dustin in a menacing manner and screamed in my head,"Collin! Dustin!"

As I thought, they could not hear me. I carefully took the locket from around my neck and clasped my hand around it tightly. This wasn't the time to freeze up. My acting would need to be superb. I took one last deep breath and stepped forward, "Dustin, so glad to see you finally got what you deserve."

"Bethany, we thought you got away," Collin stated sarcastically as he turned to face me giving a menacing look. "And decided not to join us. We have punished Dustin while we waited. Would you like to see us continue?"

"Maybe, after I say I'm sorry to you, Collin," I answered. "I owe you an apology since my two friends attacked you. Really, you shouldn't be mad at them, be mad at me. I asked them to deal Dustin some tough justice. You just happened to get in the way."

"And why would you want your friends to do this?" Asked an older, rough man as he stepped out of the crowd. "What did he do?"

"He made me mad!" I screamed at him hoping my act was believable. "I wanted them to hurt him," I continued as I walked to stand in front of Collin. Poking his chest I spewed, "Only Collin got there first." I hesitated while trying to look sincere. "We pulled Dustin out and all of you interrupted us. Then he disappeared. However, I did trick him and sent Tilly with him."

I strutted over to Tilly with Collin close behind me. I held out my open hand for Tilly and pulled her close to me and gave her a hug whispering, "Use it." The uncertainty of my message made her pull away and I grabbed her other hand passing the locket from mine to hers. I glanced directly into her eyes and could see the indecision behind them.

"I now see I was hasty, you took care of him for me," I stated while turning to grin at Collin and the old, unkept man. "He does look weak now. Collin, do you think he has learned his lesson for making me mad?"

"That is not why we are punishing him," another guard stated in my head.

"You don't wish us to punish him more?" Asked the old man in return.

"If I tell you too," I retorted staring him down. "Besides, who are you to question me?"

"Whoa! Did you hear what she just said to Geren," a female guard stated from behind Tilly.

"Hush!" Geren demanded in his head.

"I'm Geren," the old man introduced himself. "Head royal guard."

"Geren, I realize I have caused all of you a great deal of trouble," I stated firmly and then hesitated. "He is my guard and I think he is adequately punished. I fear if you punish him more, he won't be worth much. Besides, he didn't cause your bad evening, I did. You can punish me later if you wish."

"Punishing you is not up to us," replied Geren in my head.

I felt a small sense of relief.

Then Collin stated, "You don't seem like yourself." Every eye in the room was intently focused on me waiting for my response. For the first time, Dustin was looking at me. I knew I could not return his gaze or he would break my concentration which I needed to get us out of here.

"Well Collin, you like to gaze at the world outside the grounds. You have seen first hand what that world does to a person. Am I mistaken?" I questioned.

"Well... I don't talk about that," he growled back at me with eyes pitch black seething with anger.

"She will not disgrace Tina by talking about this!" I heard Collin yell at the others as he grabbed my shoulders, squeezing them tightly.

"Calm down," replied Geren.

I had hit a nerve. "Well, the horror of what happened to Tina, you did to me," I growled back to him and struggled to be free from his grasp. "Being outside the grounds will harden a person, won't it?"

One of the other guards stepped forward saying, "I still don't understand one thing. Why has Dustin not brought you home to the Dwellers? It was his duty!

Knowing they could not hurt me I replied with a smirk, "You can't blame him for that. I simply refused. I didn't want to go back into the world outside the grounds. Really, Dustin is faithful and doing his duty. Eventually, he stopped pressuring me so much. He recognized my fears."

"He has a greater allegiance to Venema House," disagreed Geren.

"Oh yes, that's what it is all about. You," stated Collin.

"Yes, it is about me!" I screamed at him like a spoiled brat. "A guard is to protect me from what I fear! If he didn't constantly watch my back, you would have allowed Tina to send me back out. If he can't trust you, then he felt I was better there."

"Enough," stated Geren.

"Dustin tell me, now that the air has been cleared. Is it best that we go back?" I kneeled down and asked him.

Dustin looked up at me with pleading, fearful eyes. He closed his eyes saying what the room needed to hear, "Yes." Then, as if he must communicate and verify his true feeling, he mumbled, "My true princess... because together we..."

I could finish his sentence together we would draw unwanted attention. He was conveying that he could not stay with me in the world of the Keepers. He also knew I could not live in the world of the Dwellers. I had intended to give myself up for Tilly. Dustin was conveying I needed to find my inner strength. The true princess would need to pick the time for the battle, not give up. My choice suddenly became clear. "Very well, the choice has been made."

"Don't," stated a weak voice that I hardly recognized as Dustin's.

I could not respond. No matter what happened to me, I had to take all the blame. They had to think I orchestrated Marvin, Anthony, and Trevor attacking Collin. They had to think I sent Tilly off with Dustin to tell me his whereabouts. Most importantly, they had to think Dustin was doing my bidding, not the Keepers. They had to believe Dustin had told me to go with them, not run! My disappearing with Tilly needed to rest on my shoulders as well.

"Tilly can I have one more hug goodbye, I will miss you dearly." I said as I stood and held my arms out.

"Oh no," Collin stated. "She's my new toy if you don't want her."

"Toy?" The lady guard repeated in my head.

"Yeah," another guard chimed in. "Why does Collin get a slave?"

Intently ignoring Collin, I grabbed both Tilly's hands in mine.

"Back off," Collin growled in his head. "I just brought home the biggest fish in years!"

Fully able to feel the locket, I began to rub as I closed my eyes and murmured, "Keeper House."

I felt the cool breeze swirling before we fell in the hallway, outside of our room, with a thud.

Scrambling to get up off the floor and out of the hallway before any of the other girl's dorm doors opened, we hurriedly entered and slammed the door to our room behind us. As I flipped on the light, I could hear Tilly gasp as we confronted Mrs. Farris sitting on my bed waiting for me or possibly us.

"You," Mrs. Farris spewed in a venomous tone. "You ruined the opportunity I had!" She stood and suddenly launched herself at me hitting me hard in the chest with her shoulder. I flew into Tilly's makeup table with most of her precious makeup hitting the floor. Gasping for the air that had been knocked out of me, Mrs. Farris again grabbed and shoved me off into the floor by the door.

Before I could move, Mrs. Farris had two hands firmly gripped on my shirt. Tilly grabbed her from behind squealing, "She has a locket!"

"Let go, or I will take you with us," Mrs. Farris growled at Tilly. I did my best to roll out of the way of the door which someone was attempting to open.

"Mary, stop," Professor Zirak said as he rushed through the door.

"How nice to see you Ruben," said Mrs. Farris in a sarcastic icy voice peering at him like he was temporarily the new target. "You're too late to protect your protégé. They have already taken him. I'm sure you had something to do with Elizabeth's opportunity as well."

"My involvement or non-involvement is none of your business," Professor Zirak stated. "You have not changed at all."

"Ruben, surely you have forgiven me and are not still holding grudges for all of those funny situations you found yourself in during our training," Mrs. Farris taunted with a sly, feline giggle.

"Yes, I have forgiven you, but I have also grown up," Professor Zirak retorted.

"Oh yes, so grown up you could never leave the Hall of Knowledge?" Mrs. Farris stated with another devilish grin.

"So grown up, I realize actions have consequences. I have known about your coming and going between the Hall of Knowledge and the Hospital for a long time. I have permitted it," Professor Zirak sternly added.

"You did not permit me to do anything," retorted Mrs. Farris in defiance.

"I did by never turning you in," countered the Professor. "A mistake I now regret because of your obvious meddling in my trainee's lives."

"It is a family situation I am handling. You know, being a good aunt," said Mrs. Farris.

"You don't fool me, Mary," Professor Zirak countered.

Tilly with me in her grip had backed up to stand under the door frame of our room. We silently watched the conversation unfold. Then, we were suddenly pushed aside as Mr. Solliday entered followed by a group of men that included Rhett and Marvin. Tilly and I backed out of our room and peered back through our door. Gawkers in the hallway pushed and shoved to get a peek.

Mr. Solliday glanced around and began, "Mrs. Farris, may I inquire as to why you are here?"

"Don't be coy, you know why I am here or you would not be confronting me," Mrs. Farris replied.

Tilly began to combat the crowd of girls who were pushing the two of us roughly trying to get a better look inside at the unexpected scene. That was when I noticed a smiling Destiny. Returning her smile, I understood she had sent the professor up and maybe got Mr. Solliday involved as well.

Mr. Solliday gave a small wave and the group of men sprung into action. From what I could see, over the blur of men in our room and the arms of Mrs. Farris flailing around, she was quickly subdued.

They dragged her through our door with her spewing, "It will come, Solliday… It will come. They will find a way."

As I watched the men dragging Mrs. Farris down the hall, I turned to mouth to Destiny, "Thank you!"

Destiny smiled and flippantly went into her room, closing the door.

"Imagine that," Tilly stated from behind me. "Nosy doesn't want to know what's going on."

I couldn't tell my best friend that Destiny already knew exactly what was happening. She had a front row seat without having a front row seat.

With the majority of the men gone, Mr. Solliday ordered, "Miss Cantrell and Miss Bradford, please join us." Then he turned to one of the men who came with him, "Please see to it that the door is guarded and that no one is eavesdropping."

Tilly and I exchanged places with the man who now would be guarding our door. The guard closed it once we were inside. Rhett, Marvin, and Mr. Solliday were all attempting not to stare at Tilly's face which was badly bruised.

"Are you okay?" Marvin asked as he crossed the room, attempting to look over every inch of me.

"Rhett, please escort Miss Bradford to your home immediately for the evening," Mr. Solliday interrupted. "Put something cold on that bruise as soon as you get there. Call for the doctor if needed."

"Absolutely," Rhett answered. He walked over to Tilly and put his arm around her shoulder.

"Oh yes, Miss Bradford, your friends from Lakeland and Mr. Stillholm will arrive at Rhett's shortly," Mr. Solliday continued. "We have had enough turmoil for tonight. See if you can keep those two boys of yours from hurting each other." He paused, "They are both crazy over you." Tilly looked at him like a deer that had been caught in a headlight. As she shot me a look, I shrugged at her. He continued, "Tomorrow you and Mr. Stillholm are welcome back at Keeper House and your friends from Lakeland will be escorted home."

"Mr. Lagedge," Mr. Solliday called.

Marvin was intently staring at me and didn't seem to hear him.

"Mr. Lagedge," he called again.

I pointed towards Mr. Solliday as Marvin said, "Huh."

"Mr. Lagedge," Mr. Solliday said with a displeased look across his face. "Please wait downstairs in Professor Zirak's office. I would like to speak to you privately."

Marvin gave me one more glance as he began to move towards the door.

"One more thing," Mr. Solliday sternly said causing every eye to turn to him. "None of you are to speak to anyone about this. Understand?"

"Yes, sir," Marvin replied as he stared at me. He turned to leave the room. Tilly shook her head as they exited the room. With the door open, I could hear the mumbling of the disappointed girls who were being turned away. I caught one more longing glance from Marvin before Mr. Solliday blocked my view. Marvin moved through the door. He closed it behind him without saying a word to me. Now it was only the professor left and I to face Mr. Solliday.

"Professor Zirak," Mr. Solliday called. "I trust you will stay with Miss Cantrell while I visit with Rhett and Mr. Lagedge?"

"Yes sir," Professor Zirak answered. With that Mr. Solliday made his way out the door and it closed behind him. "Elizabeth, should we sit and wait for Mr. Solliday?" Professor Zirak asked as he held out his hand to point to the chairs over by the windows. As we plopped down into the chairs, the professor appeared genuinely sad as he asked, "Dustin didn't make it back, did he?"

"No," I simply replied. I hadn't had a chance to think about how I felt about Dustin not returning.

"I knew he would do anything to protect you," Professor Zirak stated in a sad tone. "I should probably start at the beginning. When I was in training, Mary was in training in the Department of Administration. She was a character to put it politely."

"Mary is Mrs. Farris?" I questioned.

"Yes," Professor Zirak stated. "Once working for the Department of Administration, she began to use the information she was privy to as blackmail material. She eventually went too far and the Council transferred her to the Department of Keepers. She was a Keeper assigned to her first Humling to assist on the Earth Plane. Early on, she did not like her appointed Humling, so she hatched a plan to let bad things happen to him. She did not pass along helpful information. She was negligent in fulfilling her duty. After many warnings, she was sent before the Council who ruled that she no longer would be a Keeper."

"Whoa," I hummed.

"Instead, she would live with the Humlings and be forced to live a lower class life, as well as lives on the Earth Plane," Professor Zirak continued. "Her best friend, Rose, from the Department of Administration always agrees to be her Keeper each time she goes to the Earth Plane. Do you know who Rose's daughter is?"

"Tiffany," I replied.

"Yes," said the Professor. "Dustin was dating Tiffany so that she would not expose you."

After a short silence I interjected, "You told me you have known about her coming and going through the Hospital corridor..."

"You want to know if I know about your adventures as well?" Asked the professor. He watched me nod my head and continued, "Yes, I allowed it because I thought that like Mary being drawn to us, you would be drawn to the Humlings. I just thought letting you visit would curb the craving."

"If you knew, why did you not help Marvin?" I asked.

"He is a full Keeper, an adult, and as a mature responsible Keeper he is fully aware of the consequences to his actions," said the professor.

"Would you have helped Tilly and me if we had been caught?" I asked.

"I would have assumed you would be sent before the Council," answered the professor. "However, I don't know now since Marvin didn't end up before them." The professor began to tap his fingers nervously on the arm of the chair while pondering his previous statement. "Let me tell you about my training. I was the brunt of many pranks at the hands of the Department of Administration. Mary was the leader and Rose was never far behind. They were Tiffany and the cronies of my day. Can you think of times when I came to your rescue this year?" Asked the professor.

So you knew?" I asked.

"Yes," Professor Zirak answered. "Although, I could not have held off Professor Presnell any more times. Also, I never lied for your benefit."

The door opened and Mr. Solliday walked back into the room, "Thank you for waiting."

Professor Zirak got up from his chair saying, "You can have my chair sir."

"Thank you Ruben," Mr. Solliday graciously stated as he moved towards the windows. "Elizabeth, do you know why the events of this evening transpired?"

"Yes," I replied deep in thought. "Dustin was my Keeper and I now understand his need to protect me. He was also my Dweller guard."

I couldn't help but notice the professor's demeanor falter. He thought I was simply a Humling. I closed my eyes and shook my head. Why did I say that? Now he knew. Not only about me, but about Dustin.

Mr. Solliday ignored the professor as he began, "We discovered that Mrs. Farris was working with the Dwellers and intended to…"

I held up my hand to stop him, "I know."

"Will you be down?" Professor Zirak asked Mr. Solliday as he opened the door.

"Shortly," Mr. Solliday answered.

"Thank you professor," I said as he left the room.

"Marvin found me this evening after you were almost captured. He gave me this folder of journal entries," Mr. Solliday said as he handed me back the folder. "I had no idea Mrs. Farris's plans were so extensive." Mr. Solliday paused seeming to have regrets. "I'm sorry. When Marvin explained you had gone to save both your friend Tilly and Dustin," Mr. Solliday replied pausing again. "I knew I owed you an explanation."

"This," I said as I held up the folder. "Explained it all."

"I regret not telling you myself," Mr. Solliday simply stated. "I also wished I hadn't read it."

Anyone, who had read it, would understand why. Grace. Somewhere in the depths of his mind, he had to know what she faced. However, reading about it couldn't have been easy.

"It is only fair you hear what happened to our family," Mr. Solliday stated. "Your mother, my daughter Christy was in training when she met your father, Walter. He was indeed a dweller who was intent on ruining everything a Keeper stood for. Then one day they met and she simply melted the dark away into one of those shades of gray you once asked me about. He did indeed come to me to confess what I already knew. He wanted my trust and the price for me was high. With time, I began to see your mother was his entire life and they were very much in love.

Shortly after, they declared themselves soul mates and married. The Dwellers always were breathing down Walter's throat. When you and Christina came along, your parents knew it was time for a drastic change."

"So we went into hiding," I threw out.

"Yes," Mr. Solliday agreed. "All of you went to live as Humlings. This meant living in their world, beyond the dome."

"I assume this is where Mrs. Farris came into our lives," I interjected off the top of my head.

"Unfortunately, she ended up being your next door neighbor," Mr. Solliday answered. "Mary Ann Simmons, now Mrs. Farris, was once a Keeper. However, she didn't take care of her Humling which was assigned to her. The Council sentenced her to live as a Humling, beyond the dome. It was a mistake in hind sight!" Mr. Solliday paused deep in thoughts of regret.

"We unknowingly moved next to her, didn't we?" I asked.

"Your parents moved once a year," Mr. Solliday began to answer. When you moved to Shell Ridge, your mother wrote me how the neighbor next door was mesmerized by you and your sister. Then she wrote saying Mrs. Farris had cornered your mother asking about her true identity. Your mother denied it, but Mrs. Farris knew."

"She probably started plotting then," I stated.

"You're exactly right," Mr. Solliday admitted. "Mrs. Farris began attempting to blackmail your parents."

"Why didn't we just move?" I questioned.

"Moving would only confirm to Mrs. Farris what she believed," Mr. Solliday answered. "They had no choice but to stay and act as if she were crazy."

"It must not have worked out very well," I stated negatively shaking my head slightly.

"The sins of a father," Mr. Solliday sighed. "I arranged for her and Wendell Farris to meet. Wendell wanted a wife and I knew Mary Simmons would attach herself to anyone she thought was in a powerful position and able to give her status. I thought at the time it was a perfect match. When they were married they moved off into Stonehenge."

"You no longer consider it a perfect match?" I asked.

"Mrs. Farris has had track of you since then. She moved and you did too," Mr. Solliday began to explain. "Then, Mr. Farris was granted the position in the Hospital as a social worker. Mrs. Farris took the job of running the processing desk. When your mother went to the Earth Plane, it became apparent she couldn't return home without Mrs. Farris knowing."

"Where is my mother now?" I asked.

"She's a ghost," Mr. Solliday answered with sadness behind those wise eyes. "She has been one for awhile."

"She's trapped as a ghost," I repeated thinking about the ghost society. "Is it true what I read about my father and sister?"

"Yes," Mr. Solliday answered. "When the Dwellers found you, it was only the three of you since your mother was visiting me. Your sister laughed and spit on your father as they carried out their justice. They left you and your sister, figuring we would send both of you to them through the black arch."

"You only sent Christina to them," I stated. "Why did you keep me?"

"As it often goes, you and your sister were polar opposites, Mr. Solliday stated. "She was dark and you have always been full of light." He looked off into the room as he continued, "Your mother had already left for the Earth Plane and you were at a boarding school. You started writing me letters. I enjoyed reading each one."

"Did I know who you were to me?" I questioned.

"I never met you," Mr. Solliday stated. "I only had pictures and stories of you that your mother had sent to me." Mr. Solliday gave me a warm smile. "That is why I treasured those letters."

"What did I write to you?" I asked.

"It was as if you knew your place was within the dome as a Keeper," Mr. Solliday stated giving me one of those warm smiles. "You wanted to be a Keeper."

A knock came at the door as a guard opened it slightly peeking in.

"Yes?" Mr. Solliday asked.

"Sir, the Council has sent for you," the guard answered.

Mr. Solliday let out a sigh.

"It's okay," I stated to relieve his worried look. "I'm very tired."

"Of course," Mr. Solliday agreed as he started to stand. "The ramblings of an old man can wait until tomorrow."

I began to say, "That isn't what …"

Mr. Solliday held up his hand to stop me mid sentence. "I know." As he neared the door he said, "Until tomorrow."

I nodded as I watched him exit the door. I could see Marvin leaning against the wall opposite of my door when Mr. Solliday passed him. Not one word was spoken between them.

The guard allowed Marvin to ask, "Elizabeth, may I come in?"

I nodded, exhausted. "Marvin, don't." I crawled into my bed fully dressed, turned my back to him, and pulled my pink comforter over me. His steps faltered at the end of my bed. "Shut the door, will you!" I growled.

I could hear the door shut and assumed since I hadn't heard Marvin walk back to the door, it was the guard who was still posted at my door. I was very surprised when he crawled under the comforter next to me, placed his arms around me, and gently held me. His arms were always gentle and I felt a huge sense of relief as I felt the first tear stream down my cheek.

"You're tired," Marvin started. "I'm staying all night, you can sleep. Everything will seem better in the morning."

I did not respond. Even though he was so warm and I felt so safe, the tears continued to quietly stream down my face. He seemed content to let it all sink in and let my tears flow. I was so selfish to do this to him, but I needed him to stay and comfort me. However in the back of my mind, I did not know if there was any hope of a renewed relationship with Marvin. I would bring him more pain than good in his life. I couldn't put into words the desperation I felt as I left Dustin alone. I had already done to him what I didn't want to do to Marvin. Somehow, it seemed both had an unnatural attraction to me. However, I didn't have to decide how I felt about all of this tonight. Soon the warmth of Marvin's arms overtook me.

CHAPTER
TWENTY-THREE

Elizabeth

When I awoke, I found Marvin lying next to me, fast asleep. With my head clearing, I felt very restless. Marvin's arm was securely holding me. I struggled out from under it while trying not to wake him. I tip toed to sit in a chair before the windows which had brought the darkness into my life.

Marvin looked peaceful, just like a sleeping angel. There were so many things left unsaid. All I could dream about was having him in my life. However, now I knew this wasn't to be. I had to stand firmly between my Dweller family and Marvin, just as a mother would do to protect her children. After all, a life with me wouldn't be a life. Anyone attached to me, would constantly be looking over their shoulder. My Dweller family was relentless. There would never be a peaceful, little home where we could invite our friends over to have diner parties. I couldn't ruin his life.

My thoughts drifted to Dustin. Although I couldn't remember dating Dustin, he remembered dating me and thought he was in love with me. He too should realize I'm trouble and not good for him. I could only imagine the torture he was receiving due to my deception. Dustin had always been there for me. When the chips fell, I wasn't there for him. I let him be the fall guy. Why had Dustin not buried the eerie notion of me in a deep place never to see the light of day? The answer came to me simply as my head cleared. Looking back was always 20/20. He should have known I was unhealthy for him. Now, I knew I couldn't cause Dustin anymore trouble.

As I looked at all the makeup staining the carpet, my mind drifted to Tilly. She risked everything to draw the Dwellers away from me last night at great personal risk. I never should have agreed to send her with Dustin. Trevor was right, Tilly shouldn't be in their cross hairs. It was my place, not hers. Her concern was for my safety rather than her own. She truly was more of a better best friend to me, than I was to her.

Marvin was stirring. As his hand noticed I was missing beside him, he sat straight up. The glare of the light coming through the window caused him to squint and rub his eyes with his hands. He caught sight of me and appeared relieved as he ran his hand through his hair. As he, sleepily peered at me, a relieved grin crossed his swollen and bruised face. He said, "Good morning."

"Good morning," I repeated in response smiling.

He pulled himself up to lean against my headboard and patted the spot next to him, inviting me to sit with him. Reluctantly, I moved to sit next to him dreading what was to come. It was really wrong of me to let him stay last night. Startling me, I felt Marvin's hand push my hair behind my ear after I crawled up next to him.

I glanced up at him knowing exactly the conversation I wanted to finish. I wanted to ask, "So, you knew me before?"

"No," Marvin corrected. "I saw you once while I was in training."

"There's a difference?" I questioned.

"Yes, I didn't know who you were," Marvin explained. "It was a Tuesday evening. I made my way to my uncles, but found him gone. A note was pinned on his door saying he had taken a walk. I followed him to the Administration Complex figuring that was the direction he had walked. We stood and watched a door out of curiosity and that's were we saw you."

Marvin looked away and seemed to be deep in thought.

I was impatient, "What was I doing?"

"You were simply standing with Mr. Solliday," Marvin replied. "I watched him put a locket around your neck."

"This one?" I asked as I held it up from under my shirt. "It must have been the night I went to the Dwellers with Dustin."

"I didn't realize its significance at the time or what you were being asked to do," Marvin said as his voice and thoughts trailed away. "I just thought I had seen the most beautiful girl ever. And yes, you gave your watch to Mr. Solliday and then you disappeared with Dustin."

Looming over us was Dustin, so I decided to start, "I guess you knew Dustin was my guard?"

"No," Marvin corrected. "Until Lakeland, I only knew that Dustin was an acquaintance of yours."

"Why didn't you tell me?" I asked as he looked away.

"Elizabeth, I honor my promises," Marvin replied.

"You promised not to tell me?" I asked.

"I made a promise to my uncle that I would not tell anyone about what I saw that evening," Marvin corrected. "I just didn't know how hard that promise would be to keep. I wanted to tell you everything, especially when I understood how you longed to remember."

"You should have trusted me," I responded.

"I couldn't understand why you couldn't remember," Marvin stated. "I thought your lack of memory was protecting you from something. I worried that whatever it was, Dustin was included."

"You were both right and wrong," I stated.

"Right, it did include Dustin. Wrong, that he would hurt you," Marvin agreed. "I only understood this after that night in Lakeland."

I never gave Marvin credit for what he was capable of. I spent too much time burying what I knew while worrying it would all be too much for him. I was as much to blame. If I had leveled with him, maybe he would have leveled with me. What happened that night?" I asked.

"Dustin saved me from the Dwellers once he knew you were safe," Marvin stated.

"Then why?" I asked.

"After Uncle Rhett and Mr. Solliday explained it all to me, I knew it had to be," Marvin stated. "I had to step aside so you would allow Dustin to be close to protect you. My stepping aside was my decision."

"You wanted me to be with Dustin?" I questioned feeling utterly shocked.

"Every moment spent without you has been hell. Thinking of you with him has made me want to die," Marvin responded. "My only reason for wanting you to be with him is that I realized, after Lakeland, I could not protect you. I would never be able to fend them off the way he could."

"Rather than tell me," I huffed. "You chose to break my heart."

"You know you truly love someone when you can walk away letting them have what is best for them," Marvin stated as he grabbed my hand. "I can't tell you how many times I have said that to myself trying to convince myself that my decision was right."

"Oh, you did it all for me," I said sarcastically as I pulled my hand from his.

"It wasn't for me," Marvin replied. "I walked away from my life! I moved so you wouldn't try to see me. I gave up my job so I could stay away from you at the Keeper Complex. But worst of all, I gave up the moments with you. I have been lost without you."

"As I was without you," I replied.

"But you had Dustin comforting you," Marvin said with a hint of anger.

"And you had Tiffany," I countered.

"No," Marvin replied. "You kept hinting to others you did not believe we were over. Each time I was in the same room with you, I couldn't stop myself from craving to take you into my arms. I wanted to hold you, to tell you how wrong I was. So, each time I would breathe deeply and attempt not to make eye contact. I would repeat again and again in my head that my decision had been right. However, you wouldn't give up and I had to make you believe it." I didn't know how to respond. "You must believe me, I never dated her."

"Yeah," I replied. "I guess I should have put more stock into what Jessie told me."

"Jessie?" Marvin questioned. "When did you see him?"

"One day before training at the Keeper Complex," I replied.

"He actually told you I wasn't dating Tiffany?" Marvin questioned seeming to tense up.

"Yes," I replied. "You didn't want him to tell me that did you?"

"No," Marvin replied.

"You chose Tiffany as the one, to put the final nails in the coffin to ensure I would believe it," I said feeling the heat swell from my skin.

"I only walked her to training the one day so that you would see us together. It worked," Marvin replied. "Only too well. When I saw your reaction, I knew I had gone too far… I feared I had lost you forever."

"I have never felt so devastated," I said letting my thought slip out my mouth.

"Exactly, that is how I felt watching Dustin comfort you, devastated," Marvin replied.

And it had surfaced, the only true issue looming over us, Dustin. "Honestly, I have always felt strangely drawn to him and I can't explain it."

"I understand," Marvin said.

"How can you?" I questioned.

Marvin answered, "Once I had knowledge he was your guard, I understood your bond with him." He paused trying to bury the resentful look on his face as he closed his eyes saying, "It's natural."

"Yeah. Natural," I sighed. "How can you accept how I feel about him?"

"I love you," Marvin hesitated. "All of you. Not for one day did I stop loving you or thinking about you every moment. You are my life. There is no one else I would sacrifice everything to protect."

"You love me so much that you will accept my bond with Dustin?" I asked shocked.

"All that really matters to me is being with you," Marvin began. "I can accept him as a part of our life as long as we can be together."

Why had I ever let Dustin come between us? "Marvin, I know I am not in love with him," I stated.

"I know," Marvin replied.
My thought seemed to spill out my mouth, "But was my passion with Dustin real?"

"Passion," Marvin repeated as I could see him hiding behind the pain which my words caused. "The only passion that is real is how I feel about you. How I know, deep down beyond your confusion, you feel about me."

It was all summed up. My passion for Dustin wasn't real love, only physical attraction. He always drew me in. "Is that enough to go on from here," I questioned. "Do you want to live the life that being attached to me would bring you? I will forever be tracked!"

"That doesn't matter to me," Marvin stated adamantly shaking his head.

"It should," I disagreed.

"You think you will bring darkness into my life?" Marvin assumed with a huff.

"You don't?" I challenged.

"I can understand how you would think my being with you would cause me to be tracked," Marvin stated. "However, I know if I wasn't already, I am now marked. Being with you doesn't make any difference where that is concerned."

"If you are already marked, I did that to you," I replied.

Marvin grabbed my shoulder and gently turned me to him. I tried to look away and then he turned my face to peer directly into his. As his hand gently caressed my cheek he longingly peered into my eyes saying, "Elizabeth Cantrell, none of this matters to me. I love you." He paused and I could feel his hand shake nervously. "We're soul mates!" His eyes seemed to be searching for my lips to say the same in response before asking, "Don't you know that?" He paused as his hands dropped from my face, "You are the only one I can ever be with. I can't live without you."

"But you should," I disagreed.

"Don't do this," Marvin begged.

"I don't want to," I stated.

"Then don't," Marvin pleaded. "There's no life for either of us if we are apart. We are one."

I closed my eyes not wanting to see his face as I stood my ground, "You shouldn't have stayed last night." I took a deep breath adding, "I'm sorry."

My only thought was to move as fast as possible. Marvin's hands found their way to my shoulders, stopping me as he peered directly into my eyes. He took a deep breath and again said for the world to hear, "Elizabeth Cantrell, you are my soul mate!" He paused looking away as his hands dropped from my shoulders. He questioned, "Do you not think I'm serious about you?"

There was no doubt in my mind that he was serious. I began to answer, "No…"

"Of course you don't," Marvin stated to himself. "I did this. I placed that doubt into your mind." Marvin became quiet and I could read the regret across his face. "I declared my intentions last night to your grandfather and Rhett," Marvin spit out. "Why do you think they let me stay?"

"What did you tell them?" I asked feeling caught off guard.

"I got nervous and said much more than I meant too," Marvin admitted. "I declared to them that you are my soul mate. Don't you see? There will never be anyone else for me."

"You declared me as your soul mate?" I questioned feeling flabbergasted. Marvin nodded as I again questioned, "In public?"

"Basically," Marvin agreed. "They were there, a few guards... I don't know who else might have heard."

"You can't ever make that declaration again," I stated off the top of my head.

"I will never need to declare it again," Marvin stated as his hand caressed my cheek. "You are my one and only soul mate!"

I leaned over into his arms understanding he was right. We were soul mates. Marvin held me tightly. With my head on his chest, I could clearly hear his heart beating as I began to sob.

Marvin gently said, "It's okay."

Our worlds were changed and we could never go back. Marvin had stated what I was scared to say out loud. Even though I knew I would bring darkness into his life, I couldn't deny that we were soul mates. My heartbeat felt as if it were his, not mine. There were two hearts living in separate bodies but beating as one. I had to give in. All of a sudden, my existence finally felt right. In Marvin's arms, my thought came out my mouth, "Marvin, I love you too."

His head leaned down against mine. He gave me a small hug and kissed the top of my head. I looked up at his face and our lips met. A simple kiss not filled with raw burning passion, but an enduring love.

CHAPTER
TWENTY-FOUR

Elizabeth

We were standing in a straight line waiting for our turn to go on stage in Grand Hall. Tilly and Trevor finally showed up from their night at Rhett's. Their relationship was full of tension. I worried that Anthony was slowly driving a wedge between them. We were all to act as if nothing happened, so we hadn't discussed much of anything between us. Since our fellow trainees had taken up staring and whispering amongst themselves, no one was talking to us either. More talking about us.

"Hey, the videos loaded," Eddie said as he whispered over my shoulder.

I turned and whispered back, "Thank you."

"No problem," Eddie sighed. "You are going to tell me…"

"Later," I interrupted.

"Okay," Eddie hummed. He leaned forward and whispered again, "About that date…"

"Eddie," I stated trying to figure out a way to get out of the date.

"I have to tell you Kim discovered my date with Destiny last night," Eddie said. "Actually, she showed up. It wasn't pretty."

"Who has chick problems now," Trevor said stepping up and grinning.

"Kim demanded I choose on the spot," Eddie said rolling his eyes.

"Her or Destiny," I assumed. At least I didn't have to worry about Eddie demanding that date with me. Kim had her thumb on him.

"Yeah," Eddie said. "I'm just giving you a heads up. She's mad at you too."

"Why is she mad at you?" Trevor asked.

"I talked Eddie into going on a date with Destiny," I explained.

"Why?" Trevor asked.

"Later," I hummed.

"Right, later…" Eddie said with another roll of his eyes. "I better get to my spot in line." Eddie looked at Trevor adding, "You better get to your spot too. Tilly seems to be in a foul mood."

"She certainly has a sunny disposition today, doesn't she," Trevor huffed as Eddie chuckled and wandered off.

Trevor leaned over and again asked, "Why?"

"The less you know the better," I whispered back.

"Spit it out," Trevor demanded. "No more secrets."

"Tiffany took it too far," I answered.

"What do you mean she took it too far?" Trevor seriously asked. "What did she do?"

"It doesn't matter," I assured him. "All that matters is that you aren't involved."

"This doesn't sound good," Trevor stated with worry crossing his face.

"After what happened…" I stopped giving him a look. "This is a cake walk."

He let out a huge sigh, "Okay."

I could tell he wasn't totally satisfied as he shuffled to his place as the line began to move.

"How, how, how… c… c… could yo…you?" Kim half stuttered, half yelled as she grabbed my arm from behind.

I pulled my arm out of her grip returning, "How could I what?"

"Set Eddie up with that s… s… stinky, nosy D… D… Destiny," answered Kim.

"He doesn't like Destiny," I countered.

"He… he… he's n…not g… g… going!" Kim retorted.

"He was doing me a favor," I admitted to the visibly angry Kim. "Taking one for the team."

As if a button had switched inside Kim she spewed at me, "Eddie is mine! I'm going to marry him one day. Don't ask him to do favors for you." She shoved me back a step adding, "Keep your hands off!" Again she moved to shove me, so I simply stepped back. "You'll keep your distance if you know what is good for you! Got it?"

Mild, meek, Kim had just come unglued! If only Tilly were here to see this. She would be proud and was simply never going to believe me. Who would have thought Kim would find her voice over Eddie.

"Got it?" Kim again repeated.

"Sure," I replied shaking my head wondering if she had ever seen him eat.

Satisfied with my lack of rebuttal, she walked past me and climbed the three stairs onto the stage in Grand Hall.

Those passing me were staring, wide eyed as I stepped back into line. More for them to gossip about. I climbed the three steps and stepped out onto the stage and into the glaring lights. Eddie had insisted the very large video screen was to play a video behind the band. Only I knew what was really going to show on the screen. I tried not to appear guilty. I took my place

275

with the girls who would be singing the back up chorus. The room was full, anticipating Tilly's repeat performance with her band.

Marvin was sitting in the first row, smiling broadly at me. There wasn't a soul at the Hall of Knowledge who didn't know that Marvin had stayed last night. We were clearly gossip bait this morning. Marvin stood with me all morning and never left my side until we lined up. I could only assume he thought he was taking the brunt of the stares, but I really no longer cared what the others around me thought. Clearly, I had bigger concerns than the other girls gossiping or getting busted for helping Janelle get revenge on Tiffany.

I tried not to look at Tiffany's crew who were now all sitting in a group not far behind Marvin. However, I couldn't miss the bits of paper they were tossing at Marvin to try to get his attention. I knew he was intently ignoring them. Helping Janelle would be one thing I wouldn't regret.

As Jay hit the first chord on his electric guitar, without looking, I knew the screen behind us came to life. The lights from the screen, flashing behind us, were causing our shadows to dance on the stage floor. Wasting no time, it was Janelle's voice I heard instead of Tilly's.

I turned to view the screen listening to an amplified voice of Janelle say, "Tiffany Raderton, this video is for you and about you. Since you always want to be the star, I hope this satisfies your egotistical need to be the limelight!"

Janelle stood on the video with microphone in her hand. From the video she announced for the suddenly drop dead quiet crowd in Grand Hall, "Welcome to Tiffany Raderton's version of the Friend Feud." The crowd gasped as we watched Janelle walk across the room to a line of fellow trainees standing behind a counter that appeared to be somewhat familiar to me. "Please state your group name for the video audience at home."

"We're the moronic freaks," a tall, lanky young man answered.

"State your names as we go down the line," Janelle said.

"Derek," a tall, lanky young man answered.

"Seth," the next answered.

"David," said a young man as he winked at Janelle.

"Oh my," a girl standing near me whispered to another. "Aren't those all Tiffany's old boyfriends?"

"James," the next answered.

"Fred," said the last in line as he wielded an air fist pump.

Trevor moved over to me and asked under his breath, "Is this is what I was better off not knowing about?"

I shrugged not looking over at him.

"Moving right along," Janelle stated as she walked to the other side of the room. "The opposing team! What are you calling yourselves?"

"We're the wenches," the first young lady loudly stated.

"That's not a very nice name?" Janelle countered.

"We know," the young lady answered. "We all were surprised to be included in this club."

"Very well," Janelle sighed. "Tell our video audiences your names."

"Brittany," the first young lady answered.

"Stacey," the second answered.

"Susan," the third answered.

"Wendy," the fourth curtly answered.

"Karen," the last responded.

"Now for the face off question," Janelle stated as she smiled for the camera and walked to a podium between the groups. "Come on up Derek and Brittany."

Both ran up and automatically placed one hand behind their back.

"The first to know the answer to my question, please slap the buzzer," Janelle stated. "What were the top two responses when 100 people were asked, what does Tiffany use to make herself cry on demand?"

The slaps sounded simultaneous. Janelle pried the first hand up revealing that Derek had slapped the podium first. Janelle smiled a devilish grin as he stated, "Yawning."

"Let's see," Janelle sighed. "Was yawning one of the top two results. Yes, yawning was number two with forty-seven of those surveyed choosing that response." Janelle then looked at Brittany, "Ladies, now it is your time to steal. Do you know how Tiffany really makes herself cry on demand?"

Brittany peered back at her fellow teammates and it was clear they all shared the same thought without it needing to be spoken. "Onions," Brittany answered.

"For the number one response of those surveyed," Janelle stated in pure theatrical manner. "Number one with fifty-three votes. Onions." Then she peered at the camera, "Oops, watch out for those big purses she carries with her. They are likely full of raw chopped onions!"

At this point, Professor Presnell shoved me aside as she ran for the cords powering the screen which were behind the chorus singers. She yanked and pulled to no avail. They weren't plugged in, but hard wired into the wall.

"Sorry fellas," Janelle stated as she moved to the girls. "The ladies have the floor. Question two goes to Stacey. How many people out of the 100 asked stated this was Tiffany's worst character flaw which made her untrustworthy?" Janelle asked as she stepped up to the second young lady.

"That's easy," Stacey matter of fact answered. "Stealing."

"Stealing?" Janelle questioned.

"Anyone who lives in Administration House knows she rummages through everyone's rooms and takes what she wants when you're not looking," Stacey answered in the same nonchalant manner.

"Well, you're in luck," Janelle stated. "Stealing was our number four response with thirteen votes. Imagine, thirteen unhappy people with something missing."

If I wasn't mistaken, that was everyone who lived on the girl's hall at Administration House. I couldn't help but hear the crowd behind me gasp as Marvin's warm hands grabbed my arm. A mass of adults were rushing the stage intent to turn off the video. Marvin pulled me to the side of the stage and whispered in my ear, "You didn't have anything to do with this, did you?"

"Susan," Janelle called moving down the line. "What would you think Tiffany's worst character flaw is making her untrustworthy?"

"Backstabbing gossip," Susan quickly answered. "Which Tiffany will never say to your face."

"Ooo..." Janelle hummed. "Gossip was our number three response with fourteen votes. Ladies, you know Tiffany too well." She then looked to the next player, "Wendy, tell me your opinion."

"Doing ones own class work," Wendy replied.

"You must explain this one for our video audience," Janelle seriously stated.

"If I must do my own class work," Wendy huffed. "Tiffany should too!"

"Yes," Janelle stated appearing to console Wendy. "We all understand we don't have a class nerd... Sorry Ruthanne... to push around and black mail into doing our class work for us." Then Janelle peered right into the camera, "Number two response with twenty-five people voting this way. Tiffany, guess the gigs up on that one." Not missing a beat Janelle stepped down to the last girl calling, "Karen, why do you think Tiffany is untrustworthy?"

"She's a snitch," Karen answered. "You know she uses any opportunity to brown nose the professor."

"Let's see," Janelle hummed. "Dear, the ladies are running away with it. Snitch is response number five with eleven votes." Janelle then walked back to Brittany. "It's all up too you. What do you believe the number one character flaw Tiffany has that makes her untrustworthy?"

"Boyfriend stealer," Brittany stated.

"Ooo..." Janelle again hummed. "Well, this has taken a serious turn of events. How many people could actually think that?" Then she peered right into the camera spewing, "I'll give you a hint. At least one thinks so... Me. Oops, sorry Rodger, I assume you didn't want your mom to know about your cheating ways." With a devious grin at having burned both Tiffany and Rodger, she continued, "Number one with thirty-seven of those surveyed believing the number one flaw of Tiffany is boyfriend stealing."

Trevor had migrated towards me and said under his breath, "Are you crazy? Or just delusional to think you're going to get away with this?"

Janelle walked back to the podium, picking up a ratty covered book. I knew exactly what it was, Tiffany's burn book.

"Gentleman," Janelle called holding up the burn book. "Do you know what this is?"

"A diary," Derek answered.

"Not just any diary," Janelle answered. "Now is your opportunity to steal the show back. Seth, according to the hundred people surveyed, what are the top five subjects recorded in this burn book of Tiffany?"

"Parents," Seth replied.

"Let's see if that is one," Janelle taunted. She flipped through the book and seemed pleased with the passage she was reading. "Mrs. Bradford thinks she's a big fish, but really she's a small fish which others work around. The only thing gained from kissing up to her is the priceless look which I occasionally see cross Tilly's face. What a shame to have a mother that hates you." She peered into the camera saying, "Sorry, Tilly." Then she looked back at Seth saying, "Parents came in fifth with six people voting this way."

"You don't have to ask," David piped up from beside Seth. "My answer is the professors."

"Of course," Janelle agreed. "Who doesn't complain about their professor?" With a devilish grin she again flipped through the book. "Oh dear." She shook her head as she began to read, "Being seen with Professor Presnell is worse than being seen with my parents. Who ever taught her how to dress, or put on makeup? She walks around like she's the talk of the town. In reality she is old, used up, and mentally deficient. Not to mention, she is obviously color blind." With a slight smirk Janelle said, "Good answer. Professors were forth on the list with twelve people saying this was in the book."

At this point Professor Presnell instantly turned a deep shade of red. As if her feet were suddenly glued to the stage, she was too red faced angry to continue attempting to stop the video. She just stared at the screen.

Janelle moved down and asked Fred, "Do you know one of the remaining three subjects recorded in this burn book?"

"Boyfriends," Fred answered as all five guys smirked.

"Well, that's something all of you know about," Janelle smiled as she turned to a pre marked passage. "Rodger is fun to play with, but he is as dumb as a block of wood. To think he actually thinks we are going to date. How gullible and dense can you be?" With a satisfied look she then turned back to Fred saying, "Good guess. Boyfriends rated number two with thirty-three votes."

Janelle then stepped down and asked, "James, what do you think is in the burn book?"

"Classmates," James answered as if reading Janelle's thoughts.

Janelle instantly flipped to a page and took a deep breath before beginning, "Coming in at number one with thirty-four of those polled, Classmates. All those useless, simple minded classmates of mine. They don't have enough vision to see the big picture." She flipped a few more pages and read, "It is painful to sit in study group. They aren't smart enough to wipe their noses without me."

"Wow," the last young man said. "If that is what she wrote about her classmates, tell me did friends make the cut."

"Your answer is friends," Janelle said as he nodded. "James, you are right. The number three answer with fourteen votes." She smiled and flipped through the book.

The screen suddenly went dark. Professor Presnell stepped up to the mike saying, "If you are in Administration House, Keeper House, Records House, or Ghost House, please do not leave."

"Excuse me professor," Janelle stated as she seemed to step up to the mike from out of nowhere. "I take full responsibility for this."

"Teaming up with Miss Bradford," Professor Presnell spewed clearly very angry.

"Actually, Tilly had nothing to do with this," Janelle disagreed.

"How could you betray me?" Tiffany said standing before the stage and looking up.

"All the members of the two teams suddenly strolled up behind Janelle. As if Derek was speaking for the group he said, "We too take credit. And how dare you ask how she could betray you! Everything you wrote in this book, betrayed anyone who at one time trusted you."

"I suppose all of you will say Miss Bradford had nothing to with this as well," Professor Presnell again prodded.

"Is it so hard to believe we did this without Tilly," Janelle challenged.

"I want the names of all one hundred people who you surveyed," Professor Presnell stated.

I watched as one by one, all of the Administration House stood. Destiny had wandered up from somewhere. She grabbed my hand demanding, "Come on!" I looked over at her and she gave me a solid smile.

I let her pull me away from Marvin until we were beside Janelle. "We take credit too!"

"You do?" Professor Presnell mused.

"We do too! So do we! Me too!" Said countless other trainees as they began to step forward.

Slowly all in the houses were standing leaving Tilly and Trevor as the lone wolves standing alone. Trevor peered over at Tilly and offered his hand to her. I watched as she stared up into his eyes and took his hand. In that instant I knew their disagreement had ended. Their commitment to each other went well beyond all rational thought. They too stepped forward. When it was all said and done, everyone was standing.

"Are you going to punish all of us?" Janelle asked. "We just pointed out the truth."

Derek handed the burn book to the Professor as he added, "Read it for yourself."

Destiny looked over at me and smiled. Destiny knew we weren't in trouble.

"The disrespectful conduct of this group of trainees will no longer be tolerated," Professor Presnell loudly stated. "The expectation while in training is that you will lead with integrity. What you did here was under-handed. I won't tolerate any more pranks." In a swirl she turned on Janelle spouting, "I will see you and all those on the video in my office immediately."

THE KEEPER SAGA
SMOKE AND MIRRORS

BOOK SIX
SNEAK PEAK

Dustin

I found myself chained to a dirty dungeon wall. Apparently, I had been here for days. No amount of struggling freed me. I yelled but no one came. Then suddenly, I was surprised when Geren entered the small room which held me captive.

"I must ask you," Geren started as he pulled the guards chair from its position by the door and sat down in front of me. "Why do you believe you have been allowed to come and go at will, to make your own plans?"

"Because it has been my duty to do what was necessary to find Bethany," I replied.

"Wrong," I heard his mind say.

"Then enlighten me?" I shot back.

"One day, you will take my place as head guard," Geren stated.

Who was he kidding? Only a son of his could take his place. I watched as a smirk crossed his face. He stared at me as possible awareness of my parentage become apparent across my face.

"Yes, I am your father!" Geren stated. "Your mother is Mary Farris."

I felt sick. The idea I used to be accepted by the Keepers inside the dome wasn't a rouse at all. Just the opposite, it was true. I had been fooled along with everyone else. Why didn't I see it before now?

My earliest memory was sitting alone in the hospital. Geren came for me explaining he was going to take me home. That is where my life in the world of the Dwellers began. I lived with Geren until I was old enough to start my training. Ingrained in my memory was how proud Geren was as I was welcomed as an official member of Venema House upon the completion of my training. He wasn't proud because I was a lost kid he took in, I was his...

"My son, how long do you plan to rebel against Deward's demand?" Geren asked.

Deward had requested that I bring Elizabeth here at all cost. He intended to send her through the black arch for an eternity of reincarnations on the Earth Plane. The moment she would die on the Earth Plane, her soul would recycle right back into an Earth Plane baby. She would cease to be Elizabeth in the world of the Keepers or Bethany in the world of the Dwellers. The simple thought made me crazy. She was the light in my life.

"Tell me why you refuse to follow his order," Geren begged. "Let me help you."

"I am in love with her," I whispered.

"I see," Geren said as he stood and began to pace across the damp and muddy dirt floor. "Deward can be dealt with when he understands the reasoning behind what we do. I once felt the same about Mary. I knew from the moment I looked at her. Did you know from the moment you saw Bethany?"

I nodded.

"Affirmatively my son, if it is her you desire, I will talk with Deward today concerning a possible union," Geren stated. He then stopped directly in front of me. "I need to know I can trust you."

I sighed and began, "I don't have anything to give or any way to prove to you..."

"Actually you do," Geren interrupted as he sat back on the two legs of the stool. "I will arrange her safety for as long as you want her. However, if you betray me, I will ensure she is granted travel through our black arch." His voice turned icy as he added, "I want your loyalty to me and me alone! Don't ever cross me."

The line in the sand was drawn. His threat made the consequences quite clear for betraying his trust. "There is still another problem," I added under his steely stare. "She is in love with another."

"I am aware of the Keeper you talk about," Geren stated. "What do you propose to do about him?"

"I need to get rid of him!" I stated firmly grasping that this was the corner I was backed into. Elizabeth would never give me a chance if Marvin was standing in my way.

"Yes! Now you're scheming like my son," Geren replied with a chuckle. "Then, your problem is making her stay. You have your work cut out for you. She is already the scandalous talk of Venema house. She's cunning and might even give her sister, Tina, a run for her money."

ALSO BY JJ HULL

The Keeper Saga
Smoke and Mirrors (Book 6)
Letting Go (Book 7)

Order these titles from
www.paranormalcrossroads.com

VISIT THE SAGA

WWW.THEKEEPERSAGA.COM

www.ingramcontent.com/pod-product-compliance
Lightning Source LLC
Chambersburg PA
CBHW071311170626
46809CB00001B/396

* 9 7 8 0 9 8 4 9 8 7 9 5 5 *